NIGHTS

OF THE

MOONLESS SKY

NIGHTS

OF THE

MOONLESS SKY

*A Tale from the
Vijayanagara Empire*

N. S. VISHWANATH

Archway Publishing books may be ordered through booksellers or by contacting:

Archway Publishing
1663 Liberty Drive
Bloomington, IN 47403
www.archwaypublishing.com
844-669-3957

ISBN: 978-1-4808-9576-8 (sc)
ISBN: 978-1-4808-9574-4 (hc)
ISBN: 978-1-4808-9575-1 (e)

Library of Congress Control Number: 2020917321

Print information available on the last page.

Archway Publishing rev. date: 12/9/2020

To
You

"There is nothing stronger than a broken woman who has rebuilt herself"

- HANNAH GADSBY

OVERTURE

Mid-16th century, Vijayanagara Empire.

In the capital city of Vijayanagara, the emperor Acyuta Raya, who had succeeded his illustrious brother Krishnadeva Raya to the throne, has died. Acyuta Raya's brother-in-law Salkaraju has declared himself caretaker ruler. Opposing him is Rama Raya, a longtime aspirant to the throne. As Krishnadeva Raya's son-in-law, Rama Raya was once considered a favorite to rule as the guardian of Krishnadeva Raya's infant son, but the child died, leaving the throne to Acyuta Raya after Krishnadeva Raya. Following several failed machinations to outmaneuver Acyuta Raya, Rama Raya is now no more than a rebel commanding a burgeoning insurgency with support across the empire.

Neither Salkaraju nor Rama Raya are of royal blood and cannot ascend the throne legitimately. The only bona fide heir of royal blood is Sadasiva, a nephew of Krishnadeva Raya. But Sadasiva is a teenager, too young to rule…and he has disappeared. Whoever among Rama Raya and Salkaraju prevails and can produce Sadasiva can claim to be the boy's regent and rule on his behalf.

Far away from the capital, in the splendorous estate of Madhuvana, destinies collide as events paralleling the churnings in the royal corridors unfold …

1

WHEN AADARSHINI WAS FIVE, HER left eyelid flickered incessantly on the *amavasya* afternoon when she lost her favorite doll. Then later that year, it fluttered all day, when her parents drowned during a stormy river-crossing. That a twitching left eyelid was a portender of bad luck, the young Aadarshini had come to embrace as a law of nature. The appearance of the *ghoshaka*, the village crier, on the other hand, had over time established itself as an omen of good tidings, with the magical ability to countervail the unwelcome consequences of a blinking eyelid. So when Aadarshini heard the faint rumble of the *ghoshaka*'s drum this morning, she ignored her trembling eye and smiled at the azure sky and the green expanse ahead.

She was glad she had come out into the plantation. Sarala, her maid, kept an eye on the farmhands harvesting bananas. The jasmine bushes, ubiquitous across the majestic Madhuvana estate, *her* Madhuvana, of which she was veritably the queen, were gloriously in bloom. Aadarshini took a deep breath. She loved the smell of jasmine and the wanton pang it seemed to set off within her. She plucked a flower and tucked it into her hair, bending down to adjust her silver anklets. The flower fell off, and she grunted in frustration.

"Let me help you with that," said Sarala.

Of all her maids, Aadarshini trusted Sarala the most and rarely ventured far into the plantation without taking her along. Although serene and naturally fortified, with the Amruta river running along one edge and a half mile swath of paddy fields, coconut-palm groves, wild woods, banana orchards, and other plantings that encircled the magnificent family home, Aadarshini knew Madhuvana wasn't always safe, what with the snake-infested vegetation, the confusing mazes of trails, or the occasional leopard she had smelled but happily never sighted. So Aadarshini heeded her husband's advice and took along Sarala and a male farmhand or two whenever she stepped out. But there had been times she'd stolen off by herself, and had relished the thrill.

Sarala delicately braided Aadarshini's tresses, which reached below her knees. She then rolled the hair into a neat chignon which rested elegantly on Aadarshini's nape. "There. Now it'll sit without falling," she said and tucked the jasmine back in.

Aadarshini walked over to the lily pond and stooped over.

"You look like the goddesses in the temple, Akka," Sarala said with visible pleasure.

Aadarshini smiled. The goddesses Sarala referred to were the stone sculptures carved on the temple pillars: flawless female figurines, dusky, slender, with playful eyes and perfect breasts. She took another look at her reflection and blushed.

"Come," she said. "Let's walk to the gate. I haven't been there in a long time."

They walked gingerly across the paddy fields on skinny footpaths, Aadarshini in front, waving to the farmhands as they passed them. Beyond the fields, tamarind trees lined a trail that led to the gates of Madhuvana. This was the edge of Aadarshini's universe, she felt, for beyond the gates sat the rest of Maravali. The same sinuous dirt track ran through the village, then traipsed away, following the Amruta to lands unknown to her. A peepul tree and a Rama temple stood guard at Maravali's borders, as if keeping watch over its residents, about a thousand in all. Aadarshini stood at the other edge, the gates of Madhuvana.

The *ghoshaka*'s drums could be heard louder from here.

"Have I told you," she said to Sarala, "that in all the years I have been his wife, Rajanna has never once taken me to the village to see the *ghoshaka* perform." Aadarshini could never understand why, despite being one of the wives of the most prominent man in Maravali, she wasn't allowed out of Madhuvana without an entourage. *For your own good*, Rajanna had impressed upon her.

"What would you do there, Akka?" said Sarala, sounding surprised. "Rajanna was right. What happens there is only for men. And children."

Aadarshini knew her son Raghu, just eight, had gone to listen to the *ghoshaka* with the other Madhuvana boys, likely doing what she had done as a child when the crier came to her village.

"I'd call out to my friends no sooner than I heard the crier's drum. We'd follow him as he shrieked out bulletins in his squeaky voice: *Hear! Hear! O' citizens of the great empire of Vijayanagara...*"

She giggled as she mimicked the *ghoshaka* from her childhood. But then, with a touch of melancholy, she added, "But that seems so long ago."

Faded memories of life at the Navagiri *ashram* came to her. The ashram, a sanctuary for orphaned Brahmin girls and widows, had been built as an annex to a temple. She was often told her parents had gone to visit Lord Narayana in *vaikunta* and would come back someday to take her with them, but she knew they had drowned. In her memories, the ashram was a happy place, where she played with friends and heard stories from the Puranas from caring widows, many of whom had been widowed as children. *Don't despair, child, Lord Narayana takes care of us all*-the elders would tell them when someone was sad, and then they'd cry themselves, and Aadarshini had never understood why. On occasion grown-up priests would visit and talk with the older widows well into the night, after the children had gone to bed. She could hear the women laughing, and felt happy for them.

Then one day when she was twelve, Aadarshini was told the village astrologer had arranged a matrimonial alliance for her with a prosperous businessman from a place called Maravali a seven-day bullock cart ride away, where she would live like a princess. The residents of the ashram had bid her a tearful farewell when she boarded the festooned cart, Rajanna appearing to her like the kings she had heard about in stories. She had asked him if he would bring her back to visit her friends. He had said he would. That was ten years ago. But though he had not taken her back, she idolized him. Rajanna was wise, powerful, kind to her to a fault, and nothing less than an emperor as far as she was concerned.

A breeze tousled Aadarshini's hair, making her aware of the fragrance of jasmine.

"Sarala, when is *amavasya*?" she diffidently asked on their way back.

"Why, Akka?" replied Sarala. "What's on *amavasya*?"

Aadarshini realized she had already asked the maid about the next night-of-the-moonless-sky several times that morning. She was expecting Rajanna to return by then.

The farmhands were almost done with the harvest back in the banana grove. "That should do for us now," Aadarshini immediately said to Sarala. "Tell them to take the bananas home and put them out on the portico."

She watched them haul up the bananas and followed them at a leisurely pace. Walking down the trail, Aadarshini stopped and savored the sight of the Madhuvana rooftops as they came into view. Four sloping terracotta roofs, one at each corner, surrounded another in the center. Coconut-palms towered high into the sky and swayed mischievously in the wind between the homes. If the gates of Madhuvana were the edge of her universe, this was the center.

"The five homes," she said as she looked at Sarala, "all of them looked the same when I first came here as Rajanna's bride. The portico around the sunken courtyard and its swing, the large rooms, the *tulsi* plant in the center of the courtyard – and then that one, over there…" Aadarshini pointed to a roof in the northeast corner, forgetting that Sarala knew where she lived, "…I was told I would live there with my husband and his two wives. I soon discovered I could go from one home to the other without getting wet in the rain. I had never seen anything like it. What an ideal place to play hide-and-seek, I'd thought. Oh, how I wanted to join the children here. But I had to watch my behavior as a newlywed. And the flower gardens, outhouses, cowsheds, stables, barns! 'Ammamma! I am sure even heaven isn't as splendorous as this,' I told Rajanna."

Once back home, Aadarshini asked Sarala to inform the family about the harvested bananas. She went into the courtyard and smiled at her sister wives Cheluvi and Kalavati who were lounging like a pair of doves on the swing. *Such a matched pair*, she thought. Kalavati's thin and tall frame complemented Cheluvi's diminutive and buxom physique perfectly. Kalavati, in her forties, so full of chatter and Cheluvi, in her fifties, so soft-spoken except when she was arguing with Rajanna.

"Akka, here," she said and playfully tossed them a few bananas.

"Come here, child. Rest a while. You seem to have worked hard this morning," said Kalavati.

Aadarshini didn't mind them addressing her so. When she'd first come to Madhuvana, she had indeed been just a child. An orphan at a young age, she had felt blessed to be a part of Rajanna's bustling household. Overwhelmed by the size of the family, she had asked Kalavati who was who and who lived where within Madhuvana, and had received light-hearted advice that still came in handy.

"Don't waste your time trying to remember names," she'd said. "Rajanna doesn't have siblings, and neither does Cheluvi. Rajanna's parents are no longer alive, and neither are Cheluvi's. Now, *those* would be the names I'd have taught you to remember. I have a brother, Shamanna, but he doesn't live here. Everyone else is some sort of relative - granduncles, grandaunts, uncles, aunts, cousins, nieces, nephews. At first most of them were all Cheluvi's relatives. After I came here, my relatives joined the family. Rajanna is magnanimous like that. Right now, other than us, there are two old widows, one old widower, seven married couples, ten boys and thirteen girls all younger than you and ready for marriage, four unmarried men, twelve cows, twenty buffaloes, fourteen maids, countless farmhands, and who knows how many goats. Just call the older women 'akka', avoid calling the men by their names, and make up names for the rest, as I have learnt to do."

"What about our husband's relatives?"

"His family died a long time ago in the plague. He doesn't have any other relatives," explained Kalavati.

"I don't either," Aadarshini had said.

Aadarshini chuckled as she recalled Cheluvi, who looked elfin alongside the towering Rajanna, reprimanding Rajanna for having taken a third wife, that too one so young.

"What made you do this? She is just a child, you old fool," her silver hair fluttering in the wind as she taunted him. "Look at her, she still has breasts the size of lemons."

The young Aadarshini had later asked Cheluvi if it was wrong of her to have lemon-sized breasts. Cheluvi had laughed and embraced her.

"Don't worry, child. Mine were once smaller than yours. Look at them now," she'd laughed and had pointed at hers, big relative to her stature and, as Aadarshini would find out later, ogled by one and all.

Both Cheluvi and Kalavati, despite being decades older than her, had taken her under their wings and mentored her through puberty, sexual awakening, childbirth, and the odd ways of the household. The two of them had borne three daughters each, all of whom were married and had moved far away. Rajanna, at sixty, had taken her as his third wife in hope of a son. Aadarshini had expected her sister-wives to be mean to her, undermining her at every step, as she'd been warned by the widows at Navagiri. But no, they had doted on her and been happy that she was providing Rajanna with the excitement they feared they no longer could. And when at fourteen she had delivered Raghu, Madhuvana at last had an heir. Cheluvi and Kalavati had danced around her, which deepened her love for them.

"Unusually vivacious today, our Aadarshini, smelling of jasmine and so perky," noted Cheluvi. "What's the matter?"

"I went all the way up to the gate," replied Aadarshini. "It felt so liberating. The three of us should go beyond Maravali sometime by ourselves."

"Yes, yes," said Kalavati, not taking her suggestion seriously. "The next thing you know she will propose we go with her all the way to take a look at the emperor in Vijayanagara."

They all knew that the capital city was a fifteen-day cart-ride away west.

"Maybe someday," said Cheluvi, "after Rajanna is back. He should be returning soon. Come here. Sit with us."

"If he is not back soon, I will go out by myself to the riverside if you two will not come…just wait and see." The two older wives laughed as she joined them on the swing, nestling herself between them. She rested her head on Cheluvi's shoulder, and gently rocked the swing with her feet as Cheluvi massaged her forehead.

Aadarshini's reverie was broken by a boisterous din of boys who had returned from Maravali. They flocked to her, each eager to tell her what he had seen. Among them was Raghu. With his effulgent face, her eight-year-old son stood out despite being the youngest in the group. Momentarily she visualized him as a grown-up: well-built, with a distinguished mustache and with a lion's gait, just like his father.

"My prince has been playing in the dirt too long and needs his mother to clean him," she said to Raghu, pulling him closer and wiping his brow clean with the edge of her sari.

Cheluvi and Kalavati got off the swing and left for the kitchen to supervise the cooks. Aadarshini could hear them yelling out instructions. She rearranged herself to be more comfortable and turned to the boys.

"So," she asked Raghu, "what did you do in Maravali?"

"We played by the tamarind tree, Amma," he replied. "We wanted to play with the *ghoshaka*'s drum but he asked us to wait. He said he would be here soon."

Aadarshini didn't know the *ghoshaka*'s name, or of the other criers who passed through Maravali. For her, they had always been the *ghoshaka* – those who went from village to village, town to town, and announced bulletins on behalf of the emperor and his authorities. *What exciting lives they must lead, the places they must have visited, the people they meet*, she often thought. But dreaming of wandering as the *ghoshaka* did was all she could do. 'Women don't wander,' the widows at the ashram would explain when she would ask to go to places they'd hear about in stories. 'Only men are meant to be adventurers, to go to places far from home.' It remained the same after her wedding too.

Aadarshini shifted her attention to the other boys. "So," she began asking the boys, "What else did the *ghoshaka* say? Is the governor coming to Maravali? Will our temple get a new elephant? Will the evil *Turka* kings invade us? Will our emperor invade them? Did Vijayanagara get enough rain? When is the next cattle fair? Is the *nātakā* troupe coming by any time soon?"

The boys, delighted at receiving her attention, spontaneously put on a show.

"Hear! Hear! O' residents of Maravali, loyal subjects of the mighty empire of Vijayanagara whose lord and master...," Raghu mimicked the *ghoshaka* just as Aadarshini had earlier. She let out a laugh.

The boys then began to jostle each other to impress her.

"Listen, citizens! The governor will come to Maravali on the next full moon on his new elephant," said one boy.

"Be warned! It will appear as if an elephant is riding another elephant," added another. Aadarshini giggled and patted the boy's behind in mock reprimand.

"Those who mock the governor will have to marry his one-legged daughter," yelped another.

Aadarshini squeezed each boy's cheek in appreciation, causing them to blush. She asked Sarala to fetch a bowl of tamarind as a reward for their performance.

"Only one each," she said.

"When will the *ghoshaka* be here, Amma?" a restive Raghu asked her.

For as long as Aadarshini could remember, the *ghoshakas* who came to Maravali always stopped by to pay respects to Rajanna.

"Soon," she promised him and got off the swing. "Why don't you go play outside and let me know when he arrives?"

Later, closer to lunch, Aadarshini heard the boys shout joyously.

She hurried out to the portico to see the *ghoshaka* being followed by the boys dancing behind him. He had been coming here for years. A small fellow about her age, wiry, with a turban on at all times, the unfurled end of which he'd use to wipe off sweat and blow away flies. His clothes, Aadarshini noted, were dusty as always.

"Come, *ghoshaka*," she said. "You must be tired."

She then gestured to Sarala who brought him a pitcher of water.

"You look thinner than when I last saw you, *ghoshaka*. Has your wife not been feeding you?" she asked, making him blush.

"What wife, Akka?" the man replied. "I barely see her for a few days when I go home. I am away for so long. I owe it to the generosity of people like you to stay healthy and well fed when I am travelling."

The *ghoshaka* had already relinquished control of his drum to the boys. A dozen shrill voices now argued about who would first get to beat the drum. Their racket made her cover her ears.

"I heard your drum earlier," Aadarshini said. "It sounded so benign, like distant thunder."

The *ghoshaka* beamed.

She watched as he poured water into his mouth, taking care not to let the pitcher touch his lips. He then splashed it on his face and dried it with his turban.

"I see the skies over Madhuvana are clear as always. No clouds. No thunder. Just enough rain," he said, reciprocating Aadarshini's compliment.

"Yes, indeed. It's the grace of God," she said. "These are tranquil times at Madhuvana."

The crier peeked behind her into the courtyard.

"No, Rajanna is not here now," said Aadarshini. "He is away. But the others are all here. They will summon you after they have eaten."

She asked the *ghoshaka* if he had eaten.

"Yes, I ate at Prabhakara Swami's home. He too is away from Maravali, but his wife made sure I ate well. They are kind people, like all of you here."

She knew that the priest insisted weary travelers who stopped by the temple not leave without dining at the temple, or at his home. This was a Maravali tradition. Though Rajanna was friendly with Prabhakara Swami and the two men often indulged in long conversations, Aadarshini's interactions with him were limited to mostly superficial exchanges at the temple when he would ask if all was well at Madhuvana and she would nod and attribute it to the grace of the gods, just as her sister wives had taught her to. It was not lost on her that the handsome priest was enamored with her ankles, for he'd often stare at them in a manner that made her uneasy.

"You may rest here then," she said to the *ghoshaka*. "I will let you know when the men are ready for you."

Aadarshini rushed back in and asked Sarala to place two dozen banana leaves along two rows on the portico floor, enough to accommodate the first batch of lunchtime diners. The women would eat after the men.

After the men had eaten, Aadarshini asked the *ghoshaka* to come into the courtyard where the family conducted business with outsiders. In the center was a large *homa* pit where the family proffered rituals to a consecrated fire. The enormity of the pit, so wide and deep that if one fell in they would need a helping hand to clamber out, both impressed and terrified Aadarshini.

"Be careful. Don't fall in," she jested with the *ghoshaka* and left the courtyard to the men.

Though she sometimes eavesdropped, Aadarshini usually found the crier's bulletins boring, mostly of interest to men. They were usually about new levies, upcoming visits from provincial officials, royal births and deaths, plague advisories, and such. Then, whispering, he'd share rumors about the succession struggle at the capital, hearsay he had picked during his meanderings. Aadarshini had often overheard Rajanna and others talk about the rebellion, but had never cared to know more. Such matters didn't affect her. She and the other women of Madhuvana wanted to hear not about politics or rebels or succession struggles but of gossip about strangers from far away, strangers they would never meet but in whose lives they got invested. Aadarshini hurried back into the kitchen to pack *akki-rotti* and mango pickle for the *ghoshaka*. She knew how much he appreciated this kindness and showed it in various ways, like letting the children play with his drum.

Before long, Aadarshini could hear the laughter of women from the courtyard.

"Wait for me. I'll be right there. I don't want to miss a word," she shouted from the kitchen and rushed out. The men had left. A dozen women, both old and young, were now sitting around the *ghoshaka*.

Cheluvi and Kalavati were absent from the courtyard. Aadarshini assumed they had gone to rest in the quiet of the *zenana*, a concept she was not familiar with till she came to Madhuvana. Not normally a part of the culture in these parts, she found it fascinating. Rajanna, impressed with the homes of his Mohammedan friends from the north, had long ago decreed that the southwest section would be set aside exclusively for women and children, where even he was expected to announce his presence before entering. It was a private place for women, a place to rest and be with other women, and to get away from the men. *Ze-naa-naa*! Aadarshini liked the way the word rolled off her tongue.

"Are we going to wait for Cheluvi and Kalavati? Where are they?" one of the younger women asked.

Aadarshini smiled. She knew where the two were, and what they might be up to. She had known since when she'd been Rajanna's wife for less than a year. On a monsoon afternoon, she had followed a kitten into a room in the *zenana*. The door was slightly ajar, enough for the kitten to sneak in. She was about to go in too when she noticed Cheluvi and Kalavati, both oblivious of her presence, in a far corner, naked, and in each other's arms. They had smeared the pulp of a ripe mango over each other. She had watched with bated breath as they held each other. Then, embarrassed at invading their privacy and shocked at what she had witnessed, she had backed out and stood in the rain before sinking to the ground, trying to make sense of the feelings now stirring within her, her heart pounding. Now, nine years later, her innocence having deserted her a long time ago, Aadarshini too had on occasion sensed such feelings.

"No," she told the women, "we will not wait for them. They are tired and need to rest." She turned to the *ghoshaka*. "So, *ghoshaka*, what juicy news do you bring us this time? Tell us."

As expected, the women had their questions ready.

"Did the temple priest of Sharapura find out who ran away with his wife?"

"Did they find a groom for the mad daughter of the headman of Choomala?"

"Is it true that women in the northern lands don't cover their breasts?"

As always, the *ghoshaka* did not disappoint. *Yes, she had run away with the priest's brother; yes, her own maternal uncle has agreed to marry her; some of them do, some don't.* By the time the *ghoshaka* had answered all the questions and was ready to leave, the waning half-moon was visible in the early evening sky. Aadarshini asked the boys to return the man's drum. Cheluvi and Kalavati came out to the courtyard, and the three wives saw the *ghoshaka* off at the front door.

"It is *Krishna Janmashtami* tomorrow," noted Aadarshini. "The coming days will be full of chaos among the *nakshatras*...so I've been told."

Tales about the chaos of the planets following the celebration of Lord Krishna's birth were legendary in Maravali.

"Yes, indeed," said Kalavati. "It's difficult to travel in the rains. Journeys like this are not good for Rajanna at this age. With the unrest around Vijayanagara, it's not safe for him to be away from here for so long."

"With Azam Khan by his side, no harm can come to him. That boy will protect Rajanna with his life," Cheluvi reassured her. "Come. Let's go back in."

The mention of Rajanna's trusted bodyguard caused a quiver to run through Aadarshini, for she alone knew he was not by Rajanna's side.

Aadarshini had been struck by Azam Khan's fair skin, towering height, and green eyes unlike the other men in Maravali the first time she saw him. She was just twelve then. At the time he was thirty-two. Rajanna explained that Azam Khan's ancestors had come from a land far away where people looked different. She hadn't understood what that meant, for any place beyond the tamarind trees at the edge of Maravali seemed far away. Whenever she accompanied Rajanna into the village or on walks by the riverside Azam Khan followed them, alert, and ready to assist. She never spoke directly to him, but always asked Sarala to convey her instructions. He had treated Aadarshini with deference too, rarely making eye contact, walking a fair distance behind them, never transgressing the boundaries of propriety.

But all that had changed one afternoon three *amavasyas* ago, just after Rajanna had left on his journey. Aadarshini had gone into the plantation by herself, walking along a trail when she had come upon Azam Khan napping in the sun at a secluded clearing. She watched him silently from behind a jasmine bush. Sweat glistened on his sunburned skin like dewdrops. A gem-encrusted dagger in its bejeweled sheath dangled from a belt across his bare chest. Seeing him in Madhuvana had stunned her. She thought Rajanna had taken Azam Khan along. After all, his sole purpose in life was supposed to be protecting Rajanna and being by his side outside the gates of Madhuvana, at his beck and call. Inside Madhuvana, Rajanna did not need a bodyguard or a helper; there were servants and farmhands for that. Besides, Azam Khan, on account of being a Mohammedan, a *Turka*, was not allowed to enter Madhuvana, a Brahmin household steeped in tradition. In all the years she had been here, she had never seen Azam Khan inside its gates. She reasoned that Azam Khan, on account of being as special to Rajanna as a son, must have been granted dispensation to go in and out if circumstances demanded, as long as no one detected his presence. Based on what Rajanna had told her, she knew he could slip in and out of anywhere at will, with stealth being as second nature to him as to a leopard.

Aadarshini couldn't take her eyes off the man. A pit began to form in her stomach, and the helpless attraction she now felt towards him collided fiercely with who she was: a married woman. Amid the chaos in her mind, the words of Cheluvi from a long time ago edged into her conscience.

"When you selflessly care for your husband, your family, and

everyone else you are responsible for – that is love, that is devotion…
and *that* is morality. Everything else is not. Don't feed the feelings you
may have for other men. The gods will never forgive you."

Shuddering, she'd turned to slip away quietly from the plantation
when a mouse being pursued by a mongoose rushed past Aadarshini's
legs, causing her to yelp and dart out of the bushes towards the
clearing. She'd stumbled and landed on him, coming to rest with her
hands on his shoulders and her face on his bare chest. She'd wanted to
apologize and run. But she just could not. She'd stayed, momentarily
paralyzed, her lips on the crescent moon tattoo around his nipple. As
though possessed by an unseen force, she had pulled him against her,
hungry, demanding, and had held the embrace. She could feel his
calloused fingertips moving down her back till he reached to undo the
knot that held her sari in place. The dagger, in its bejeweled sheath,
pressed just below her navel. Something about the dagger excited her.
A bead of sweat trickled down her back to her thigh, arousing fierce
longings she'd never known. And then, struck by a bolt of conscience,
she sprang up, draped herself and hurried away from the scene without
taking another look at him, aware that if discovered, the two would
face dire consequences: for him, death; for her, banishment from her
perfect life at Madhuvana and a lifetime of ostracism.

On her way back to the well to wash herself, she had run into
Cheluvi.

"You smell different," Cheluvi had noted, "like damp grass."

"I stepped on something," she'd replied as she hastened away to
wash off his scent.

Ever since, she'd often wake up feeling exhausted, unable to
ward off the wanton dreams about a man about whom she had never
harbored promiscuous thoughts previously.

Aadarshini looked around her. It had been yet another happy day
at Madhuvana. Her life indeed was perfect, and there was nothing
anybody could do to shatter it. Anxious, she rushed out into the open
to breathe free, dragging Raghu along. She pulled the boy close to
her and prayed.

"Lord Narayana, please continue to keep us in your protection.

Please don't take this away from us. I know the feelings I am having are wrong. I am devoted to Rajanna. I will chant your name a thousand times before I sleep. O Lord Narayana, please bring Rajanna back to us soon."

She turned to go back in when, against the setting sun, she noticed a palanquin coming towards Madhuvana.

Rajanna, she sighed, and rushed in to inform the senior wives.

Because the gods had chosen to thrust him time and again from one uncertain future to another, questions of morality rarely entered Prabhakara Swami's mind. *I will shape my destiny,* he had resolved a long time ago. *I will do what needs to be done to serve the interests of my family and, most importantly, my own. Where is the question of morality here?* So, was it right to have someone killed? *Of course, as long as it was for the right reasons. There is nothing immoral about self-preservation. Even the lowly mouse and the mighty lion know this.*

Prabhakara Swami unfurled the braided *shikha* on the back of his clean-shaven head, and surrendered to the breeze under the shade of a peepul tree. He had much on his mind, and it was quieter here at the temple, a simple stone structure atop a hill a little beyond the village of Jokhandi. It had taken him more than fifteen days to get here, some on foot, some on a cart, and some on a coracle down the river. He'd now been here for a little more than two new moons. He had sent word to his host, an unmarried temple priest named Vasu that he would be coming, but hadn't indicated how long he would stay. He simply didn't know himself. With each passing day, he had become progressively restless as he waited for the message to arrive, a message that would confirm his mission had succeeded. He had deliberately chosen to have it delivered to this invisible *agrahara* of a few hundred people, mostly farmers. No one knew him here. And he had kept to himself. That a stranger appeared here, lingered for an *amavasya* or two at the temple, then left, would be forgotten quickly. He briefly considered giving in to the impatience gnawing away at him and returning to Maravali. But that wouldn't be prudent. What if the target of his planned assassination had survived? What if he was implicated as the puppetmaster? What if the intended victim lay in wait for him in Maravali?

No, he'd just have to wait. It didn't matter how long it took for the message to come to him. It wouldn't be easy, he knew. If all went well, the message would traverse a grid, pass from one runner to another, and eventually make its way to this temple in Jokhandi. Till then, he was here. He had to be more patient.

The priest Vasu shut the temple door for an afternoon break and joined him under the tree. The man had been hospitable and had not pried into why Prabhakara Swami was here.

"So, Soorya," said Vasu, after they had sat in silence for some time. "Where in Vijayanagara are you from?"

Prabhakara Swami chuckled at the fake name he had given the priest.

"Nowhere," he replied abruptly, and continued to stare through the peepul into the clear blue sky, reflecting on his passage from a vapid existence as the son of an impoverished Brahmin priest in Pushpagiri, the *nowhere* he once called home, a nondescript village several *amavasyas* journey east of the capital unmotivated by the endless opportunities the empire afforded, a *nowhere* waiting for *nothing*.

When a plague wiped out Pushpagiri, a then young Prabhakara had watched helplessly, perhaps even with a touch of glee, while the only home he had known till then was expunged from the annals of history. But he alone was spared, and he had to wonder why. *Destiny,* he reasoned, *it was my destiny to survive.* He gave himself a new name, Bhaskara, when a caravan of theatre performers let him travel with them. In exchange for food and shelter, he'd write plays for them and on occasion play bit roles. Weary of a nomadic life, he had walked away from the caravan, ending up in Varnali, a few days from Vijayanagara, where an aged priest took him on as an assistant, occasionally letting him deliver the discourse at the local Vittala temple. One rainy afternoon, when he thought he was alone at the temple and was uninhibitedly rehearsing a fiery patriotic speech which he planned to use in his discourse, he'd heard the uncontrolled coughing fit of a man and had rushed to help him. The man was choking, his face turning ashen and his eyeballs bulging out of his face. Grasping him tightly from behind, he had squeezed the man's abdomen and helped dislodge the betel nuts that were making the man choke.

Veeranna, the man whose life he had saved, was a spymaster in the service of Salkaraju, the *pro tem* emperor. Shortly thereafter the spymaster, ostensibly impressed by the speech he had overheard and in gratitude for being alive, had offered him a commission as the temple priest in a nearby hamlet, which he'd readily accepted. His real job, he soon discovered, was to collate scraps of information faceless couriers would bring him from time to time and develop plausible hypotheses about the burgeoning rebel insurgency. Thus began his exciting métier as an itinerant temple-priest in the service of the emperor's spymaster. He took his orders from intermediaries and rarely met with Veeranna after that first time. Happy with his performance as a reliable provider of insights, his superiors had asked him to move often. With each move he gave himself a new name, each name an epithet for the Sun, the 'light giver'. It was during one of these stints that he had married Jahnavi, a fetching woman whose astrologer-father had prophesied she would one day live in a magnificent palace within an enchanted kingdom. He had guffawed at the man's simplemindedness.

And yet, around two years ago, he'd received orders to move to Maravali, a ten-day journey south of the capital, and a possible hub of activity for mercenaries loyal to Rama Raya. He had arrived at Maravali with a new name, Prabhakara. The honorific 'swami' came when Rajanna, a prominent citizen of Maravali who had arranged a grand welcome for him at Madhuvana, started addressing him thus. He'd gasped as his palanquin entered Madhuvana, for he had never seen anything so enchanting. Almost all of Maravali had gathered to pay the customary obeisance to their new priest. It was then that he first saw Aadarshini. He had stumbled awkwardly the moment he'd laid eyes on the youngest of Rajanna's wives, much in the manner he'd gasped when he'd first laid eyes on Madhuvana. He had to have both. Lusting for another man's possessions was futile, he knew, especially a man as powerful as Rajanna. So he'd been content visiting him often and lingering long, stealing glimpses of Aadarshini, and imbibing Madhuvana's erotic aura.

"Ah yes, *nowhere*! I should know that place. I used to live there," said Vasu with a sneer, and left. Prabhakara Swami wondered if Vasu too was one of Veeranna's many pawns.

After mid-day, Prabhakara Swami got up to stretch his limbs upon hearing a bullock cart halt at the bottom of the hill. A thin man jumped off the cart and huffed up.

"There's no one here. The temple is closed now," Prabhakara Swami told him.

"I am looking for a Soorya. I have a message for him. Do you know where I can find him?"

Prabhakara Swami felt his heart race.

"I am Soorya," he said. He tried to keep his emotions under check. "What is the message?"

"The deed was done," recited the messenger, paused for a moment, then turned back.

"Good," noted Prabhakara Swami with a straight face. "Which way are you going?"

The messenger pointed south.

Prabhakara Swami looked out into the horizon. There was enough daylight left for him to travel until nightfall.

"I'll join you," he said, and followed the messenger down the hill.

On his way out, he stopped at Vasu's to thank his host. No one was home. He picked up his bundle of clothes and his palm-leaf umbrella. The bulls seemed to know where they were going, hardly needing the occasional prod of the messenger who steered them. Prabhakara Swami had to adjust his posture often, alternating his weight from one side to the other. He didn't mind. He was going home.

Azam Khan had felt uneasy ever since he found out Rajanna would travel east to the port city of Masulipatnam without him. Rajanna had impressed upon him that the journey, though long, was routine in nature, and that Pratipa, one of the many men he had at his disposal, would travel with him. Azam Khan hadn't known him, but Rajanna said Pratipa knew the Masulipatnam area well. Instead, he was to stay behind and carry out "an errand of utmost importance".

"Stay invisible…or better still, disappear after I leave. Let people think you are travelling with me," Rajanna told him. "Midway between the second and third new moon from now, reach Honnavara."

Once in the port city of Honnavara, Azam Khan was to go to Dilawar's tavern every evening and linger till everyone had left. Someone would come to him sooner or later and ask him about Rajanna's well-being. Once his identity was confirmed, the man would give him a "priceless" satchel. Azam Khan was to head back to Maravali only after acquiring the package.

"You should return by the third *amavasya*. If I haven't returned by then, go to Sidappa and give him the satchel. Remember, give it to no one but him," Rajanna had emphasized. "In the wrong hands, it could change the course of Vijayanagara history."

The mention of Sidappa was enough to underscore the importance of the mission. Sidappa, Azam Khan's mentor and once Rajanna's bodyguard, had taught him everything he needed to know. Although now aged and blind, Sidappa clandestinely assisted the rebel cause along with his son Venkata and nephew Rudra by giving refuge to rebels in his nondescript village that wasn't marked on any map. He had been guiding Rudra to run and intercept messages across Vijayanagara, a system Sidappa and Rajanna had established over their decades-long association. Sidappa's invisible hamlet was a full day's trek from Maravali, and few people knew the route to it. Azam Khan was one of them. But he hadn't been there in years, and as far as he knew, Rajanna too hadn't visited his old friend in a long time. Sidappa too had last come to Maravali when Raghu was born eight years ago.

Azam Khan knew Rajanna's dealings with Sidappa were now

conducted via Rudra, who lived in Champanhalli, a day's ride from Maravali. In any case, few knew of Rajanna's aid to the rebels in Maravali, where he maintained a low profile and carried out his business away from the village. In Maravali, Rajanna's reputation was that of an elderly intellectual and Madhuvana patriarch who everybody could lean on for advice. Rajanna's support for Rama Raya was ostensibly based on considerations of common geographical moorings and a simple belief that Rama Raya was better for Vijayanagara than Salkaraju. Few in Maravali were privy to Rajanna's commitment to Rama Raya's insurgent cause; it was a clandestine participation. So when Rajanna asked him to go to Honnavara, he knew it was because Rajanna himself couldn't be seen in the port city.

There was something seductive about the morning Azam Khan was to disappear from Maravali. He wanted to enjoy it in solitude before he left the village. He knew just the place. He sneaked into the Madhuvana plantation and came to one of the many secluded clearings he was familiar with. He had dozed off longer than he wanted to, and was startled awake by a woman falling on him, as if she had dropped out of the sky. She knocked the wind out of him. At first he couldn't make out who she was, with her face on his chest. He tried to wiggle out from under her when he felt her grasping him and pulling him towards her, her tongue running around his nipple. He pulled her hair up, and saw it was Aadarshini, his master's wife. A moment's shock gave way to an overpowering feeling of passion, and he had surrendered without much of a struggle. He had hesitantly reached for her sari when she sprang up, as if offended, settled her clothes, and hurried away, leaving him drowning in guilt.

She was just twelve when he had first seen her. He had accompanied Rajanna to a village whose name he couldn't remember, where Rajanna was to take a third wife. There was no wedding entourage, just the two of them. Azam Khan was asked to wait outside the village while Rajanna rode in for the ceremony. After the wedding, a bullock cart festooned in bright colors came rolling out, Rajanna riding alongside on his black stallion. Sitting in the cart was Rajanna's new bride. "This is Azam Khan. He is like a son to me. He serves me and looks after my safety," was how Rajanna had introduced him. She had smiled coyly. Azam Khan had mouthed a silent *namaskara*, his hands folded respectfully. That was ten years ago.

Now he wondered if the sacred covenant he had with Rajanna's family had been soiled. He got up and left the scene, glad he was going away to Honnavara. Rajanna had given his horse to the new bodyguard Pratipa, so Azam Khan would have to make the journey on foot.

Azam Khan set out early. He walked briskly at first, then ambling, before resting and repeating the cycle. All through his walk images of Aadarshini and the smell of jasmine from her hair tormented him. He reached Periyappa's serai around nightfall. The serai hadn't changed much since he had passed through a few years go. He washed up, but didn't bother washing his face. The muck on his face and the dagger dangling from his waist would discourage others from striking up a conversation. There was a group of riders who ferried messages speaking loudly in a corner. Easy targets for brigands otherwise, all messengers spent their evenings drinking in the safety of a serai. Azam Khan remembered when he too had been a messenger-boy like them, running messages for Rajanna and Sidappa along with Rudra. Together, the two protégés ran messages across the empire, staying at unknown serais, facing brigands, and learning how to look danger in the eye and not blink. Now Rudra had taken over the service, while Azam Khan stayed with Rajanna and watched the empire convulse amid the succession struggles at the capital.

Azam Khan paid for the meal in advance, ate alone in a corner, and exited quietly. Outside the serai, the messengers' horses were tied to a banyan tree. Looking at them, his feet began to hurt. It would take him more than ten days to reach Honnavara if he walked. He simply had to steal one. He quietly untied one of the horses, shushing and calming the animal before it could raise an alarm, and began to walk away, the animal following him calmly like a known pet. He was confident the drunken messengers would not notice the missing animal till he was long gone. After he had walked a fair distance from the serai, he climbed up the animal, riding under the light of the crescent moon and enjoying the susurrus of the river next to the path. He'd now reach Honnavara in less than five days.

He smelled the sea well before he reached the port-town, a bustling coastal nerve center for traders of all kinds coming from lands that he had never heard of. The crowds, like ants that crawled around with a specific purpose, seemed unchanged since he had accompanied Rajanna here years ago. At the time, pointing his finger towards all directions, Rajanna had explained to the wide-eyed Azam Khan how goods "from there and there and there" got "to there and there and there."

"People like me, son, make it happen," Rajanna had said.

Rajanna and others like him 'made it happen' by dint of decades of relationships with traders across the land and the support of the rulers of Vijayanagara. Though a rebel now, Rama Raya was once the right-hand man for his father-in-law, the emperor Krishnadeva Raya, and in charge of all influential administrative positions. Rajanna and others like him had prospered under Rama Raya. But Salkaraju's claiming of the regency had forced Rama Raya to oppose the throne, and until the child Sadasiva was found, neither's claim would be validated. Reasoning he could be of more help by supporting the cause as best he could without seeking visibility, Rajanna had remained tight-lipped about his position, which was known only to a few confidants.

"Root judiciously. Never wager everything on one side. Stay unseen. Fortunes shift as the sands in the desert, but you need to prevail regardless of which rooster wins the fight," Rajanna told them.

In Honnavara, Azam Khan spent most of the day away from the bustle. He could see a few ships and several smaller boats lined up on the shore. He knew that most of the ships belonged to Afaqis, Shiite Mohammedans from Persia and Turkey, just as he was the descendant of one such Afaqi too. His grandfather from Persia had been a stowaway on one such ship, and when they had ported on the western coast, he had got off to explore the town. By the time he returned to port, his ship had sailed. Like so many others, he ended up as a laborer in Bijapur where Afaqis wielded influence under the Sultanate. The old man never made it back to his homeland, having died during one of the internecine wars of the times. But in Azam Khan, his descendants had survived the many wars that plagued the region.

He arrived at Dilawar's tavern after dark. There was no telling when his contact would show up. Two torches, one by the door and one on the far wall, struggled to light up the drinking hole. The place reeked of melancholy and cheap liquor. Sailors, all of whom looked like they'd been away from home for too long, sat sulking and drinking. The one next to him began talking about his home in Persia and how much he longed to go back.

"How long have you been away from home?" he asked Azam Khan.

Azam Khan listened attentively. He couldn't comprehend much of what the man was saying in his strange Farsi dialect, but he understood the question. He thought of the place he now called home, Maravali: a place with traditions as old as civilization itself, and unambiguously stratified. Brahmins, the highest of the classes, discharged the sacred duties. The nobles and administrators were next in line. Then came the merchants and traders. At the bottom were the farmhands, artisans, weavers, potters, oil pressers, washermen, barbers, fishermen, and tanners. Then there were those who were beyond this stratification, the lowest of the castes, and the Mohammedans like him, who lived beyond the edge of Maravali, a place simply known as the 'other side'.

"All my life," Azam Khan replied. The sailor returned his sardonic smile with one of his own.

The toddy continued to flow, and the voices began to grow louder. A little while later, an old man with a flowing white beard entered the tavern. Azam Khan watched him crouch in a corner and adjust the frets on his lute. Then he commenced a prolonged wail and began playing a tune that made his audience break into applause. Azam Khan knew of the wandering minstrel tradition of his ancestors. He was not familiar with the songs the minstrel sang, but based on what the newly befriended sailor told him, the minstrel seemed to sing about beautiful women, citrus groves, scented breeze, and love.

"Of all the lands, mine is the undoubtedly the best," the minstrel sang. Azam Khan watched hardened sailors break out in tears. Then one by one, they dropped some coins in front of him and stumbled out the tavern. The minstrel kept singing till most of the drunken sailors had left. He then packed his lute and nodded at Azam Khan on his way out.

"It's late," he said. "Go home."

Azam Khan looked into his mug without giving him much thought. Someone tapped on his shoulder. He turned around.

"So how is the old coot Rajanna? Still soaring?" the man said emotionlessly, a voice that was much unlike the melodious singer's.

Azam Khan had killed men who were far less insolent about his master. But he knew the man's question was part of the protocol.

"Who lives forever, friend? But *inshallah* he will," he responded, as he was supposed to.

The man smiled and handed him a satchel. Azam Khan noticed the wax-sealed black ribbon that ran around. It was meant to be opened only by Rajanna. *No wonder he didn't trust this errand to anyone else.*

"Go with God," the man said and walked out.

Azam Khan waited for a bit, then walked to the shore. A strange feeling of longing had invaded him ever since he heard the minstrel. He rested against a boulder and listened to the sea all night. *Sounds from home*, he thought, as his mind conjured up endless expanses of cherry blossoms and date palms.

He began his ride back to Maravali the next morning, anxious, even fearful of what he would do when he faced Rajanna or Aadarshini. He resolved to fall at Rajanna's feet and confess, accept whatever punishment his master would hand him. But a niggling feeling ate away at his insides. The pounding in his heart grew louder as he neared Maravali.

Something is wrong, he thought as he kept riding. *Something is wrong with Rajanna. I can feel it.*

2

WHY DO YOU STILL FLUTTER?
Aadarshini asked her left eyelid as she ran in to tell Cheluvi and
Kalavati that Rajanna was back.

"Are you sure it is him?" they asked.

"It's Rajanna. It must be," she replied. "Who else would come to
Madhuvana in a palanquin at this time?"

Besides Rajanna, only two other people in Maravali used a
palanquin to get around. There was no reason for Prabhakara Swami
to visit when Rajanna was out of town. And Chandrabhanu, the head
of the village council and the man responsible for maintaining law
and order, never came without sending word.

She saw Srikanta, Cheluvi's nephew, rushing out to the front door
to greet Rajanna, Sarala behind him. Aadarshini hurriedly rearranged
her sari. She reached behind her back and parted her hair, letting it
hang over her right breast. She felt the *kumkuma* on her forehead to
make sure it was centered, then took a deep breath and waited in the
portico with Cheluvi and Kalavati.

Sarala came running in, babbling unintelligibly.

"Akka, a holy man is here! Akka...Anna...Anna is gone."

Aadarshini saw Cheluvi and Kalavati bolt towards the front door.
She shook Sarala with both hands to snap her out of her hysteria.

"What are you talking about, girl? What holy man? Who has gone where?"

Rather than conjecture, she rushed out too.

Outside the front door, Prabhakara Swami's apprentice-priest Giridhara stood by the palanquin, his expression somber. Cheluvi and Kalavati were sprinkling water on Srikanta who had collapsed.

"He said something to Srikanta Anna," Pandu, a farmhand, told Aadarshini, pointing at Giridhara, "Anna then fell to the ground. I rushed to get water."

Aadarshini invited Giridhara to come inside, but he refused.

"It is proper that I stay outside, Akka," he stammered. "I have just conveyed inauspicious news."

As Srikanta regained his senses, Aadarshini asked him, "What inauspicious news, Srikanta?"

She waited as Srikanta composed himself. He was trembling now.

"We have been orphaned. Rajanna has left us. Giridhara says he has passed away in some village called Loconda. His last rites were performed by local Brahmins."

Cheluvi slumped to the ground. "How does he know this?" Kalavati asked with a shock in her voice.

"A messenger…"

"A messenger?" shrieked Cheluvi. "Why? Why hasn't Azam Khan brought us this news? Wasn't he with Rajanna? How can we trust a messenger?"

Aadarshini was speechless. She knew why Azam Khan hadn't brought them the news. *He wasn't with Rajanna.*

"Where is the messenger?" a distraught Kalavati yelled at Srikanta. "Let us find the man. We must speak to him directly."

Giridhara slowly said the messenger had left Maravali.

"You imbecile," Cheluvi began to scold Giridhara, "This is Rajanna we are talking about, not some ordinary person. You shouldn't have let the messenger leave."

"Yes…I realize that now," Giridhara appeared apologetic. He was stammering again. "I was at the temple. I…I was traumatized when I heard the message. I couldn't ask him. The man came to Prabhakara

Swami's home… Jahnavi Akka sent for me. He didn't stay long. I got myself together then hurried here."

They all knew that messengers always brought messages straight to the temple, handed them to Prabhakara Swami or Giridhara, occasionally ate a hot meal, and moved on. They never lingered.

Aadarshini told a distraught Cheluvi there was no point in further badgering Giridhara. Kalavati had cradled Cheluvi in her arms. Both were sobbing. Aadarshini, her heart throbbing, mouth dry, watched as Giridhara walked to the palanquin and returned with a wooden box that he held reverently with both hands. Before she could ask him, Giridhara handed the box to Srikanta.

"The messenger…he brought this with him. Before he passed away, Rajanna had apparently asked that these be sent here."

Srikanta opened the box. "Rajanna's turban, his silk tunic, his eight rings, his gold necklace…" He stopped abruptly without going through the rest, and broke into tears.

"These are indeed his," he handed the box to Aadarshini.

Aadarshini quickly looked through the box. All this while she had wanted to challenge the premise that the dead man was Rajanna, but that didn't seem necessary now. The personal effects were all Rajanna's. Cheluvi didn't bother looking into the box, neither did Kalavati.

Aadarshini heard Giridhara tell Srikanta, "I wish Prabhakara Swami was here to give your family guidance at this time of grief. Alas, he is away, but he is expected back any day. It is now up to the elders to provide direction about the rituals to be performed by Rajanna's widows. I am sure they know what they have to do. Please summon me as needed. I am at your service."

Aadarshini felt her chest throb. She staggered back inside, collapsing twice before she reached the courtyard as she thought of what was to follow. She had grown up among Brahmin widows and was aware that they lived a life of severe austerity and self-denial. Widows in Madhuvana too spent most of their time in the *zenana* watching over children or in prayer. Inside, she ran into Lakshamma, one of the oldest women living in Madhuvana, and a widow. Aadarshini expected her to break down upon hearing of Rajanna's demise, but she was remarkably composed, and ran her hand over Aadarshini's head sympathetically. Aadarshini suggested that Lakshamma gather the children of the household, including Raghu, and take them to the *zenana*.

"Better that they are away from here."

Back in the courtyard, Aadarshini saw Cheluvi banging her head against a pillar on the portico. "O Ishvara, O Krishna, O Rama," Cheluvi shouted incoherently, exhorting the gods to take her away too. Kalavati had fallen to the floor and was pulling at her hair, wailing "Ayyo" over and over.

Other women from the family, and maids and female farmhands, trickled into the courtyard. They too began to wail. Aadarshini held back her tears. Her thoughts kept returning to the 'rituals to be performed by Rajanna's widows'. She had asked Cheluvi and Kalavati about rituals after death, but they had always said there would be plenty of time for her to learn about such things. Overcome more by uncertainty than grief, Aadarshini too began to sob. Cheluvi stepped away toward the outhouse. Aadarshini followed her.

"Akka, you have taught me much about the ways of the world. Our husband is dead, and we are widows. But what is to happen next? What rituals was Giridhara alluding to?" she demanded.

"What can I say, child?' Cheluvi explained. "We are a cultured family with reasonable traditions, unlike some where the duty of the wife to her husband is deemed to continue even in the afterlife."

Aadarshini knew she was talking about *sati*. A neighboring woman back in her childhood had to undergo the ritual when her husband had died away from home. His widow, powerless to thwart tradition, was forced into a fiery death. A cremation pit was dug near the riverbank. A platform of sandalwood was laid out in the pit. The widow, alive but sedated into unconsciousness, was laid on the platform and covered with more sandalwood. When the fire was lit, a live woman turned to ashes, which were collected the following day and immersed in the river. The men who presided over the ceremony then performed several purification rituals to ensure a smooth journey for the departed souls. Aadarshini, just ten, had listened in horror as the women at the ashram recounted the episode. "Couldn't the men in the family stop it?" she had asked, only for a bitter old woman to caustically reply, "Men? Who do you think establishes these practices, dear?"

Aadarshini, still standing by the outhouse, held a blank stare. Kalavati joined the two.

"There are several options open to us widows," Cheluvi said, "but it's our beloved Rajanna's wishes that are paramount. And I have no idea what they were. Now, isn't that strange?"

"Do you think he would want *sati* for us?" Aadarshini asked.

"I don't think he would," asserted Kalavati. "Why, even now we have widows living among us in Madhuvana, like old Lakshamma. Poor woman, she was widowed when she was just eleven. Her husband died young of a snake bite when he was defecating in the woods. Rajanna had stepped in and decreed that the family would care for her. Our traditions are most reasonable, and he was a man of reason. You, my dear, you have his young son to care for. He would not have disregarded that."

Aadarshini broke down and couldn't hold back her tears. She knew the men were now in conference, discussing the rituals that the three of them had to perform. The courtyard slowly emptied out. The children were brought back to their mothers. Cheluvi and Kalavati went back to Cheluvi's room. Aadarshini had to get her mind off the proceedings of the evening. She began preparing a meal for Raghu.

"Amma," the boy asked, "why is everyone crying?"

Aadarshini didn't reply.

"When is Appa coming back, Amma?" Raghu pressed her.

"He has travelled far away, Raghu," she replied, struggling to keep the poise in her voice. "The rains have been severe where he has gone. The rivers are flooded and difficult to cross. We must be patient. Don't believe what anyone tells you about Appa. You are his son. Be brave like him. Never let anyone see you cry. He will be back when he can," she said, holding back her tears as best she could.

Aadarshini could hear Sarala sobbing outside the kitchen. "Go home, girl," she told her. "We've had a long day. Oh, how it started out, and how it has ended. Come back tomorrow. Go back home before the sun sets."

Sarala and others like her who tended the fields or worked in homes lived in thatched huts spread across the plantation, away from Madhuvana. Aadarshini was aware that Sarala's home was across a stream on the edge of Madhuvana, but she didn't know exactly where. She had never been to her home.

Back in her room, she blew out the lamp by her mattress and lay beside Raghu. Sobbing intermittently, she told him a story from the *Ramayana*, about the exploits of the protagonist Rama. Then she sang him a lullaby, one she had sung for him since he was born:

> *Sleep well, my Rama, sleep well.*
> *You are the delight of your father, my Rama*
> *You are the joy of your mother, my Rama*
> *You are the scion of our race, my Rama*
> *You are the pride of our people, my Rama*
> *You will soon wear the crown, my Rama*
> *If misfortune befalls you, my Rama*
> *Your mother will always protect you, my Rama*
> *Sleep well, my Rama, sleep well.*

The soothing monotony of the melody never failed to achieve its purpose. The boy was soon fast asleep.

Aadarshini could not sleep. Her head hurt. She thought of Azam Khan. She was surprised, even a little disturbed, that despite her state of mind she could still recall his naked body, his scent, his taste.

"Ammaaaaa ...," Raghu called out in his sleep often that night, and as many times, she patted him back to sleep.

"Narayana! Please guide me. I must raise him to be like his father and rule Madhuvana well," she prayed through a sleepless night.

The next morning, Aadarshini came back into the portico after leaving Raghu in the *zenana* with the other children. Six men were whispering amongst themselves. They were the oldest men in

Rajanna's extended family and usually arbitrated, along with him, sensitive family matters. Outsiders were not privy to these discussions. There were no other women in the courtyard except the three wives. The servants had been asked to leave lest they eavesdropped and spread half-cooked truths. Aadarshini shut her eyes and chanted, *I am in your refuge O Narayana!* Cheluvi and Kalavati held each other, their hands trembling. Aadarshini fidgeted as she listened to the toothless Thatha Kanteeravaa, the oldest among them, who explained in a barely audible but compassionate voice that the advice he was going to deliver was a consensus arrived at after a sleepless night of deliberation.

"I had personal knowledge of Rajanna's wishes, for he had shared it with me on more than one occasion. This edict is in the interest of the eternal well-being of the Madhuvana family. It is sanctioned both by tradition and by scriptures. And it is binding," said Kanteeravaa.

"In the interest of our family's standing in the community," he continued, "everything we say here will be confidential and will not be shared outside Madhuvana. News of Rajanna's death will undoubtedly have spread across Maravali by now. The villagers will come to pay respects. They will be respectfully turned away at the gate. We must be discrete. Our traditions are our business."

Aadarshini's heart began to beat erratically.

"For in our culture, tradition is paramount. Without this, we are not any better than ..."

Aadarshini lost patience.

"Thatha," she pleaded. "Here we are, Rajanna's widows, waiting to find out if you will turn out to be a messenger of death or an angel of mercy, and you are going on about the virtues of tradition. Pray tell us what we have come here to hear. We can talk of tradition sometime else."

Aadarshini was surprised that the old man was not agitated by her impertinence and quickly pivoted to the matter at hand.

"Two days from now, dearest Cheluvi, being the eldest, you will perform *sati* to honor your late husband's wishes," he said.

Before Cheluvi could react, he added, "Dear Kalavati, you will follow the day after that."

Aadarshini felt a flash of disgust. Her tresses fluttered in a gush of wind that swept through the courtyard. She couldn't hold back her anger at the six men who sat in judgment as if they were a royal council of ministers. She roared at them, "You insensitive men, how dare you shamelessly pronounce such a vile decree? This is not some stranger Rajanna wed and brought to Madhuvana. This is Cheluvi. She was born here, in this very Madhuvana. This is *her* home. Rajanna ruled here only by her father's grace. Will you allow Rajanna to dictate from the heavens what she can and cannot do here? How dare you doom her like this?"

Madhuvana was indeed the ancestral property of Shivanna, Cheluvi's father. Cheluvi being Shivanna's only daughter, her father wanted a *mané aliya*, a son-in-law who'd live at his wife's home. A suitable Brahmin *mané aliya* was not easy to come by, and when the family finally identified Rajanna as a prospective groom, it was agreed that Rajanna would inherit all of Shivanna's property as dowry. While Cheluvi, just eight when she married Rajanna, was playing with her dolls, Rajanna learned Shivanna's business and grew to be an able son-in-law. When Shivanna died, Rajanna was installed as the head of the household and he gave Shivanna's estate a new name, Madhuvana.

Aadarshini continued to rant, not caring about any disrespect towards the men. "And how much Kalavati has cared for all of us, in good times and bad..."

Cheluvi and Kalavati looked at each other and held hands. They looked stunned. Clearly, they had not expected this.

Kanteeravaa, who seemed to have ignored Aadarshini's rant, addressed her next without missing a beat. "After that, my child, the honor is yours. I want to assure you that your son Raghu's future is secure. He will be raised by us under Prabhakara Swami's tutelage. He will grow up to be a scholar. Someday, when he comes of age, he will take Rajanna's place."

Aadarshini struggled to stand. Her world had come crashing down on her. Stunned, she now began to plead with Kanteeravaa.

"Thatha, what if what you know of my husband's wishes for us is outdated? How long ago did he tell you? Maybe his views changed after Raghu was born. We all know Rajanna was close to Prabhakara Swami. Maybe he shared his new views with the priest. Why should we rush? Shouldn't we wait for him to return to Maravali and seek his counsel? And why continue a cruel tradition? Widows already live among us in Madhuvana. Their husbands didn't decree *sati*. Why would Rajanna do so?"

Kanteeravaa and the men talked among themselves, then addressed the widows, "Aadarshini's request is reasonable and not contrary to any tradition. We will wait and see if Prabhakara Swami knew of Rajanna's views on this matter. We will wait for his return. I will then send someone to consult with him."

"No, I must go and plead with him personally," demanded Aadarshini. *I will seduce him if I need to*, she resolved, surprising even herself.

"Child, you know that Prabhakara Swami cannot meet anyone from Madhuvana till the purification rituals are complete and these homes are sanctified again. So you cannot go there. We will send an intermediary of your choice," Kanteeravaa proclaimed.

Aadarshini held back her urge to strangle him. She turned to the other men who began gazing into the ground, none able to look her in the eye. "What is the matter with you? What have we done to deserve such coldblooded treatment? Would you let your daughters go through this horror? Can't you make a reasonable decision instead of blindly following tradition? Shame on you! Cowards! Eunuchs! The wrath of God will breathe down on you."

Aadarshini realized she had exhausted her coherence. She collapsed to the floor with her face buried between her knees. She could hear the men mumbling among themselves.

"Poor girl, she is delirious."

"A demon has entered her."

"A husband's death can do strange things to a woman."

"Our ancestors were not fools. They devised sati for a good reason."

"It will be over soon. She will find peace."

"No! No! No!" Aadarshini kept shouting over and over as her sister-wives cradled her in their arms.

"Oh Rajanna, whatever have you done?" Cheluvi cried.

"No. It is not his doing," Kalavati said to Cheluvi. "It is our karma. It is our fate."

Aadarshini rested her head on Cheluvi's lap and thought of Rajanna's advice, one he'd give her often.

"Reason with people," he would say.

"And what if they don't listen?" Aadarshini would ask. "What if the stars wish it to be so?"

"Then you do what you have to do. The stars will adjust themselves."

3

"SO, GOURI," SAID AADARSHINI, "this seems to be the end of the road for your Aadarshini."

It was a little past sunrise, and she was in the cowshed milking her bovine confidant Gouri, who she had helped birth a few years ago. Aadarshini liked it here, a private refuge where she could pour her heart out to Gouri, Lakshmi, and Amba, cows all named after goddesses, and excellent at keeping secrets. She had told them about her encounter with Azam Khan, about Cheluvi and Kalavati being lovers, and a lot more. And now she told them about the parting gift Rajanna had left his wives.

"Look," she said, barely able to hold back her sobs, and showed Gouri her bare wrists and ankles and pointed at the drab yellow-ochre sari she now wore as a sign of her widowhood.

The night before, Cheluvi and Kalavati had explained to Aadarshini that since Rajanna had left for *swargaloka*, their days of indulging in the many pleasures they were accustomed to were over. With much sensitivity, they took off her silver anklets, her gold bangles, her silver sash that always hugged her slim waist, the emerald stud on her nose, her diamond earrings, her toe ring, and finally the *mangalasootra* Rajanna had tied around her neck during their wedding. The *kumkuma* on her forehead and the kohl around her eyes were wiped clean; her hair was washed till it stopped smelling of jasmine. Cheluvi then handed her a few tamarinds, a *laadoo*, and a few ripe mangoes, all Aadarshini's favorites.

"Eat them tonight when you are by yourself," Cheluvi had said.

"Here," she said as she gave the cows the mangoes she had brought with her. "I saved them for you."

She let them slurp the fruit off her hands.

"They say I can no longer eat my favorite foods, that they stimulate desire, that desire is no longer suitable for me. Have you heard anything so absurd?"

She thought of Azam Khan. *I wonder if he knows about Rajanna's death.*

Aadarshini moved on to milk Amba, then Lakshmi, but kept talking to Gouri.

"What else can I do now, Gouri? Run away? Where would I go? With whom would I go? And how would I take Raghu with me?"

She looked up at the roof and prayed.

"O Narayana, please bring Prabhakara Swami home."

She turned back to Gouri.

"What if he isn't back in time, you ask?" she said. "I don't know, Gouri. I simply don't know. But I will think of something. I must."

Back inside, she ran into Sarala. Aadarshini, who normally distributed the fresh milk herself, asked Sarala to do it. The maid stared at her, struggling to digest her mistress's new look.

"What have they done to you, Akka?" She turned away and left, sobbing.

Aadarshini was in her room when the maid returned to her. Raghu was still fast asleep.

"Don't go around weeping, girl. This is our tradition. You've seen this before, even among your people. My days of being a temple goddess are over."

She retrieved the silver anklets she had taken off the previous night.

"Here, let me give you something." She handed Sarala the anklets. "I have no use for these now. They are yours. Go ahead, put them on."

Sarala refused at first, but Aadarshini persisted.

"There, how nice it looks on you. I have plainer ones too, made of cowry shells, from when I was a child. I will find those for you."

Sarala took off the anklets.

"Does he know the truth yet, Akka?" asked Sarala, pointing at Raghu.

Aadarshini shook her head.

"Not yet. It's not easy telling children about death. What have you heard outside, Sarala?"

"Everyone in Maravali knows, Akka," said Sarala. "They gathered at the temple and prayed for Anna's soul. They are worried about the three of you. Some women came to see you but they were turned away at the gate."

It appeared that no one, not even Sarala, knew about the decision of *sati*. No one inside Madhuvana seemed to be talking about it. Rather, Aadarshini was surprised at how quickly things had returned to normal. The men had already gone off to the fields, while the women got busy in the kitchen. Farmhands and maids went about their duties. Gossip and naughty talk, albeit hushed, could be heard in courtyards. Most of the family avoided long interactions with the three widows, and when they did, they didn't look them in the eye. Someone would bring them bland insipid food several times a day. They'd talk to them from outside the threshold, say a few words of sympathy, then go away. Lakshamma had dropped by several times to reassure Aadarshini that Prabhakara Swami would return in time to rescind the sati decree.

Later, Aadarshini asked Sarala why she wore a scowl.

"All two-faced, these women," she said. "They talk sweetly to you, Akka, but many have already asked me what you and the other wives plan to do with your jewelry."

"And why should that make you sour, girl? Tell them I plan to watch them fight over it. So will Rajanna ...from up there." Aadarshini pointed at the sky, causing Sarala to smile.

"Good, you are smiling again," said Aadarshini. "If they ask again, tell them I will have it in safekeeping for Raghu's bride. Now go, don't pay attention to idle gossip."

Sarala seemed satisfied.

"Don't worry, Akka. I will be here…to serve you and Raghu."

Aadarshini stepped out into the plantation with Raghu. She planned to tell him the truth about his father. As she sat in the shade of a palm and watched Raghu play with other boys, she could hear them talking.

"Where is your father, Raghu?" a boy asked him. "They say he went away."

Aadarshini knew the older boys were aware Yama, the God of Death, had visited the family.

"I don't know," replied Raghu.

"Then let me tell you," said another boy, a few years older. "Rajanna has gone to bring Yama. They will come back together on Yama's buffalo. Then they will take you and your mother and your other mothers with them to heaven. You will all live happily together."

"There will be more than one buffalo, of course," assured one mischievous boy. "All of you cannot possibly fit on the back of one buffalo."

Aadarshini, seeing Raghu was about to cry, resisted the urge to scold the boys. She grabbed Raghu and took him back inside.

"Don't listen to them, Raghu. We are not going anywhere on a buffalo. Who travels on buffaloes these days?" she said. "Your father will return soon, I assure you." This was not the time to tell him about Rajanna's death.

Inside the kitchen, she began rearranging items in the larder to get her mind off her anxiety. She came upon three ceramic vials she didn't remember seeing earlier. She showed the vials to Cheluvi and Kalavati.

"This must be what we will drink before we…you know," explained Cheluvi. "It will make us sleep. When we wake up, we will be ash." She began to laugh maniacally.

"I wonder who put the vials there," said Kalavati. "Have they presumed Prabhakara Swami will not be back in time?"

"They must have. And they have already started preparing for the inevitable. I will throw these away."

"No. What good would that do? They'd just replace them. Keep it back where you found them," ordered Cheluvi. "We will all be brave, as we have always been. What is in these vials will make it easy."

Aadarshini couldn't resist smelling the vial. She popped open the stopper and took a cautious sniff. It had the scent of fresh rose, but then went straight up her nostrils and made her cough. She wondered how this harmless liquid with its sweet and pungent scent could do what it was meant to do.

As she drifted into sleep that night, she dreamt of Azam Khan.

Anxiety gripped Azam Khan throughout his ride back. He tried in vain to dismiss the thought that Rajanna was in trouble. The man had taught him not to speculate, but that lesson was not coming in handy right now. *Pull yourself together, Azam Khan*, he admonished himself, *and if something is not right, deal with it then.*

"This is as far as we travel together, my friend," Azam Khan told the horse he had helped himself to just days ago, gently caressing the horse before letting it free in an open field outside of Maravali. *Inshallah, you will find a home soon*. He had never considered taking the horse back home. The sight of him marching into town with a strange horse would have set tongues wagging. He also didn't want to be branded a horse thief. As Rajanna's bodyguard, Azam Khan valued his reputation.

As he sighted boys playing around the tamarind tree on the other side of Maravali, Azam Khan smiled to be home. The butcher's boy came up the trail, and he assumed the boy wanted to welcome him home.

"Azam Khan," the boy instead said. "Go home. There is bad news."

Azam Khan asked the boy to repeat himself.

"Your master has gone to heaven."

Azam Khan hurried his pace. *I was right. Something is wrong.*

Hashim and his wife Ammi, the old couple with whom he lived, were sitting on the tiny portico of their modest home.

"The butcher's son, he said something about my master going to heaven," said Azam Khan and walked right past them, not slowing down for an answer. He went in and put away the satchel where no one, except perhaps Ammi, would have the nerve to pry. He hurried back to the portico.

"What was he talking about, Abba?" he asked Hashim.

"We got word of this," said Hashim, "from one of the servants at Madhuvana. Rajanna apparently died while on a journey. A messenger came to Prabhakara Swami's home, conveyed the news, and left. The priest is out of town. Giridhara, the idiot, received the messenger and was so shaken that he forgot to ask the messenger who he was, where he came from, and where he was headed. The messenger gave him a box with Rajanna's possessions."

Azam Khan, aware of how messenger services worked, knew that the fellow who brought the message would have no idea who sent the message and where it came from; he was just a cog.

"And Rajanna's family, how have they taken the news?" asked Azam Khan, thinking of Aadarshini, Raghu, and the others.

"The family is convinced that the news is true. They are in mourning and have not permitted outsiders to enter Madhuvana."

Azam Khan knew this was customary.

"Did anyone come to inform me?"

"Why would they?" the old man said. "Everyone assumed you are with Rajanna. If they saw you, you'd have a lot to answer for."

Everyone, thought Azam Khan, *except Aadarshini Amma*.

Azam Khan let out a shriek of rage. It frustrated him that he couldn't march into Madhuvana and talk about this. All the men there had known him for decades, of how dear he was to Rajanna. They treated him like one of their own. Yet, tradition said he could not enter the estate, and he had respected it.

"Ah," he said, feeling an unbearable pain in his stomach. "Wretched me, I wasn't with him when it mattered the most!"

Old Hashim tried to pacify him.

"Grieve all you want, son. But be reasonable in your grief. True, Rajanna was like a god to us, but keep in mind that he had crossed seventy. Who lives that long nowadays? He was away for far too long for his own good. Why should you be surprised if he ran into the angel of death somewhere along the road? But do grieve, for Rajanna was a man worth grieving for. He took care of us well."

Azam Khan could see Hashim was weeping too. He rested his head on the old man's lap.

"Life is over for me," Azam Khan wailed over and over.

"Nothing is over," the old man responded, and ran his fingers through his hair.

Azam Khan looked up at the sky. An overcast and gloomy shroud of a moonless dusk hung over the other side. He needed to be alone. He walked to the riverside and washed himself. He was pensive, staring at the Madhuvana treeline to his east, thinking of what might be happening within Madhuvana, of how Aadarshini, Raghu, Rajanna's older wives and others might be dealing with their grief. Aware of his agitated state, he looked away and found himself staring at a trail leading west to Choma's den, where the burly Choma helped men clear their confused minds with several options: opium, ganja, and toddy. Azam Khan decided he could use all three tonight. He would deal with reality later. He walked west till he reached Choma's hut. His first binge resulted in a rapid loss of coherence during which he asked himself…*What happened to Pratipa? Why hadn't the bastard come back yet? He has my horse…where is my horse?* As he lost control of his senses, he sat helplessly as countless images of his adventurous life with Rajanna flashed in his head. Intermittently, he'd hear Rajanna's voice, *Promise me, son, if something were to happen to me, you will look after the safety of my wives and my son till my son can fend for them.* Azam Khan found himself blurting *I will, master, I will* as Rajanna's plea reverberated in his head. As his cerebral fog grew thicker, he began hallucinating about Persian palm trees flying in the sky. The trees kept evaporating one at a time till only a handful were left, and they were all laden with mangoes and tamarind, the native fruits of

Vijayanagara. Amidst the branches was Aadarshini as he had last seen her. He didn't notice the night come or go. When he woke up to the sound of Choma's wife yelling at her husband, the sun had reached the top of the hut.

"You've been babbling all through the night," she said to Azam Khan.

Not yet sober enough to think about what to do next, Azam Khan went back to sleep.

The journey, as expected, had been arduous. The rickety cart, the fourth one on which Prabhakara Swami had travelled since leaving Jokhandi, tossed him around and inflicted more agony on his sore behind. But he wasn't complaining. *It's better than walking*, he kept telling himself.

"You must get yourself a horse," one of Prabhakara Swami's superiors had once suggested.

"Yes, a priest riding around on a horse would certainly endear him to the devotees," Prabhakara Swami had sarcastically responded. "I am quite happy with my palanquin."

He had inherited the palanquin from his predecessor, a slightly lame man who couldn't move around the village easily. When he arrived in Maravali, the village council had agreed to extend this privilege to him. "Don't see the palanquin as a symbol of power," Chandrabhanu had cautioned him. "You have no real power. You are our priest. Do your job well. Be careful about who you cross. People are very religious and superstitious around here. Your power comes from your wisdom. Show us you are wise. Earn our respect."

And he had. The people of Maravali had sought his counsel on matters small and large, like the men under the banyan tree that fateful afternoon. The village council had received a request from the provincial governor to consider building an ashram as a sanctuary for widows and orphans. The men were debating the matter and were delighted to have him join them.

"Not in our village," Satisha, a man in his fifties, had said. "It would invite lecherous behavior from men here."

"God forbid my wife ever ends up in an ashram. It is better that she commits sati. Indeed, I will decree that it be so," said Govinda, also in his fifties.

"I am happy to have an ashram here. I would not want my wife to be burnt alive. That is nothing short of murder. Neither will I have her stay on in our home after my death. She'd be treated like a slave, an object of torment and lust," said Ganesha, much younger than the others.

"What do you think, Prabhakara Swami?" asked Govinda.

Prabhakara Swami thought the sati tradition had outlived its relevance, but he held his tongue. It was his habit to never reveal his views unless it served some purpose. He did the same when people asked him whether his loyalty lay with Rama Raya or with Salkaraju. He'd always say his loyalty lay with Lord Rama, with whatever was good for Vijayanagara, and with the people of Maravali – in that order. Maravali loved him for this.

That was when Rajanna had walked into the proceedings.

"Interesting discussion, Rajanna..." Prabhakara Swami had started to say, but Rajanna looked straight at him and gestured with his forefinger. He seemed impatient and angry.

"Come," he commanded.

They walked away towards the riverside. Azam Khan was, as always, walking behind them at a discrete distance.

"I'll come straight to the point," Rajanna began. "I know who you are. I know what you are doing here. I know who you work for. Fortunately for you, I like you. So does my family. So do the village folk. You misguided man! You have a good life here. Why are you bent on spoiling it with your warped sense about what is right for Vijayanagara and what is not? You are a good priest. Work for me instead."

Prabhakara Swami felt the urge to counter Rajanna's tirade with one of his own, for he too had recently discovered Rajanna was not just a prosperous businessman but also a Rama Raya sympathizer who provided extensive logistical support for his cause - funds, safe houses, mercenaries, and messenger services. Rajanna was an enemy of the state as far as he was concerned. He had already told his superiors he had discovered a traitor and had asked for the services of Kaala, a mercenary in Veeranna's stable of cold-blooded assassins. He hadn't told them that the traitor in question was named Rajanna; there were just too many traitors to keep track of in a time of rebellion, and neither Veeranna nor his superiors particularly cared as long as they were eliminated. Kaala had been hiding nearby, awaiting his instructions. Prabhakara Swami was conflicted, however, for he was fond of Rajanna and wanted to defer the killing as much as possible. But Rajanna's discovery of his true identity had made it easy. Rajanna had to die. Their allegiances were to different warring gods. But this was not the time to kindle Rajanna's ire by arguing with him. Instead, drawing on his experience as a theatre player, he began to grovel.

"Rajanna, you are mistaken. I swear on all the gods in heaven, I am just a priest caught in a web. Help me. Tell me what I must do. I'll do your bidding forever. I love Maravali and its people. I am nothing here without your benevolence. Take me in your refuge."

Rajanna seemed moved.

"Good. I have to leave for Masulipatnam tomorrow. I'll be back in three *amavasya*s. No one yet knows the truth. Continue serving the people, and stop all communications with your superiors. I will know if you do. Trust me, Rama Raya *will* prevail. Vijayanagara *will* prosper. If you are patient, so will you. I will find an appropriate role for you after I return."

Prabhakara Swami had swallowed his pride and stood with his head bowed as the arrogant Rajanna left without saying another word. He could see him saying something to Azam Khan. *Perhaps he is telling him about our conversation.* It didn't matter, for Rajanna would soon die, and Azam Khan, who was always by his side, would die with him.

For all the condescension he had just received from Rajanna, Prabhakara Swami had felt the urge to kill the man himself, but lines he had written for a play a long time ago came to mind: 'Killing someone you know is not easy. Get someone else to do it for you, and let him inherit the karma'.

Later that night, Prabhakara Swami gave Kaala explicit instructions. "Follow them with stealth. Be patient. Wait for the right opportunity. Both Rajanna and the bodyguard must die. Send Rajanna's personal effects to the temple here in Maravali with a message that he died a natural death and that the last rites were performed by local Brahmins. Make sure you mention the name of the village where the deaths occurred...just make up a name. I don't care what you do with their bodies. Send the message 'the deeds were done' to Soorya at the temple in Jokhandi."

Indeed, it seemed like just yesterday that all this had transpired. And now it was all over. Rajanna was dead. Shooing away the guilt of murdering a man who'd been generous to him turned out to be easier than he thought. *The man was financing rebels, he was a traitor, you discovered him, you did your dharma, and you are a patriot.* He felt sorry for Azam Khan. When their paths had crossed, Azam Khan would always step aside and bow politely. But if he'd been left alive, it was only a matter of time before he would hunt down his master's assassin. *No, the Turka had to die too.*

Prabhakara Swami woke up early and resumed his journey. The long travel gave him time to think about his future. He liked Maravali and wanted to stay, but Veeranna would probably one day send him elsewhere as he had done in the past. But Madhuvana and Aadarshini were both without a master, a protector. *Opportunity,* he thought. With the right moves, he could have them both. Several questions gnawed away at him. How would he visit Madhuvana as frequently as before, now that Rajanna was gone? Would being around Aadarshini even be possible, now that she was a widow and would likely remain out of sight? And if he did see her, would she be as delectable as before?

"We should be passing by Maravali early tomorrow," announced the cart driver, "unless it rains."

"Good. I have been away too long," said Prabhakara Swami. "It'll be good to be home."

The cart kept plodding along ever so slowly.

"I smell rain," said the driver.

It rained all night, the intermittent thunder and lightning making the cows restless. Aadarshini patted them to calm them down. The thought of Prabhakara Swami not returning in time was troubling her. Exhausted, she had dozed off in the cowshed when she dreamt of Azam Khan, as she had often since she had landed on him. By the morning, the skies were clear. She wondered if it would be possible to find Azam Khan and seek his help in finding Prabhakara Swami. She ran into Cheluvi as she walked into the house. The older wife appeared as if she hadn't slept either.

"I milked Gouri this morning. I don't have too much time left with her," Cheluvi said, and handed her a cup of warm milk. "You were sleeping in the cowshed. What's the matter?"

"I couldn't sleep in my room. I needed to think. The cows helped me sleep," she replied.

They were interrupted by a servant girl.

"Akka, someone named Sidappa was here to pay respects to you. He was blind. A boy with a limp was guiding him," she said, trying to get the words out too fast. "I ran into them on my way here. The old man said they'd walked all day yesterday so he could see you, but they were turned away by the guards at the gate. He asked me to convey his family's condolences."

Aadarshini had met Sidappa twice, once when she had wed Rajanna, and again when Raghu was born. There was something endearing about Sidappa, something grandfatherly. Each time he had whispered similar blessings to her: *May the grace of the Almighty shower upon you. May you bear sons strong of mind and body…my family is forever in your service and will lay down their lives for you.*

She tried but couldn't remember how he looked now, after all these years, and asked Cheluvi about him.

"I have known Sidappa since I was a child," she explained. "He worked as a horse groomer for my father. Then he was Rajanna's right hand till he lost his eyes in a swordfight while protecting Rajanna, saved Rajanna's life, and almost died himself. That is when Azam Khan took over Sidappa's job. After he went blind, Rajanna took good care of Sidappa. He gifted him a small hamlet, just a few huts around a pond nestled by coconut palms, and an expanse of farmland for him and his family to live with pride."

"Have you been there, Akka?"

"The journey seemed so daunting, at least the way Rajanna had explained it to me. A day-long trek on one of the trails past the last tamarind tree in Maravali. No palanquin, just walking all day in the sun. I never took Rajanna up on his offer to visit the hamlet. Besides, we don't enter the homes of Sidappa's people. If Rajanna went, it was his business. You knew him. He was always flouting norms."

"We could have used Sidappa's blessings now," noted Aadarshini, sad that the man had been turned away.

"Yes," said Cheluvi. "Rajanna would've liked that. Sidappa was one of two people Rajanna trusted without question. The other as we all know is Azam Khan. I wonder whatever became of him. I hope he is well. It should have been him to bring us news of Rajanna's death."

Kalavati came to the portico. Aadarshini could tell she had been crying. The two then embraced Aadarshini and kissed her forehead. There was a strange tranquility in their faces, as if they had accepted what was to come.

"Be strong, child," said Cheluvi.

The rain came down without warning again in the afternoon. Aadarshini stretched out on her bed and let the steady drizzle lull her into an unscheduled nap. She was startled awake by Sarala's scream. "Akkaaaaaaa," she bawled, as she often did when she had something urgent to say but couldn't come up with the words. She stood outside her door, trembling.

"What happened, Sarala?" Aadarshini asked.

Sarala grabbed her hand and led her to Cheluvi's room.

As soon as the door opened, Aadarshini covered her mouth in shock. The two older wives lay on Cheluvi's bed, dressed like brides, clad in the finest sari they owned, and bedecked in jewels. Their tresses were groomed. They held each other's hands, as if they were both sleeping in peace, a serene smile on their faces. But the pale-yellow frothy crust around their mouths told the truth. A terrified Aadarshini bent down and pressed her ear against Cheluvi's breast, then on Kalavati's, hoping to hear a heartbeat. She placed a finger under their noses, but she knew there was no hope. *Dead!* The longtime lovers, not willing to go through sati, had chosen to bring their lives to an end by themselves. She was surprised how indifferent she was to the pain that now pierced her mind and body.

"Wait here," she ordered Sarala.

She went out to the portico, moistened the edge of her sari in the rain and hurried back. She gently wiped the muck around their lips. Next to the bed, she found two small empty vials. Unlike the ceramic ones she had seen in the kitchen, these were copper vials. The women had consumed some poison, she surmised.

"Get rid of these," she said to Sarala. "Hurry back."

Sarala did as told.

"Find Raghu. Take him to the *zenana*. Stay with him till I come. Pull yourself together. Do not talk to anyone about what you have seen here. I need you to be strong."

Sarala nodded.

It was time to inform the family. Aadarshini went into the northwest section where Cheluvi's relatives lived. The news spread quickly after that. The men dispatched someone on horseback to fetch Giridhara to organize last rites.

Aadarshini returned to Cheluvi's room and sat by the bed, unable to cry, tired of repeating her tale of finding them. Before long, the room was crowded. One woman speculated on where they may have got the poison. Another said the plantation was full of plants of all virtues, and since the two had lived here so long, they likely knew where to get the poisonous berries whose juice they appeared to have ingested.

"Ayyo...*atma hatya*, the worst sin!" one of the women wailed.

"One must watch the little one carefully now," said another.

"Who knows what she is thinking of doing? Poor child, she must be so confused."

Aadarshini, not amused, glared at the women and quietly stepped out. Outside, she saw Srikanta and Kanteeravaa discussing cremation arrangements with two others. Aadarshini stopped behind a pillar to eavesdrop.

"Giridhara is on his way here," Srikanta was saying. "He will guide us. The women will pay their respects here. Those of us who want to help carry the biers as our last act of gratitude to Cheluvi and Kalavati may do so. I plan on accompanying Cheluvi to the cremation site."

Giridhara soon arrived with another priest who Aadarshini had not seen before. Aadarshini listened to Giridhara stammer what he had to say to Srikanta.

"As you know, Prabhakara Swami and I...I don't conduct cremations. Rituals related to death are performed by Shashidhara here," explained Giridhara. "He is well-versed in...in the matter."

The others nodded at Shashidhara, who didn't look much older than Aadarshini. The thin priest went into the northeast section where the bodies lay. Giridhara continued to chat with the other men, now about Aadarshini.

"This unfortunate incident could give her inauspicious ideas. The rains are here. It is unlikely that Prabhakara Swami will be back anytime soon. Why wait for him? I suggest talking to her about getting on with her *sati*. Two days from now is a most auspicious time, before dawn, around *brahmamuhurtam*. She will surely attain *moksha*. She must not miss the opportunity."

"Who will tell her?" asked Srikanta.

"I say we tell her right away, after Shashidhara leaves for the cremation," offered Giridhara. Aadarshini froze. *They do not want to wait for Prabhakara Swami.*

"Who will accompany her to the cremation ground? She has no known relatives," stated Srikanta.

"I understand," said Giridhara. "There is no need to panic. I will arrange for a few people to do the needful. No one *here* needs to be at the riverside. You can pay your respects before she is taken away... if that is what you want. It is up to you."

"I will speak to her. She will listen to me," offered Kanteeravaa.

Aadarshini felt the bile rise to her throat. She went back inside the *zenana*. The women began to wail as the bodies of Cheluvi and Kalavati were brought to the front door, Shashidhara chanting in a shrill voice behind them. She looked out a window. The corpses, fully shrouded except for their faces, were placed on a wooden platform, ready for their final journey to the cremation site by the river.

Just like you in a few days, she thought.

Aadarshini prayed for the two sister-wives as their bodies were carried away. She sat in a corner, holding Raghu close to her. Sarala sobbed nearby. With what had happened earlier today, and the drama that had followed, Aadarshini expected the servants to know about her sati too.

"Akka," said Sarala, breaking her silence. "What is about to happen to you? I heard the sweeper women. They say such troubling things."

Aadarshini decided it was time to tell Sarala the truth. Perhaps she could also use her help in what was to come.

"You need to be strong, Sarala," she asked, and began.

A shocked Sarala ran out of the *zenana* after listening to her. Aadarshini asked Raghu to stay and followed her. She found her weeping in the coconut grove outside.

"What will happen to Raghu, Akka?" Sarala asked.

"I don't know. He is the heir to all this," she replied, her eyes sweeping across the estate. "I suppose the family will look after him till he comes of age."

She looked Sarala in the eye. It was now or never.

"Sarala, listen carefully now. I need your help. Do you know where Azam Khan lives? I believe it's on the other side?"

Sarala nodded.

"Good. Go there right away. Find him. Tell him I need his help. Ask him to meet me outside the gates of Madhuvana at dawn tomorrow, by the big banyan. He may ask you about what has transpired here. Don't answer any of his questions. Tell him I will explain."

Sarala looked puzzled. "Akka," she asked. "Azam Khan cannot possibly be in Maravali. He went with Anna, didn't he?"

"No, I know he didn't. Don't ask me how I know. Just go."

She didn't know if Azam Khan was still in Maravali. But it was worth a try. *Did he know about Rajanna yet?*

"How do you know, Akka?"

Aadarshini noted Sarala's aspersive tenor.

"Sweet Sarala, just go. Do as I ask," Aadarshini cupped Sarala's face and pleaded. "This is not the time to ask questions."

Sarala obediently hurried away. Aadarshini waited on the portico outside, impatiently chewing on her fingernails. Kanteeravaa tottered over to her.

"Oh, there you are," he said.

She knew what he was going to tell her.

"It looks like Prabhakara Swami will not be back in time to give us his counsel. This is unfortunate. The burden is now on the elders to guide you on the right path," the old man said. He repeated what Giridhara had told him the previous day, but Aadarshini didn't really pay him much attention. Finally, he concluded, "It will be best if you acquiesced to what is being asked of you, for that would be the right thing to do, your *dharma*."

"Thatha, if Narayana wishes so, so it will be. Neither you nor I can change His will, can we?" she replied without looking at him, her voice unexpressive.

"Good, my child. God bless you. I knew you will make us all proud."

"Haven't I always, Thatha?" replied Aadarshini, and watched Kanteeravaa totter back inside. She could hear the sweepers outside talking about her.

"Woe to be a dead Brahmin's wife," said one.

"Do you think she will do it?" asked another.

"Does she have a choice?" opined yet another.

We all have choices, Aadarshini felt like screaming out loud.

Azam Khan washed himself three times over to rid himself of the malodor from Choma's. His head still hurt. Two angry billows of smoke rose into the sky in rhythmic bursts at the far edge of town. A strange panic gripped him. He could tell the smoke came from the cremation grounds of Madhuvana and not from a kitchen. With no clue about what was happening inside Madhuvana, he briefly considered going there to find out for himself, then dismissed the thought. Putting your nose where it didn't belong only led to trouble, Rajanna had taught him.

When he reached home, he saw Sarala pacing up and down the narrow street where he lived.

"Yes," he said to Sarala before she could speak. "I heard about Rajanna. Is that why you are here? Tell me. How are Rajanna's wives? How is Raghu? How is the family?"

Sarala shook her head. He could see she was nervous.

"I have come here at the behest of my mistress. She needs your help. She has asked that you meet her outside Madhuvana at first light tomorrow, by the big banyan. I am not supposed to ask you any questions. Yet, considering we have known each other for a long time, may I ask you how Akka knew you were here? Why were you not with Rajanna?"

Azam Khan hesitated. Telling her anything was out of the question. Yet, he liked Sarala and wanted to give her a response that would dissuade her from interrogating him further.

"Girl, I could make you promise you will not tell anyone. But you are a woman after all…who knows what you will do? If I suspected you betrayed my trust, I would have to cut off your tongue," he said and tapped his dagger. "Do you understand my dilemma? Do you still want me to answer your question?"

Sarala shook her head in fear.

"Good! Now, listen. Tell your mistress I will be at the banyan tomorrow at first light as commanded. Don't let her come alone. You accompany her to the gate. It will be dark. Be careful that no one sees you. Do you understand?"

Sarala nodded.

He wanted to ask her about the smoke, but decided he would ask Aadarshini.

"You should go back now. Give my regards to Aadarshini Amma."

It was dusk by the time Sarala returned to Madhuvana.

"Akka," an out-of-breath Sarala cheerfully reported. "I met him. He will be there as you requested."

Good, Azam Khan is in Maravali.

She now knew what she wanted to do next. She would escape. Immolating herself was out of the question.

"Come," said Aadarshini. "You sound parched. Let me get you some water."

Sarala followed her into the kitchen.

"Tell me," Aadarshini started to say, curious to know more, but was interrupted by someone calling out her name.

It was Srikanta. He stood at the far end of the portico.

"All went well with the cremation of Cheluvi and Kalavati. The ashes will be collected and immersed in the river tomorrow. Puttaraju will do the needful for his aunt Kalavati, while I will perform the rituals for Cheluvi," he said.

Surely he has not come here to tell me this. Aadarshini could sense that Srikanta was struggling to say something. He stood silently, his eyes moist. She lost her patience. "No need to give me instructions, Srikanta. Thatha Kanteeravaa and I spoke earlier today. Tomorrow's my turn, I know. I will spend the rest of my time preparing for my destiny." She was disappointed that Srikanta, who Rajanna had trusted to run his business while he was away, had stood by impotently while injustice was being meted out to Rajanna's wives. She waited for him to leave. To her surprise, he stepped back and fell at her feet, sobbing.

He bowed slightly, pressed his palms together in supplication, and then left quietly.

"First they behave like gutless eunuchs, then they feel guilt, and then they cry like a woman," Aadarshini muttered to herself. "When will they behave like men?"

At night, Sarala helped her put Raghu to bed, and the two stayed up through the long silent night, neither wanting to inadvertently sleep through first light. A little before dawn, the two quietly left via the cowshed. They held each other's hands and nimbly walked up the starlit trail to the banyan.

"Shhh," Sarala called out to Azam Khan.

"Here," came Azam Khan's response, and stepped out from behind the tree.

Aadarshini slumped to the ground, glad to see him.

Azam Khan turned to Sarala. "Stand by the trail. Alert us if you hear someone coming. Just scream. Don't eavesdrop. If you can hear us, go further away. Don't get curious. It won't be good for you. Your mistress will tell you what you need to know."

Sarala nodded and blended back into the darkness. Azam Khan gestured to Aadarshini to sit under the tree. He stood on one side, so that Sarala couldn't see him.

"Amma, what have they done to you? Look at your eyes. When did you last sleep properly? You look so frail. When was the last time you ate?"

"My life is over, Azam Khan," she replied, sobbing incessantly. "Oh, whatever will become of Raghu?"

This was the first time she was talking to him directly. It wasn't as difficult as she thought it would be.

"Nothing is over," he said, with a tone of respectful admonishment. "Stop crying. I am here to help you. Be strong. You are Rajanna's wife. You must act worthy of that."

Aadarshini looked back towards where Sarala was.

"Don't worry. Sarala can't see or hear us. Tell me everything that happened."

Aadarshini explained how events had spun out of control at

Madhuvana following the suicides of Cheluvi and Kalavati, how the men had decided not to wait for Prabhakara Swami, and that she now faced a fiery death. She wanted to ask him why he had not been with Rajanna, but decided she could ask him later too.

"What a terrible time for Prabhakara Swami to be out of town," Azam Khan finally said. "He would've put an end to this madness quickly if he was here. I wish I knew where he is now. Alas, even if I did, there isn't enough time."

Aadarshini interrupted him.

"I don't intend to go through with the sati. I do not intend to immolate myself," she said with a finality. "You must help me escape."

She could see he was taken aback. He remained silent for what seemed like an eternity.

"It'll be daylight soon," she said, pushing him for a response. "I must return before someone notices I am missing. Say something. I am counting on your ingenuity that Rajanna used to extol."

"Come away with me...right now!" he said. "We will go far away. No one will find us. I will make sure you are safe."

"And Raghu?" she demanded.

"Leave him behind. He will be safe here. The family will take care of him. When the time is right, I will arrange to have him brought to you."

"What about Madhuvana?" she asked.

"That, I am afraid, you'll have to leave behind. As will I."

"No!" Aadarshini was vehement. "Raghu must be with us. And Madhuvana is his. I have to live to make sure he does too, to get what's rightfully his. We have to remain in hiding until Prabhakara Swami is back in Maravali. Only then can we convince the rest of the family."

Azam Khan was deep in thought. After a while, he began to describe a possible approach. Aadarshini heard it out, and then asked him, "Do we have sufficient time to organize this? I am to die at dawn tomorrow."

"Inshallah...one day is enough if we have Allah's blessings. Will you remember everything *you* have to do tomorrow?"

She nodded nervously.

"Good. Now we know what we have to do tomorrow, let me tell you what you need to do today. On your walk back to the house, tell Sarala that you have opted to perform sati. She must believe you will go through with it. Tell her it is for Rajanna's honor. Tell her that I, Azam Khan, will return someday to serve Raghu. Convince her this is what you wanted to talk to me about before you died in peace. Spend the day meditating and praying. Act numb. Don't talk to anyone but Raghu and Sarala. Don't tell Raghu about our plan. Eat well. You will need the strength. Inshallah, all will go as planned."

Aadarshini was trembling, but she knew this was the only way.

Azam Khan whistled to Sarala. "You take care of your mistress now," he said to her. Looking at Aadarshini, he said, "It has been my honor to serve you and your family," bowed respectfully, then walked away.

Aadarshini and Sarala began to hurry home. The maid asked her what Azam Khan said, and she told her what she was meant to.

"Ayyo Rama, what kind of justice is this? Is this the only help the *Turka* offered?" Sarala burst out crying.

"No. That's the only help I requested of him," Aadarshini said.

They returned home unnoticed. Raghu was still asleep. Sometime later, a coterie of women entered the courtyard.

"Why are they here?" asked Aadarshini.

"They are supposed to keep you company," Sarala said, "but they are actually here to see you don't do what Cheluvi and Kalavati Akka did."

The women spread themselves around the portico. Aadarshini spent the day in her room in the northeast section with Sarala and Raghu.

"Some of the women want to see you, Akka," the maid said.

Aadarshini refused to meet with anyone. She stayed in her room all day, praying, singing hymns, invoking the gods to watch over her and Raghu, often leaving the women in the courtyard in tears. Around midday, Aadarshini went to the cowshed. *All will be well*, she whispered to Gouri, Lakshmi, and Amba, *I'll return soon*. She prepared a meal for Raghu in the evening and fed him. After dinner, she gave him a glass of milk with herbs that would make him sleep soundly, then took him to the *zenana* and sang his favorite lullaby:

Sleep well, my Rama, sleep well.
Your mother will always protect you, my Rama
Sleep well, my Rama, sleep well.

"You don't need to be so strong, Akka," said Sarala. "Be like other women. Cry. You will never see your son again. You cannot possibly be so coldhearted. I know you."

"Sarala, the wise don't grieve," said Aadarshini, quoting something she had once heard at Prabhakara Swami's discourse at the temple. "The wise just don't grieve. What is to happen is already ordained by Him."

"Raghu spoke to me earlier, Akka," Sarala said. "He knows you are to die tomorrow. He knows what is to happen to you. I don't know who told him. The boy seems to have blocked out his emotions just as you have. But this is not how little boys should be. I've told him that he's been told lies…that you will always be with him."

"Good. This is not the time to be emotional. You have to be strong too."

"You have lost your mind, Akka."

Aadarshini let out a laugh and went into the kitchen. There, she picked up the three vials she had discovered the other day and emptied their contents into the drain. She washed them thoroughly and refilled them with water and rose-scented syrup. The women were still in the courtyard. Sarala was watching over her son. She quietly went back to her room and waited for the auspicious *brahmamuhurtam*.

All night she could hear the rumble of rolling thunder from somewhere far away.

AADARSHINI WOKE UP A LITTLE past midnight. She went to the cowshed and patted the cows affectionately before laying fresh grass in front of them. She bathed and ate a small helping of *ragi mudde* soaked in warm milk, which Sarala had prepared for her. The maid followed her everywhere, as if she had numbed her own senses. She helped Aadarshini lie down on the wooden platform that had been placed on the portico, and sat by her mistress. After Shashidhara arrived, he began to chant mantras Aadarshini wasn't familiar with. Four men he had brought with him stood by in a corner. Aadarshini shut her eyes and silently chanted *Rama! Rama! Rama!* Someone gently parted her lips and poured several spoonsful of a liquid into her mouth. She hoped nobody had replaced the vials. She could hear gasps as she feigned a wild convulsion, rolled her head backwards a few times, and then pretended to lose consciousness, just as Azam Khan had instructed her.

Men and women soon began to touch her feet to pay their respects. Some of them wailed, but none asked the elders to stop. She could hear Srikanta apologizing again. There were times she wanted to spring up and tell everyone to go home, that she didn't want to go ahead with it. Then she remembered that Cheluvi and Kalavati had both passed, and that there was no one in Madhuvana who could help her. After what felt like several lifetimes, she heard Shashidhara finally say, "It's time to leave. We should reach the cremation ground before *brahmamuhurtam*."

She could feel Sarala's head on her chest, and her arms tightly holding her. It was clear Sarala was not yet ready to let go of her. Her arms were wrapped around her, while her hair was all over her face. *Stop, Sarala, you are tickling me*, Aadarshini said to herself.

"I can't hear her heart," said Sarala.

"She is unconscious," Aadarshini heard someone else say. "Let us move this along."

"Wait," she heard Sarala say. "My mistress gave me these the other day. These are hers. They must go with her. Please!"

She wondered what Sarala was pleading about.

Aadarshini felt something being put around her ankles. *The silver anklets I had given Sarala.* Sarala clasped Aadarshini's feet and began to cry.

"That's enough, girl," someone said to her. "We must go now."

"Akka!" Aadarshini could hear Sarala scream. She felt the platform being hoisted. "Gently," she heard a man say. At the door, she could hear Srikanta and old man Kanteeravaa. "May the blessings of Narayana be with you," the old man said. "Come back and tell us all went well," she heard Srikanta tell Shashidhara.

Aadarshini staved off an urge to sneak a peek. Everything had gone off well so far, and she knew what was supposed to happen next. The rocking motion of the platform reminded Aadarshini of when she had entered Madhuvana as Rajanna's bride in his exquisitely festooned palanquin. "Sit still. Don't rock it," Rajanna had scolded her, as Aadarshini peeked out. Farmhands eager to catch a glimpse of their new mistress had lined the trail all the way up to Madhuvana. Aadarshini parted her eyelids slightly and saw the now desolate trail leading away from Madhuvana. Once it was out of sight, she shut her eyes and waited. It wouldn't be long now.

When she heard the river, Aadarshini squinted. The cremation ground was barely lit up in the morning twilight. *Where is Azam Khan?* A stack of sandalwood lay neatly arranged as her pyre, while she could see the silhouetted outline of a burly man next to it, the chandala who would light her pyre. A torch flickered in the wind. The chandala asked the men to place the platform on the pyre. Aadarshini wet herself. *This is not supposed to happen. Where are you, Azam Khan?*

"You may leave," Shashidhara dismissed the other men as he sprinkled consecrated water on her face. Aadarshini could hear Shashidhara chanting the final rites. She lay still, just as Azam Khan had instructed her to, but terror soon overwhelmed hope and she resolved to take matters into her own hands. *Five times, O Rama, five times I shall call your name...then I will jump off this pyre and run.*

"Rama ... Rama..." she began counting.

From somewhere behind her, the terrifying sound of a kettle-drum and a tambourine filled the air. This was followed by a series of throaty shrieks and unintelligible incantations. The sounds grew louder as the din came closer to them. *Azam Khan,* she sighed, her eyes now wide open.

A stark naked man approached the pyre, a dagger dangling from a belt around his chest, his face and body painted in intimidating black and red stripes, and dancing like a madman. He flung his tambourine which rattled all the way till it struck Shashidhara's shaven head.

"Ayyo, *pisachi*," she heard a terrified Shashidhara scream. He dropped the chalice of water on her midriff and ran into the woods without looking back. The chandala fell to the ground, his throat slit wide open by Azam Khan's dagger that had struck like lightning without warning.

Azam Khan then helped her off the pyre. She felt an immense rush of gratitude towards him.

"Keep this with you." He put back the dagger in its sheath and gave it to her. "You know what to do next. Raghu and my man Dilshaad should have reached the river bank by now. I have kept some fruits in the coracle. Give the boy something to eat. I will join you after I finish here."

Despite her nervousness, she couldn't help notice that Azam Khan had painted his penis in black and red stripes too, making it glow in the torchlight. She couldn't contain her nervous giggle.

"Now, go…please!" he said politely, pointing her in the direction of a trail that ran by the river.

Aadarshini didn't look back. She ran until she reached a bend in the river where a coracle had been tethered to a tree. Inside the boat was a small bundle of clothes, a few bananas, and a satchel. She scanned the area and called out softly for Raghu. Dilshaad was supposed to bring the boy to her.

It didn't take long before an unpleasant emotion gripped her. *Something is wrong*, she thought. *They should've been here by now.*

Azam Khan placed the chandala's corpse on the pyre, piled more sandalwood on top, and set the pyre ablaze. He knew this blasphemous act of burning the body would not go unpunished in the kingdom of Allah. He washed himself in the river, said *tauba* over and over in penitence, then walked back to where he had left a set of fresh clothes. He waited for the fire to grow so that it could stand up to the wind or a light drizzle. The priest would come by later. A dying pyre with a half-charred corpse of a man would spark outrage. Everybody would know that Aadarshini was alive, and they would hunt her down. He waited till he was content the fire had consumed the chandala's body entirely. He was about to leave when he heard indistinct chatter in the forest. He hid himself, and as expected, Shashidhara had returned with a few farmhands. They stood at a distance from the pyre. The heat and the smoke would make it difficult for them to come any closer. He quietly left the scene.

He could see Aadarshini pacing nervously near the bend. She was alone.

"He is not here. Your man is not here. Something has happened to Raghu. You didn't think this through," she immediately chastised him. "You were never in favor of Raghu coming with us. You intended to take me away and leave him behind. What was this coracle for? Would we even fit into it? What were you thinking?"

Azam Khan raised his hand.

"Quiet, Amma…I need to think."

He sat down on the river bank, hands on his head. "For the love of god, let me think," he repeated.

"Maybe I should just go home and throw myself at their mercy," said Aadarshini.

"Sure, they'll welcome you back with open arms. Then they'll give you a fresh set of vials to drink from…"

"I am sorry. I am upset. I'll be patient," she said.

"I have known Dilshaad a long time. He is an honorable man. If he has Raghu with him and could not bring him here, he will have an explanation," Azam Khan said. Dilshaad was part of a team Azam Khan had built to protect Rajanna's trade interests by safeguarding shipments, intimidating those who needed intimidation, and eliminating obstacles.

"Above reproach," he said, "all of them. Trust me, I will bring Raghu to you," Azam Khan reassured her. "Let us wait till daybreak. Something must have happened for him to delay."

"What if Dilshaad couldn't pull it off?" said Aadarshini. "Raghu could still be at Madhuvana."

"Possibly," replied Azam Khan. "In that case, the only way to find out is by going there."

The two of them sat under the tree, until Aadarshini felt fatigue overpowering her. Azam Khan stayed up, waiting for the dawn. He decided he had waited enough as light broke through the mist on the river.

"I will go back to Madhuvana. You stay here. Don't wander. Keep an eye on this satchel. It was meant for Rajanna. I have to give it to someone else now." She didn't need to know he had to give it to Sidappa. Rajanna had taught him to share such information only when it was absolutely necessary. He could see Aadarshini wasn't particularly looking forward to being left alone. "Don't worry. No one comes here. Keep the dagger handy, and stay near the coracle. Inshallah, I'll be back before dark."

He wrapped his turban around his face and left.

When he reached Madhuvana, Azam Khan was cautious as

always. He hid in the plantation and took the back-trails, which he knew very few used. A crowd had gathered outside the front portico. Sarala wasn't there at the gathering. Shashidhara was relating the events of the previous day, but there was no mention of the spectral encounter.

"Everything went well without incident," the priest declared. "God bless the chandala. He did his duty. After I left, he stayed back to make sure the fire didn't go out. He must have left after that, for when I went back later, he wasn't there. I will arrange for someone to go back and collect Aadarshini's remains."

"May Lord Narayana bless Aadarshini," Kanteeravaa chimed in. "She has upheld our honor and bravely embraced her destiny. We must be sensitive when we talk about this to Raghu. Let him sleep for now. I will talk to the boy when he wakes up."

"Thatha, about that…" Srikanta said, and called out for a sobbing servant girl. "Tell him, woman. Tell him where the boy is!"

The girl fell to her feet and began to cry hysterically, and between her sobs, said, "I can't find him. I can't find Rajanna's son. He was sleeping in the *zenana* last night. But he wasn't there this morning. I looked for him everywhere!"

Azam Khan was relieved. *Raghu is not here. Dilshaad had done his part.*

"What?" Kanteeravaa exclaimed. "How can this be?"

Another maidservant came forward and claimed to have seen a hooded figure hurrying away into the plantation sometime in the night. "I was sleeping on the portico and thought I had dreamt it. After all, who would go to the plantation at night? But now that I think of it, it appeared like he was carrying something. It could've been the child."

"Fool," said Kanteeravaa. "You should've raised a din. What good does it to do tell us now?"

Dilshaad!

Kanteeravaa immediately organized a search party. "This is an assault on the prestige of our family. We'll hunt down the abductor.

He can't have gone far with the boy," said Puttaraju, a nephew of Kalavati.

But why didn't Dilshaad come to the river? Azam Khan asked himself as he quietly left the scene. The only reason could have been that he had sensed danger and was hiding somewhere with the boy, somewhere where no one would come looking. He wondered if Dilshaad had taken the boy to Hashim's place. He crept out the same way, and rushed towards the other side. He was pleasantly surprised to see Dilshaad on the portico.

"I didn't expect to see you so soon," Dilshaad said. "Did all go well?"

"Yes, yes, she is safe. Where is the boy?" demanded Azam Khan.

"There is no boy," he said. "There was no boy in the *zenana*, let alone one with a green tunic."

Aadarshini had told Azam Khan Raghu would be wearing a green tunic and sleep by the door.

"Did someone else take him away before you got there?"

"It looks like that."

"My friend, we must find him. I cannot go back to his mother without him."

"It could take days to find him, especially if someone smart enough took away the boy," Dilshaad offered. "And there are so many possibilities. It could be anyone, someone in the family eager to get the heir out of the way, or an enemy of Rajanna seeking vengeance. Who knows? If they went on horseback, they are far gone by now. We can track them down, but it will take time, Azam Khan. We cannot go door-to-door in the village or comb the plantation either. You, my friend, are not even supposed to be in Maravali."

Azam Khan felt the earth shift under his feet.

"What will I tell Aadarshini?" he wondered aloud.

"You have become soft, Azam Khan," said Dilshaad. "Don't explain anything to her. Reasoning with a woman is difficult. Reasoning with a woman in grief is impossible. There is plenty of daylight left. Let's first take her away to one of our hideouts and keep her safe. We will then start looking for the boy. Inshallah he is still alive."

The proposal seemed reasonable. Azam Khan said they should return to Aadarshini right away.

"Rest a while," exhorted Dilshaad. "I have a horse. Let's get you one, and we can get there easily before dark if you don't oversleep. Look at you, you can barely move. When was the last time you slept?"

Azam Khan dismissed his suggestion. He was exhausted, but he had left Aadarshini alone. "I will take your horse and go ahead. Find yourself a horse and meet me at the bend," he said, and sped away.

When he reached the woods, it began to drizzle. The cold rain on his skin finally made his exhaustion real, and he could feel his grip loosen around the rein. He began to slide off the horse, but he couldn't do anything to hold on. A sharp pain in his leg shot up as soon as he hit the ground. His head hurt after it hit a rock. The horse had stopped a little distance away, waiting for him. But the pain in his leg was unbearable, and together with his exhaustion, he realized he could do nothing but wait for Dilshaad.

What a mess you have created, Azam Khan.

Aadarshini lost count of the times her emotions swung between hope and despair. After Azam Khan left her at the river bank, she'd sat in the coracle. The river had gently rocked her back to sleep. When a light drizzle awakened her, she realized she had slept through most of the day. Dusk was on its way, and Azam Khan hadn't returned yet.

The wind grew swifter, causing the coracle to bob precariously. There was no sign of the Azam Khan, and Aadarshini decided she could not wait in the coracle any longer. She picked up his dagger and the satchel, leaving his clothes behind. She walked to a banana grove to seek shelter from the increasing rain. To make matters worse, the telltale odor of a carnivore came wafting in from somewhere. *Can't linger here,* she thought. As the rain began to pelt down, she could barely see the trails. *Where do I go?* Going back to Madhuvana was not an option. But she didn't know any other place either.

She found a trail she thought would lead her towards Maravali.

It continued to rain as she walked into the village. She didn't pass a soul along the way. The lamps at the temple barely lit up the *gopuram*, but it was enough for her. She stumbled down the deserted street; she knew the front gates of the temple would be locked, but the temple walls had entrances on all four directions that led to the compound and the main shrine inside. She went around. The door on the west was latched from the outside but not locked. She pushed it open and latched the door from inside. She went to the storeroom where they stored hay, grains, coconuts, and other provisions. Raghu and other children would often use it as a hiding place when they played. In the corner of the storeroom was an old wooden trunk that contained a stack of *panchays* and some paraphernalia of the priests. She set aside the dagger and the satchel and dropped onto the hay. It was late and she didn't expect anyone to wander into the temple in the rain, at least not till after dawn when Giridhara began the day's activities. She had no idea what she'd do in the morning, or where she'd go, but for now that didn't matter. She was surprised she hadn't thought of Raghu since leaving the coracle. *My prince*, she whispered to herself, *I pray you are safe.*

Rajanna had told her about the succession drama being played out in the Vijayanagara capital – a dead king, contenders for the throne, a distressed queen, and an underage heir. She couldn't help notice the similarities with her own predicament. *At stake is all of Madhuvana*, she mused. *With me out of the way, and my son still a child, the vultures will feast.* She remembered Rajanna's words: "Remember, if you want to hold on to what is yours, you have to fight bravely, trust only a few, and try not to die!"

Now that her back was against the wall, she had decided to put her trust in two men. Azam Khan had left her by the river. Prabhakara Swami had not returned in time. Who else could she trust? Desperate, she ran across the courtyard towards the sanctum sanctorum.

She fell in supplication at the doors of the inner sanctum. "Lord Rama, let my intuition be true. Wherever Raghu is, let him be brave, like his father. Tell him his Amma must now take care of herself… that she must stay alive, that she will come back to him soon."

Then, breathing heavily, as if she had just found a second wind, she said, "And now, my Rama, guide me safely to Sidappa. Guide me there, my Lord."

She came out into the courtyard, and washed her sari in the rainwater. She strung it out on the portico to let it dry in the wind, and retrieved a *panchay* to drape herself. She split open three coconuts and using Azam Khan's dagger, she carved out the meat. It would be sufficient for her trek to Sidappa's hamlet. She settled herself in the hay and shut her eyes.

When she woke up, the light had begun to break in the east, although it continued to rain. She draped her sari and wrapped the coconut and a few bananas, Azam Khan's dagger, and her silver anklets into the *panchay*. She tied her hair into an untidy chignon to keep it from swaying in the wind, and walked out the door.

Outside, the rain and the wind bit into her. Aadarshini began to shiver. The sari hadn't dried fully, and her skin felt clammy. She kept walking, into an unknown universe. There was no turning back now.

By the time Prabhakara Swami reached Maravali's outskirts, both he and the bundle he was carrying were thoroughly drenched in the rainstorm. Both the cart driver and he were surprised to see a woman walking on the trail in the rain that early in the morning. She had stepped to the side upon seeing the cart and pulled her sari over her face. Taking pity on her, he handed her his palm-leaf umbrella. The woman extended her hand and accepted it. As the cart moved away, he shouted out to the woman and admonished her to get back home before the squall got worse, an act of kindness that pleased him.

He hopped off the cart outside the temple, glad to be finally home. He lived on a street behind the temple, where it was too narrow for the cart. On his way there, he saw the temple door on the west ajar. He was surprised. Giridhara would have entered from the front door itself. He pushed open the door, only to see the storeroom open too. Coconut shells and banana peels were strewn across the floor. Then in the hay, he saw a satchel with a wax-sealed black ribbon running around it. *Someone was here not long ago.* As he bent to pick it up, the front door of the temple creaked. He stepped out to see who it was.

"Giridhara?"

"Prabhakara Swami," the apprentice-priest said and hurried to prostrate himself. "Welcome back. I am so happy to see you."

Prabhakara Swami embraced him. He'd have to get back to the satchel later.

"So, tell me, how are things in Maravali?"

5

DILSHAAD CAME ACROSS AN incapacitated Azam Khan much later in the day. He helped him onto his own horse and walked alongside till they reached the bend in the river. The coracle still bobbed in the waters, but they couldn't see Aadarshini. Azam Khan hobbled off the horse, looking for footprints or pug marks. He noticed his dagger and satchel were missing from the boat, and sat down on a tree stump. He tried to forget the pain in his ankle and instead concentrated on where she could have gone.

Dilshaad returned from the banana grove to say she wasn't there.

"Where do you think she could've gone?" asked Azam Khan.

"Who knows? Let's first get you home. Your foot is swollen, and you need to tend to it."

Azam Khan winced in pain at the reminder. "Could she have gone back to Madhuvana? Or has some animal…"

"No," said Dilshaad. "I checked…there would be signs if a stray leopard or wild dogs got to her. The rain has washed away her footprints too. No, she must've waited for you till she ran out of patience, then left. She couldn't have gone far, maybe up to Maravali at the most."

"We must find her. She's helpless."

"What makes you say that? It doesn't look like she is. She has known what to do right from the beginning. Do you really think she is as helpless as you make her out to be, or is she taking advantage of your loyalty to Rajanna?"

"Let's go back into Madhuvana," Azam Khan said.

"No!" Dilshaad was adamant. "Not with your broken foot. You know well what they'd do if they catch us. She knows she will die if she returned home; she won't go back to Madhuvana."

"No, I insist. How about if we..." Azam Khan didn't finish his sentence, for the stump that made contact with his head made him lose consciousness. Dazed and drifting into darkness, he heard Dilshaad say, "First, brother, we have to take care of you."

When Azam Khan came to his senses he was back at home. He lay on a mattress, a pillow below his foot, now wrapped in a bandage. Someone had undressed him and wiped him clean. He wore fresh clothes, but his mouth tasted sour from the sedating herbs he had been fed. He could hear Dilshaad tell Hashim and Ammi outside, "You know what a hothead he is. I had no choice but to knock him out."

"You did well. You are a good friend," Ammi said. "His foot is swollen. He needs to rest till it heals. That woman has been nothing but trouble for him."

Azam Khan called out to them. The pain remained, but he felt much better.

Dilshaad said, "You need to be someplace where you can heal. With an amputated foot, you're not much use to anyone."

"But it's not safe here. We have to move him from here. I hear a search party is looking around Maravali for the missing boy. He can't be seen here. He has too much to explain," said Hashim.

Ammi suggested they send him to Sidappa's. "Sidappa will be happy. His family will take care of you. You'll heal quicker," she said. "Inshallah, Sidappa can guide you best on how to find the woman and the boy."

Azam Khan knew that Sidappa's place would be ideal. But his sense of pride intervened.

What will you tell the old man? That you foolishly trusted the safety of the satchel to a woman; that you lost the woman; that the woman happened to be Rajanna's wife! How will you explain what you were doing with her in the first place? How will you explain why you let Rajanna travel without you? How will you explain you lost Rajanna's heir as well? No! This dilemma was born of you. Sort it out yourself.

"No! Not Sidappa's place," he said emphatically.

Hashim sat down next to the bed and held his hand. "How about Zafar Ali's place north of the border, in Bijapur territory? He's family, a good man, and Rajanna's old friend too. He is a hakim and can have you back on your feet in no time. Dilshaad can take you there. He lives a few days ride away."

Two or three days to get there, two to get back, at least seven for the foot to heal. That's far too many days to be idle without looking for the two of them, Azam Khan thought. He then told Dilshaad, "Convene our friends right away, as many as you can. Spread out. Look in the temples. Ask around as many serais and taverns as possible...you know why."

Dilshaad nodded. The trafficking of children was a thriving business in the region, and it hadn't escaped his mind that Raghu could have fallen into unscrupulous hands.

"Assign someone to watch the temple here," he continued. "Once Prabhakara Swami is back, track his movements. If Aadarshini goes to him, he will likely keep her hidden outside Maravali. He won't take her back into Madhuvana until he is sure she will be safe there. Find out where he goes. If you find her, you know what to do. And..."

"If you don't stop talking now, I may have to put you out again."

Azam Khan returned Dilshaad's smile, then clasped his friend's hand in gratitude.

"Let us pray she is safe," he said, "wherever she is."

———✦———

Aadarshini had never expected the world outside Maravali to be so desolate. She thought she would run into villages and strangers all day. She'd hoped one of them would point her towards Sidappa's hamlet. *Surely everyone must know Sidappa.*

She had not run into a soul, except the bullock cart in the morning. She tried to recall Cheluvi's description of the trail to Sidappa's place, and didn't expect to reach till the end of the day. Walking briskly in the rain, she had passed the tamarind trees that lined the only trail out of Maravali. When she saw the cart, she quickly stepped aside and pulled the sari over her face, waiting for it to pass.

The cart driver had handed her a palm-leaf umbrella. She hadn't seen their faces clearly, but she took the umbrella, nodding slightly as the cart kept moving. "Go home," she heard the passenger shout over the wind, "this will get worse."

There was no home for her. She had to keep walking, which she did, despite the shivers she began to get. A sharp pain in her foot made her realize she had stepped on a thorn, wincing as she pulled it out with a jerk, trying hard to see if she had left behind a splinter. She tried to forget the pain as she dragged herself along the soggy ground. Somewhere along the trail it split into four, each limb snaking away into a different unknown. She didn't know which one she had to follow. Shivering, she did what she had often done when faced with such perplexing choices, something she had learned as a child. She pointed a finger at the path on the left, and began chanting, *Sree Rama ... Sree Hari... Wise Gurus...only you can guide me now.*

With each syllable, she moved her finger along to point at the adjacent trail. After she had chanted five times, her finger came to rest on the second trail, one that seemed to run along the river and looked barely worn compared to the others. *The choice of the gods,* she said to herself, and followed the trail. The rain showed no signs of relenting.

She could hear the river a little distance, as if it was keeping watch over her. Steadily losing hope and then her mind, Aadarshini thought of Raghu, of Azam Khan, and of the comfort she had enjoyed in Madhuvana barely days ago. Sniffling in despair, her mind began to go around in furious circles. *How dare they bring me to this? Madhuvana is our home, Raghu. We will get it back. I will have justice.*

As she let her tears run their course and bring her mind some clarity, she thought of the stranger in the cart. His voice had sounded vaguely familiar. *Was that Prabhakara Swami? Could it be him? Should I turn back?* However, she couldn't trust herself. She dismissed the idea of returning to Maravali and forged ahead on the trail.

The trail began to grow fainter as first dusk, then night fell. The overgrown vegetation now appeared spectral, as if they lay in wait to pounce on her. The river had left her behind a long time ago. She realized she was lost. Overwhelmed by her hopeless situation, she let out a full-throated scream that left her breathless. The path continued to twist and turn, and she was almost about to give up when she thought she could see a flicker of light. She willed herself to follow it, more exhausted by this last effort than the entire day's walk. She walked out into a clearing with a few huts, and in the darkness she could make out there was a pond somewhere on her left. She collapsed in front of the first hut, the rain dribbling off the thatched roof and creating a miasmic veil around them.

"Anyone here?" she tried to say out loud, but could only muster a whimper.

"*Yaaru?*" she heard someone shout from inside the hut.

Two women emerged from the hut, the younger of the two ready to use the sickle she held. She felt the other's warm hands on her forehead, and heard her say, "She has a fever." She felt herself being hoisted and carried inside, the hut lit up in the warm orange glow of two small oil lamps. They placed her gently on a reed mat. From where she lay she could see that the one-room hut was spotlessly clean. The thatched roof must have been well-woven, she thought in her incoherent state, for the floor was dry.

"Raghu," she called out.

"Poor child, I wonder what she has been through," said the older woman.

"We need to get her into dry clothes," the other said. Despite her delirium, Aadarshini could tell her sari was soiled.

"I am Aadarshini…" she began to say, and then fell into darkness.

She woke up to light streaming on her face through a narrow door, an elderly man sitting in the doorway. She suddenly felt herself, and realized she was wearing someone else's sari. She remembered the women from the previous night, but they didn't seem to be in the hut. The rain had stopped, and now the skies gleamed blue outside.

"You were having nightmares all night," the man said. "I came to check on you. Padma and Sharada have stepped out to the pond. They tell me you were lost. You're also running a fever."

She urgently said, "I am Aadarshini, wife of Rajanna, from Madhuvana, outside Maravali." Her words trickled out feebly. She was still exhausted from the previous day's travel. "I was looking for Sidappa's hamlet. My husband can reward you well for that information."

The old man laughed.

"Providence was with you," he said.

She could now see his toothless grin, but he seemed to be grinning at someone else.

He is blind.

"I am Sidappa!"

Aadarshini exhaled a long sigh of relief. Sidappa walked up to her and placed his hand on her head.

"Don't despair, child. You are safe here."

"You've not bathed yet," Jahnavi playfully said, as Prabhakara Swami pulled her towards him almost violently.

"I have been in the rain all morning. Isn't that enough?" he said, hurrying, not bothering to undress her.

"Here itself?"

"I have missed you."

"I can see that."

It had been a busy morning, and Prabhakara Swami had much to sort out.

There was the mysterious satchel he had found in the storeroom. Then there was the news about Rajanna, his wives and his missing son, all of which Giridhara regurgitated in one quick outpouring. The news of the suicides, the *sati* and the disappearance had so stunned

Prabhakara Swami that he had stopped abruptly outside his home, even as Giridhara continued to speak. Jahnavi had stepped out onto the portico, looking as captivating as sunshine after a rainy day. His wide grin was sufficient to tell her how much he had missed her.

"*Ayyaaaa*...don't just stand there in the rain. Come inside," she'd told him gleefully before rushing back inside.

He dismissed Giridhara telling him he will meet him at the temple, and went inside. Jahnavi was in a small windowless room which they kept as a store, looking for a towel for him. He'd grabbed her from behind, and here they were now, making love in the cramped storeroom.

"Did you hear about Rajanna?" she asked, without interrupting the lovemaking.

"Yes, Giridhara told me. Shocking, unbelievable," he replied.

"And the wives..."

"Yes, especially the little one..."

"What's she to you?" she pushed at him in mock anger. He enjoyed it.

"Nothing," he said as they resumed a more pleasurable rhythm once again.

"She always seemed so happy," noted Jahnavi. "Imagine going through sati willingly and leaving her child at the mercy of the family. It's not what happy people do."

A burst of thunder caused her to cling to him tighter.

"Ah, Destiny's drums," he noted.

"We need a bigger place for this."

"God willing," he said, "we will someday. Your father has prophesied so, hasn't he?"

"As if you are one to leave things to the will of the gods."

Prabhakara Swami smiled as they settled into a post-coital bliss.

When he prepared to leave for the temple, he asked Jahnavi about the messenger who had brought the news about Rajanna.

"He sat on the portico and conveyed his message without emotion. It was well past lunch. He ate and left quietly. He was like most messengers – dusty, smelly, calloused feet, in a hurry to move on. Why?"

Prabhakara Swami was happy Kaala had followed his instructions and sent Rajanna's personal effects back. He had expected the assassin to appropriate them for himself. *So there is honor among those who we expect to have none.* Then just before he left, he had a thought.

"Did you notice anything unusual at the temple last night? Perhaps some strangers seeking shelter from the rain," he asked Jahnavi.

"No. It was raining. I didn't look outside. Why?"

"Nothing."

"Do you really need to go to the temple today? You must be tired. Stay here. Tell me all about your travels."

He cupped her chin lightly and said, "Giridhara is waiting for me, my love. I shall return soon however."

At the temple, Giridhara and he made himself comfortable on the portico, resting against the pillars.

"So," Prabhakara Swami began, "tell me everything I missed."

Giridhara now began to elaborate from the day the messenger arrived.

"This place where Rajanna died, Loconda, do you know where it is?"

"I have no idea," replied Giridhara. "The messenger didn't know either."

Prabhakara Swami wasn't surprised. There were countless invisible villages in Vijayanagara and one only remembered places that meant something to them. The messenger wouldn't have known either. Interconnected webs ferried messages in incomprehensible ways ubiquitously across the empire. Independent operators arranged for messages to be delivered via runners. One such operator lived about half a day away from Maravali, an old man with one leg who sat under a banyan tree. Prabhakara Swami had occasionally used him to send encrypted messages to his superiors.

"And where did this messenger come from?"

A crestfallen Giridhara admitted that he'd lapsed in interrogating the messenger as thoroughly as he should have.

"There's no point pouting now. The messenger is long gone," the priest commiserated with him. "For now, we must accept that Rajanna died a natural death and there was no foul play. Azam Khan would have been by his side and wouldn't have let harm come to Rajanna. Is there any news of him?"

"No," replied Giridhara. "No one has seen him either."

So Kaala got rid of Azam Khan too. Perfect! He prodded Giridhara to move the story along.

Giridhara told him about how everyone had been waiting for him to return.

"Aadarshini didn't believe Rajanna would've willed sati for his wives. She claimed you knew Rajanna's wishes in this regard. We were to wait for your return. But then the sad drama with the two older wives unfolded, and the family wanted to move things along. They kept telling me about tradition and prestige. So I proposed an auspicious day and time for the *sati*."

I could've saved her, a dispirited Prabhakara Swami thought. There were several places where he had stopped longer than he needed to. How he regretted that! Underneath that regret, he empathized with Aadarshini's plight in the drama that had played out in Madhuvana, as if he was mourning someone his own.

"Tradition?" he chuckled scornfully. "It sounds more like greed. They could have waited for however long it took. Someone was in a hurry and wanted to end this matter swiftly. With her gone, the boy would be easy to control. Greedy people are always in great haste."

After all, it is Madhuvana they all covet, he said to himself.

"Did you really know Rajanna's thoughts, Swami?"

"Yes," he replied. "Not long ago, Rajanna and I overheard villagers talking about this bizarre ritual. Some of the villagers appeared to approve of it. I asked Rajanna what he thought. He dismissed my question swiftly saying his son would take care of his wives, and there was no question of sati for them."

"Would you have helped annul the sati decree?"

"That's irrelevant now. Tell me about Rajanna's boy. How did he disappear...and that too on the night of Aadarshini's sati?"

"The boy could be anywhere now. We don't know who took him. It's been nearly two days, and we haven't heard a word. But although the family organized search parties, and pretend to be worried about him, I think it is all just an act."

"That priest you sent to the cremation ground, I'd like to speak to him sometime," Prabhakara Swami told Giridhara. "Meanwhile, go to Madhuvana. Give them my condolences, and tell them I've returned. They are in mourning now and we must be considerate. Tell them I understand why they will not come to the temple, that I will visit them whenever they send word, and that I will perform the purification rituals at their home. Tell them not to despair. With God's grace, Raghu will be found soon."

After Giridhara left, Prabhakara Swami locked the temple from the inside. Then he broke down, calling out Aadarshini's name over and over. *I could've saved you, I could've saved you*, he lamented. He thought of the last time he saw her, when Aadarshini had walked into the courtyard in Madhuvana, and he had heard the gentle jingle of her silver anklets. He had stared at the anklets and marveled at her slender ankles. He'd forced himself to look away, but now that image came back to haunt him. He couldn't imagine how the Madhuvana family could have condoned burning her alive. *She was so innocent, so gentle...so beautiful!* Filled with rage, he vowed never to let any of Rajanna's relatives possess Madhuvana.

Prabhakara Swami wiped his eyes and turned his attention to the storeroom. The satchel was where he had left it earlier. The black ribbon was tightly wound around it, while the end of the ribbon had been knotted into a braid before being wax-sealed. The seal came apart easily. He tried to pry loose the knots with his teeth when he felt something on his tongue. He pulled out a strand of long black hair from his mouth. *A woman's hair*, he thought at first, then reconsidered his premise. It was more likely the strand belonged to one of the faceless informers who came by here from time to time to drop off information for him. But he wondered why someone would leave a satchel behind so carelessly.

Prabhakara Swami patiently unraveled the knots and pulled out a stack of scrolls. He carefully unrolled them. The first was a map. He could tell the river towards the north was the Tungabhadra. The capital-city on the river was marked with the royal insignia of the Vijayanagara kings: a boar, the sun, moon, and a dagger. Other places were marked by unfamiliar symbols, but he could make out that the map showed northern part of the state extending south all the way to Chandragiri.

The next few scrolls contained names that meant nothing to him. His inspection was interrupted by voices. Villagers who had heard of his return had come to pay respects. He put the scrolls back and listened to them all morning as more and more people continued to trickle in. He had expected to enjoy the lazy idyll of Maravali first and then ease into his priestly duties, but that was not to be. He spent most of the day meeting more people, listening to all that had transpired in their lives during his absence, and concocting anecdotes about the places he had visited and the holy men he had conferred with during his travels.

He did not tell Jahnavi about the scrolls when he reached home in the evening. He kept them in a box he stored his religious paraphernalia in, knowing she wouldn't pry there. Whether it was the fact that he ate a heavy dinner, or that he hadn't slept in his own bed in a long time, he dreamt about the boy all night, Rajanna's specter telling him he was responsible for the current state of affairs. He woke up sweating and thirsty, and Jahnavi whispered into his ear sleepily, "It is all right. You just had a bad dream."

"The boy, I have to look for him. I will find him."

Jahnavi said, "Yes, you should," and went back to sleep. But Prabhakara Swami didn't have the same luxury. He began thinking. *If the boy was abducted, where would they stay along the way? Surely not at a stranger's home or at a serai; they would likely have stopped at some temple. Where else could a stranger with a boy not be asked too many questions?*

The following day Prabhakara Swami summoned a weaver named Avadesha, who also received and sent messages for Maravali citizens. He sent messages to over fifty priests who lived within a few days' ride from Maravali, requesting them to let him know if strangers, a man and boy, had passed through their temple recently.

"Don't tell anyone about these messages," he instructed the weaver. "We don't want to alert the boy's abductor."

6

AADARSHINI SLIPPED IN AND OUT of consciousness for the next few days. The fever burned high, and Sidappa's wife Padma and daughter-in-law Sharada, the two women who had helped the night she stumbled into the hamlet, took turns wiping her down with a wet cloth several times each day. She remembered being fed insipid *ragi mudde*, and slowly her strength regained as her fever finally broke.

She woke up early that morning, feeling more vigorous than before, and slowly tiptoed out of the hut to the pond that lay beyond. The water was warm, and she walked in until it came to her waist. A canopy of coconut palms circled the pond and rose up into the heavens, and she could see blue skies between their fronds. She couldn't tell how long she had been ill; ten days, maybe more. She joyfully washed herself and smiled as droplets landed on the lotus leaves and scampered around like pearls at play. She ran her hands over her body. Her cheeks, usually chubby, had sunk in. Her breasts felt lifeless. She stepped out into the sun when Sharada and Padma came looking for her.

"You shouldn't have come out here by yourself. What if you had slipped?" said Padma.

Sharada carried a dry sari with her. "You shouldn't go into the water. You'll get sick again," she said as she draped the sari. "But it is nice to see you getting stronger."

They sat by the bank.

"How long have I been here?" Aadarshini asked. "I have given you so much trouble."

"You have not been well, child," said Padma. "You had bad dreams, screaming in your sleep, talking to your son Raghu as if he was here beside you. You scared us. I thought the fever wouldn't break."

"My son!"

"There, your hair feels so much nicer," said Sharada, who had untangled the long tresses sitting behind her. "Sidappa will be happy to know you are feeling better."

"May I speak to him now?" asked Aadarshini, feeling the exhaustion creep back into her voice.

"No," said Padma, sternly. "Not yet. Talk to him after you are well...and more coherent."

Padma walked back to the huts. Sharada threw a stone into the water. "Don't mind my mother-in-law. She is protective of her aged husband, and doesn't want him agitated."

"But I must see Sidappa," Aadarshini insisted.

"I'll see what I can do. Perhaps I'll bring him out here later in the day."

Aadarshini smiled. They began a slow walk back to the hut.

"I notice many huts around the pond," said Aadarshini.

"Yes, I will walk you around when you've regained your strength. We have a few relatives here. The rest are for strangers who occasionally pass through. We don't talk to them...or about them. They come and leave mysteriously."

Pointing to the hut where Aadarshini had been recuperating, "That's my home. Venkata, my husband, should be back any day. We have a cowshed beyond the fields. One milch cow, two bulls, some goats...I will take you there sometime."

Aadarshini could feel her vigor dissipating in the short walk back. She lay down on the mat, feeling weak. *Get well soon, woman.*

In the evening, Sharada walked her down to the pond.

"I'll be right back with Sidappa. Don't go wandering off," she said.

The light breeze and fresh air made her feel better. She sat by the bank, tossing pebbles into the water. Sharada soon came back, guiding Sidappa to her. Sharada whispered into his ear when she saw her.

"There you are," said Sidappa, sounding full of cheer. Aadarshini watched Sharada help him sit comfortably on a large flat boulder by the pond. Despite his lack of sight, it seemed as if Sidappa remained aware of his surroundings.

"I will leave you alone," said Sharada, and asked her to bring Sidappa back before dark.

"Nice breeze," Sidappa began. "I come here to listen to the birds. So soothing, so compassionate."

"Yes," said Aadarshini and tossed more pebbles into the water. She wondered how long she should wait before asking him to take her back to Maravali.

"Have you ever wondered why the pebble always creates waves in circles and never in other shapes?" Sidappa asked.

Aadarshini shook her head. Then, realizing Sidappa couldn't see, she said, "No."

"Good. Keep life simple. Don't seek answers to all of nature's mysteries. Let philosophers drive themselves mad trying to unravel those. People like us should simply marvel at such splendors without seeking too many answers."

Aadarshini giggled.

"You sound healthier. My wife tells me you came to the pond all by yourself this morning. I think that was both foolish and good, but you must be getting stronger. Eat well. Don't allow your fever to return. You must remain strong of body and mind."

"How long have I been here?"

"What does it matter? You are here now. You are better. That's all that matters."

Aadarshini moved closer to him.

"I wanted to talk to you about my son, and so much more," she said.

"Yes, of course," said Sidappa. "I have waited to listen to you too.

After all, you managed to evade sati, and yet all of Maravali thinks you are dead."

Did he send someone to Maravali to check?

"Not many people can find this place unless we want them to find it. Yet, you braved a storm to get here. You have Azam Khan's dagger with you. You've held on to your silver anklets. Yet, you've left your son behind. You have a lot to tell me."

"I don't know where to begin," Aadarshini said.

"From the beginning, as all good stories do," Sidappa chuckled.

Aadarshini took a deep breath and, despite her narration being disjointed, she moved from event to event and told him everything, including Azam Khan's role in her escape. She expected Sidappa to ask how she knew Azam Khan wasn't with Rajanna. *I took a gamble...I had nothing to lose,* she would have said. She was relieved he didn't ask. She didn't want to lie to him.

"That is how I lost everything – Madhuvana, Raghu, everything. I had pinned my hopes on Prabhakara Swami but he didn't return in time. What was I to do? Rajanna had once said that we could count on you and Azam Khan in any calamity. So I followed my instincts and looked for you when Azam Khan didn't return. I'd lost hope," she said and burst out into tears.

Sidappa reached for her hand and patted it softly.

"Take heart. You've been brave, and you're worthy of being Rajanna's wife. I know of no woman with your courage. When I last met you, you had just given birth to Raghu, but you were still a child. Look at you now, so brave, so determined. Rajanna would have been proud."

They sat quietly while he listened to the birds and she threw stones into the water.

"I need to see Prabhakara Swami," she finally broke the silence. "He would have returned to Maravali by now. He has influence over the family. I know he will help me."

"Yes, you said that you waited for the priest. What makes you think he would have saved you from sati?"

"I just know."

Sidappa chuckled. Aadarshini thought she could smell derision in his laugh. "Unfortunately, Prabhakara Swami didn't return on time and I had to reach out to Azam Khan. I am confident I can use the priest to regain my rightful place at Madhuvana."

Another chuckle.

"Yes," he finally said, "one must do what needs to be done in times of distress. Yet, I must caution you about trusting strangers who appear out of nowhere, as this priest has."

Aadarshini had no idea what Sidappa was insinuating. True, the priest had recently come to Maravali, but she didn't consider him a stranger.

"Rajanna and I once tried to find out about him, but we don't even know where he is from. I believe he is not what he appears to be. Rajanna found him interesting and intelligent. He liked such people. But even he didn't trust this priest. You did well by choosing Azam Khan between the two."

"A lot of good that has done," Aadarshini bluntly said.

"You are alive, aren't you?" said Sidappa, irritated. "Don't let your frustration cloud your judgment. You'll need Azam Khan more than this priest."

"As I see it, Prabhakara Swami is the one I need now."

"It will not be easy with him either," Sidappa argued. "Do you think you can march back into Madhuvana with the priest and Chandrabhanu by your side? What if, despite whatever favors you offer them to buy their support, they negotiate an inconsequential and subservient role for you at Madhuvana? Will you settle for it? Is that what Rajanna would want? No, we need more information about Madhuvana and Maravali. I will not permit you to go to the priest right now."

"But..."

"No. Let's not continue this discussion. I've learnt what I needed to know, and now we will wait for Venkata to return. He will find out what's happening in Madhuvana. Maybe Azam Khan will have reached here by then too. I am surprised he isn't here yet. I ask you to be patient and not to despair. We will get you back to Madhuvana someday, but not with a begging bowl and a dubious priest by your side. You may well have to ride in with an army behind you and stake your claim. That's what Rajanna would have liked you to do," said Sidappa.

The old man is crazy, she thought. She clutched Sidappa's hand and smiled. She liked his audacity.

"And Raghu?" she asked.

"If he is in Madhuvana, he will be safe. Trust me."

"And if he is not?"

"I do not have answers to all your question right now, but trust me, we'll find Raghu wherever he is. You have to get better first."

"When will Venkata be back?"

"Who knows? It's getting darker. I can tell by the sound of the birds coming home to roost. Take me back now," said Sidappa.

He placed a hand around her shoulder while they walked back.

"We could go to the governor," Aadarshini said, "as a last resort. I hear he is fair."

"No, the governor and Rajanna had a history. A long time ago, before you were wed to him, Rajanna and that terrible man had a falling out over a courtesan they both patronized. Paths were crossed, and tempers flared. Rajanna was lucky to escape with his life. Thankfully the governor was distracted by matters of state at the time and didn't pursue it much longer. But I doubt he would take highly to your presence at his court. If you introduced yourself as Rajanna's widow seeking justice, the man would gleefully oust the whole lot of you and take over Madhuvana for himself. Who knows what he'd do with you? No, we cannot go to him for justice. We'll have to look for that ourselves. Let us talk tomorrow. I am tired now."

"Yes, tomorrow, where God hides the answers to today's dilemmas."

"Hmm. Rajanna said that a lot too. Impatient man, he wanted everything done in a hurry."

That night Aadarshini asked Sharada about Venkata.

"Doesn't he tell you when he goes…or comes?"

"Do men ever? Did your husband ever tell you?"

"Don't you miss him?" asked Aadarshini, "How do you, you know..."

"How do you?" Sharada replied.

They each let out an understated titter. Aadarshini thought of Azam Khan, and in the stillness of the night, she felt his presence all over her.

The following morning, she saw Sidappa in conversation with a one-legged old man near the pond. She stood a little away and listened, waiting for Sidappa to finish.

"My dear friend Kunta, looks like you haven't been very busy," she heard Sidappa say.

"No, Sidappa," the man replied. "The usual mundane exchanges – 'I have made extra pickle'; 'my uncle's son can be a good match for your daughter'; 'the harvest this year hasn't been great' – messages with no intrigue."

"Mundane can be good at our age," said Sidappa, laughing off the old man's lament.

"But some time ago," the one-legged man now had a sparkle in his voice, "the priest of Maravali came to see me. I saw him swimming in the river once, masturbating. I assume holy men too have their needs like the rest of us."

Sidappa guffawed.

"I suppose so," he said. "Tell me more."

"He sent a message to another priest in Nagara, asking for two elephants right away. The message seemed harmless, but why does he need two elephants? The Maravali temple courtyard isn't large enough for even one."

"Hmm…He came a long way from Maravali too, to Jayapura, to send such a simple message," noted Sidappa. "He could have sent that message from Maravali itself, through Avadesha."

"Yes, I asked him the same. But he said he was passing through, which is why he sent the message through me."

"Did you believe him?"

Aadarshini couldn't hear what the man said, but he picked up his crutch and walked away. She joined Sidappa and expressed surprise at his interest in messengers.

"Rajanna recognized that the art of delivering, intercepting, interpreting, and manipulating messages was critical to his trade. Over time, we set up an elaborate web of runners in Vijayanagara, who were often capable of outrunning even the emperor's messengers. My nephew Rudra runs that operation now. He keeps track of all the messages that pass by him, and comes to me for advice when something strange crops up, especially if it has anything to do with the events unfolding in the capital."

She asked him if Rajanna and he had met often.

"Alas, I am old and blind now. I hadn't seen him in a long time. I miss serving him. He was a busy man, and I didn't leave this place very often. He'd send a message discretely at times if he needed anything. Of course, we had to be discrete, especially in this current environment. A lack of discretion can lead to your death. I will not be surprised if he didn't tell you about his involvement with the politics of Vijayanagara. And just as well. It's not a suitable subject for a woman."

Aadarshini chuckled.

"Now, why your Prabhakara Swami asked for two elephants is definitely interesting. I must have Venkata look into it."

"I still think I can use Prabhakara Swami to fight for me," said Aadarshini.

"Yes, perhaps," said Sidappa, a sternness creeping into his voice. "But it's a man's job from here on. You have to be patient. Don't think about sneaking away from here either. Sharada is keeping an eye on you. If you do something foolish, it could spell harm not just to you, but to all of us. Do you understand?" The last bit was delivered as an admonishment, and Aadarshini hadn't expected it. She could only nod.

"Say something," ordered Sidappa, now impatient.

"I understand," she said with a quiver in her voice.

"Things take time. You cannot rush into battle just because you think your plan can vanquish the enemy. We need to ensure victory for you. Be patient. You are my responsibility now. I cannot let you do anything impulsive."

"I understand. I am sorry for alarming you."

A group of boys dived into the pond at the far end and began to splash water on each other.

"Simple joys," said Sidappa upon hearing them.

Aadarshini found herself thinking about Raghu. "If I hadn't been so cursed, Raghu would have been here too, playing with them. That boy with the limp reminds me of him."

"That's Keshava. He is older than your son, almost fourteen. I am teaching him how to run errands into the Maravali area. Precocious little monkey, he never does what he is told to do. Boys are coddled too much for their own good nowadays. At his age, Rajanna had run away from home, travelled with the emperor's troops, and washed horses for a meal and a place to sleep. Trust me, whatever Raghu is enduring right now is making him strong."

Aadarshini listened wide-eyed about Rajanna's past. She had an inkling of what he did, but he hadn't revealed too much about his younger days. *Oh, how I wish I could have learnt more about this side of yours, Rajanna*, she thought.

That evening, while Aadarshini helped Sharada with the cooking, a tall, muscular man entered the hut. A delighted Sharada dropped the ladle she held and ran towards Sidappa's hut, shrieking joyously, "Your son is back!"

The man smiled and introduced himself to Aadarshini. Venkata seemed like a slightly younger, duskier version of Azam Khan.

"I know who you are. I can tell by her joy. She missed you dearly," she said to Venkata.

That night, Aadarshini moved out of Sharada's home into Padma's. The next morning, Venkata washed up and came to meet Sidappa, who politely asked Aadarshini to leave them alone.

They are going to talk about me. Good!

When they sat down for lunch, Venkata told Aadarshini, "Sidappa told me about your adventure. You've done admirably, but we must be patient."

Venkata then turned to Sharada.

"I will be stepping out now," he said and watched a crestfallen Sharada going about her chores without responding. "I will be back tonight. Some men I know are passing by a nearby serai. Dacoits, but decent people. They may have information about the boy or Azam Khan. It is worth finding out before I go into Maravali myself."

Aadarshini was delighted at Venkata's sense of urgency, but took a look at Sharada's disappointment and tried to dissuade Venkata.

"Can't this wait? Can't you see she's been waiting for you?"

"Let him go," ordered Sidappa, putting an end to the conversation.

Aadarshini waited up with Sharada into the night. As they waited, she helped Sharada braid her hair and applied kohl along Sharada's eyelids. They sat silently around the pond, impatiently looking down the trail, hoping for Venkata to appear in the moonlight. When he finally did, Sharada looked at Aadarshini, blushed, and then gingerly followed Venkata into their hut.

Aadarshini remained outside and watched the palms sway in the breeze. She reflected on Sidappa's statement that it was a man's job from here on. She had heard this all her life. But men had always taken control of her destiny, and look where that had got her! She decided to ask Venkata if he could take her back into Maravali to meet Prabhakara Swami. If he didn't agree, she resolved to take matters into her own hands. But she had no idea how.

Prabhakara Swami hadn't expected opportunity to come walking to the temple the next morning.

"Welcome, Chandrabhanu. What brings you here?"

From the village chief's listless demeanor, he could see there was something on the man's mind other than welcoming him back.

"Prabhakara Swami," said Chandrabhanu, "the mourning period for Rajanna and his wives has barely passed. The boy is still missing. I went to discuss the matter in Madhuvana, considering Rajanna has always borne the expenses for *Vijayadashami* and *Deepavali*. But the family lost no time in reminding me they have incurred significant expenses in the post-death rituals and cannot do so this year. What a shame, Swami, as if the gods haven't given them enough to last several lifetimes! Can you imagine Rajanna doing so?"

Chandrabhanu continued, "I talked to Kanteeravaa, their eldest. With tears in his eyes he told me that rather than searching for Raghu, Madhuvana's legitimate heir, the relatives have been squabbling about taking over the reins of Rajanna's estate. Some want Srikanta, Cheluvi's nephew, to take over. The damned fool is a weakling! Then there are those like Puttaraju, Kalavati's nephew, who are beholden to Shamanna, her brother. He too has an eye on Madhuvana. No one knows where Shamanna is, or whether he even knows of Rajanna's death. Fortunately, none of Rajanna's daughters have yet staked their claim. But who knows when they will surface? This is a family in turmoil, much like our beloved Vijayanagara!"

Prabhakara Swami chuckled to himself. He hadn't spoken with anyone from Madhuvana, although Giridhara had delivered his condolences. He had also met with Shashidhara who had recounted the tale of Aadarshini's cremation vividly enough to convince him that Aadarshini was in *swargaloka*. But this was the first he heard of the events at Madhuvana.

"Yes indeed, these are difficult times for the family, Chandrabhanu," he commiserated. "They must ride through this storm and come out strong or perish, as Vijayanagara will if the royal family doesn't remain strong. Let me see what I can do. I will visit them as soon as I can."

"And the festivals," asked Chandrabhanu, "what do you suggest we do?"

"Let's request the citizens to celebrate *Vijayadashami* solemnly at home. Giridhara will guide them. I will deliver a sermon at the temple on the auspicious days. The children can sing devotional hymns. We will keep the event austere to respect Rajanna. We can then see how we want to celebrate *Deepavali*."

Chandrabhanu agreed with his proposals and left. Once he was outside, Prabhakara Swami spoke in the direction of one of the pillars, "You can come out now." Jahnavi emerged from behind the pillar, having slipped there quietly while Chandrabhanu hadn't seen her. She had eavesdropped on their conversation, as she had a propensity to do.

"May I come to Madhuvana too?" she asked coquettishly. "I hear it is beautiful. I've never seen it."

Prabhakara Swami pulled her to him and whispered yes into her ears.

Two days later, Jahnavi sat inside the palanquin while Prabhakara Swami walked alongside her. He had sent word ahead to Madhuvana with Giridhara, and as they approached the estate, he could see some family members gathered outside. He took in their greetings, and led everyone into the central courtyard, where other members already waited. A few farmhands and servants watched from a distance. The women got up after the necessary courtesies, leaving only the men behind. He noted that the women hadn't paid attention to Jahnavi, who sat alone, away from the men, near the northeast section, once the domain of Rajanna and his wives. Pigeons fluttered in the courtyard behind her.

Prabhakara Swami began by complimenting the family. "Giridhara tells me all the funerary rituals were performed with great reverence. You were generous with your offerings to the Brahmins, and the citizens of Maravali are all praise for you. You have fed the entire village, and have brought great honor to Rajanna, his wives, and to your ancestors. They will be grateful."

"We only did our duty as family tradition dictates," said Srikanta.

The others nodded behind him. Prabhakara Swami noticed the men had separated into two groups, with Srikanta and Puttaraju leading them respectively. The latter, he presumed, was loyal to Shamanna.

"Good. Tradition is important. But as the scriptures tell us, we must get past our grief to continue our journey on the path of dharma."

"Indeed," said Kanteeravaa, who sat by himself at the back.

"I hear that there is much turmoil in the family," he continued. "This is to be expected. Even royal families have to endure such tussles after the death of an emperor. Our dear Rajanna was no less than one, wasn't he?"

The men nodded.

"I am given to understand that Rajanna's heir Raghu is still missing. Some of the villagers believe the family has sent him away to be in safe custody till the mourning period passes. If that is so, I commend you on your foresight. It is my opinion that you can bring the boy back now. Once he's home, the boy can resume his childhood and study the scriptures, under my tutelage if you wish. Any of you can take on the role of a mentor, a regent, to groom the boy in the workings of Rajanna's business till he is old enough to take over."

He paused to see how the men would react. As expected, both groups were taken aback.

"This is surprising," said Srikanta. "We have not seen the boy since the night before Aadarshini Amma's sati. None of us has taken him anywhere. It would be outrageous if someone did so without informing us."

Srikanta looked at Puttaraju.

"Neither have we," Puttaraju raised his voice. "Are you implying, Srikanta, that one of *us* took the boy?"

"I didn't say..." Srikanta started to say when Puttaraju and his group got up and stormed out of the courtyard.

Prabhakara Swami waited for them to leave.

"I think they misinterpreted you, Srikanta. They are emotional. Let them calm down. I will talk to them then."

He asked Srikanta to dismiss the others so that they could talk in private. Everyone except Kanteeravaa left the courtyard.

"What a tremendous responsibility you now have, Srikanta," said Prabhakara Swami. "It is a burden you must bear. You must keep this family together. Do not overlook the fact that Rajanna's trading partners and employees were no less than a family to him. You need to keep that family together too. I suggest you focus on ensuring the continuity of Rajanna's operations, for, besides Shamanna, you are the one who best understood it. Visit his partners. Assure them of your leadership. You will need their support to fend off any adversaries. Start doing this right away or risk losing the empire Rajanna worked so hard to build. *Shubhasya sheeghrum.* One must initiate auspicious missions swiftly."

"What about Raghu? You must believe me when I say that I don't have him," Srikanta said.

"I believe you. We must all look for Raghu, and we will."

Prabhakara Swami paused as a maidservant walked across the central courtyard and disappeared into one of the homes. He asked about her.

"That is Sarala, Aadarshini's maid, completely trustworthy," Srikanta said.

Puttaraju now returned to the courtyard.

"Prabhakara Swami, on behalf of all of us, I apologize for having disrespected you by leaving without your permission. I want to assure you we had nothing to do with Raghu's disappearance. Srikanta and I have our differences, but we both want the boy to be safe."

"I agree," said Srikanta.

"Good. I am glad to hear that," said Prabhakara Swami. "I could feel tension the moment I stepped inside. Evil spirits threaten to destroy this family. We need to repel them."

Kanteeravaa got up and walked to them. "I too have had a bad feeling about malevolent spirits," he said. "There must have been some fault in the way we performed the rituals. Swami, would it be appropriate to perform a purification rite?"

"Yes," said Prabhakara Swami. "One must never underestimate the power of evil forces."

Srikanta and Puttaraju discussed something between them, then addressed him, "Prabhakara Swami, we have a request." It was Puttaraju who spoke. "It would be our honor if you can officiate over the purification rituals. After that, we'd like you to stay on at Madhuvana until we can arrive at a peaceful conclusion regarding matters of succession. As you can tell, we could all use your guidance here. You are the only one everyone will listen to. You can also help direct the search for Raghu."

"I will be happy to conduct the *homa*," Prabhakara Swami replied. "As for staying in Madhuvana, I have my responsibility as the priest and need to be among the people of Maravali. Besides, my wife and I are simple people, not used to such opulence. Give me time to think. I will send word with Giridhara soon."

He then looked around for Jahnavi but she wasn't in the courtyard.

"My wife, where is she? Can you please see if she went in with the women?"

The men went to look for Jahnavi, while Prabhakara Swami went into the northeast section. Inside, he saw Jahnavi on the swing, rocking herself back and forth as a playful child would. She sprang off the moment she saw him and followed him back to the courtyard, where the family had gathered to see them off.

"So," he asked her when they were well down the trail, "what do you think of Madhuvana?"

"I don't like the women. They are arrogant and don't deserve such magnificence."

Prabhakara Swami laughed.

"They asked me if we were willing to..."

"I know. I heard everything," interrupted Jahnavi.

A sudden burst of thunder startled Prabhakara Swami. He felt drops of rain on his head.

"Listen," said Jahnavi, "destiny's drums." A little while later, she asked, "Are you really going to think about Madhuvana?"

"No. I will send word with Giridhara as soon as we get back home. We will move here tomorrow. I'll tell them it is an auspicious day."

"What's the hurry?"

"*Shubhasya sheeghrum.*"

The following morning, two burly men greeted Prabhakara Swami in the temple courtyard. Similar in stature, with matching bushy mustaches, they introduced themselves as Narasimha and Nanjunda. "You had sent for us, Prabhakara Swami. We are at your service."

Prabhakara Swami smiled. "My elephants!" he said to himself with some glee.

Prabhakara Swami had been dreaming of a blood-soaked Rajanna and Azam Khan mutilating him in his sleep ever since he'd received Kaala's message. Further, there could be reprisals from unknown quarters if his role in their deaths was ever known, considering Rajanna had been a supporter of Rama Raya's. Convinced that his nightmares portended danger, he had stopped at Jayapura on his way back to Maravali where a one-legged old man named Kunta ran a messenger service from under a banyan tree. He had asked his superiors to send two men to him until the festival season was over. He was pleasantly surprised they had arrived so soon.

When they moved into the northeast section of Madhuvana, the two men were instructed to guard the door and run errands for him. Jahnavi looked pleased to no end as they unpacked their things. A few maidservants were sent to serve them. Among them was Sarala. Prabhakara Swami remembered her as the one skipping across the courtyard the other day.

Azam Khan reflected on the parting words of Zafar Ali. "Go with Allah. You seem to be the kind of fellow who puts his nose in places it doesn't belong. This is the bane of boys of your ilk. Beware, unless you want to die young."

He had often heard this from Rajanna too. But he couldn't help himself. His nose began to twitch as soon as he crossed the Krishna into Vijayanagara territory, anxious to resume the search for Aadarshini. Now on his way back to Maravali, he had found a spot where the Tungabhadra was shallow enough for his horse to cross. As he soaked his foot in the cold waters, he couldn't help think of the bloody history of where he now stood, the northern rim of Vijayanagara. Across the river to his south was home. Beyond the Krishna to his north was the erstwhile Bahmani Sultanate, now splintered into five feuding challengers. In between the two majestic rivers basked a tract of land known as the *doab*. Picturesque, fertile, and soaked in blood, the *doab* had exchanged hands between Bahmani and Vijayanagara rulers several times in the past. Each takeover had resulted in senseless bloodshed during which lives were disgorged into uncertain futures. But for entrepreneurs like Rajanna and Zafar Ali, the *doab* had represented opportunity. With Zafar Ali in Bijapur,

Rajanna supplied to both sides of the border. It was here in this doab that he, freshly orphaned at the hands of marauders, had first met Rajanna a long time ago, and thereon had found a place to call home.

The stay at Zafar Ali's home had been restorative. He was accorded the hospitality he had never enjoyed in the Brahmin bastions of Maravali. He was amused by the merchant's frequent use of "our people" and "their people" to refer to Mohammedans and Hindus. Quite robust even at his advanced age, the man was an Afaqi version of Rajanna, with his imposing personality, his large home, three wives, and the authority he exercised over his family. Following his arrival, Azam Khan had been confined to one room in the courtyard, where he rested most of the day. His meals were brought to him. When he needed to answer nature's call, or bathe, one of Zafar Ali's sons helped him. A shelf full of mortars, pestles, and medicinal herbs lined the walls and stank up the place with a green and fetid odor. Zafar Ali's sons applied a green salve to his foot several times a day. The bitter medicine he ingested several times made him sleep a lot. Zafar Ali himself had come to see him twice a day, once in the morning, then again in the evening. He'd inspect Azam Khan's foot then talk about subjects ranging from poetry to philosophy to politics. Azam Khan briefed him about Rajanna's death and of Raghu's disappearance, but chose not to go into the wives' ordeals.

"They probably had to commit sati," Zafar Ali had said. "Some Hindus practice the strange custom even in these modern times. Strange people, strange customs...but then, we too have our strange ways, don't we?"

They had spent a lot of time talking about Rajanna.

"Good times or bad, we always prevailed, him and I," Zafar Ali had said with tears in his eyes. "He was a good man. I will miss him. Something doesn't smell right, though. It's not like Rajanna to die in a place where he knew no one or no one knew him. There is more to this. Rajanna was in the thick of the politics of succession in Vijayanagara. He may have taken sides. I hope my friend didn't pay with his life for his choices. Look into the matter, son. Find the miscreants. Slay them. It's what they deserve. Then leave Vijayanagara. You are young, go back to the home of your ancestors. Vijayanagara is headed to *jahannum*."

Now sitting ankle-deep in the Tungabhadra, hell wasn't how Azam Khan viewed Vijayanagara. Religion, trade, art, politics, war, bloodshed, treachery – there was something here for everyone. He had always seen it as an accommodating land full of paradoxes. He had met marauders, traders, seafarers, intellectuals, ordinary foot-soldiers, mercenaries, pious men, refugees, craftsmen, assorted lowlifes and interlopers of all flavors, but the land had taken them all in and made them her own. Mohammedan and Hindus fought side by side against Mohammedan and Hindu adversaries. Mohammedan governors hired Brahmins to administer their forts and provinces to the north, and Hindu governors did the same with Mohammedan mercenaries in Vijayanagara. Soldiers from as far away as Egypt and Persia fought for anyone who could afford their services, their allegiance to their paymasters and not to their gods.

Azam Khan had asked Zafar Ali what might have happened to Raghu.

"The boy is probably dead," he had stated without hesitating. "You are wasting your time looking for him."

In deference to his age, Azam Khan did not rebut the man's assertion. But he couldn't say the same about Raghu with the same conviction. The boy was far too valuable alive than dead, and whoever had him must know this.

When he got better and sought Zafar Ali's blessings to leave, he had given him the horse. "This is a gift for Hashim. Give him my love. Go with Allah, son. Stay safe, and stay alive."

Here he was, happy to be back in Vijayanagara. *The most beautiful place I know*, he said, as if talking to the land. *You will never be hell to me.*

The ride back to Maravali took a little over two days from the spot in the river. When he arrived home, neither Dilshaad nor others had returned. When Azam Khan told Hashim about Zafar Ali's assertion that Rajanna could have been murdered, Hashim was quick to dismiss it.

"The man was old. His time had come. He was much too active for his own good."

Azam Khan then asked about Prabhakara Swami and Madhuvana.

"The priest returned the day after you left. Apparently he and his wife have been asked to move into Madhuvana. I don't know why though," said Hashim.

Azam Khan was not surprised. *This is exactly as I had predicted. Had Aadarshini gone back to the priest?* But something else didn't make sense to him. *Why would the priest and his wife live in Madhuvana?* He realized he was asking too many questions, and it was best to go see for himself whether Aadarshini was in Madhuvana too. *If all is well, your work here is done. Find a new life as Zafar Ali advised you to.*

A little past midnight, Azam Khan entered the plantation unseen. Intimately familiar with the grounds, he moved cautiously and made his way undetected into the cowshed. The cows mooed upon sensing the stranger amidst them. He waited till he was certain they hadn't alerted anyone, then tiptoed onto the portico. A sari drying in the courtyard shivered in the breeze. He knew that Rajanna's wives lived in the house on the northeast, one room belonging to each of the wives. He wondered if the sari belonged to Aadarshini. He entered the first room. The moonlight trickled through a small window, and he could tell that it was unoccupied, the floor bare except for a wooden trunk in a corner. *Is she in the zenana?* He briefly contemplated, then dismissed the idea of going there. He turned to leave, when his hand brushed against and dislodged something hanging on the wall. He caught it before it hit the ground and made a sound. His face lit up as the moonlight revealed what it was. *The satchel! So she did come back home. But the seal is broken. Why? Perhaps she got curious?* Puzzled, he slung the satchel across his shoulders, relieved that it was back in his possession. He began to tiptoe back to the cowshed when he felt something hit the back of his head. He reeled in pain and fell to the ground, but before he lost consciousness, he saw a man with a bushy mustache staring down at him.

7

HIS HEAD FELT HEAVY FROM THE herb he and Jahnavi had ingested the night before to sleep. They had already endured several sleepless nights getting used to the night sounds of Madhuvana. At first, they slept in Aadarshini's spacious room, but Jahnavi thought it was haunted by her spirit, so they had moved out to a room diagonally across.

Prabhakara Swami found that Madhuvana was indeed a pleasurable residence, but the act of shifting homes was tiresome. He was exhausted by the countless number of times he had walked back and forth from Maravali, directing his two elephants to haul back some of their pots and pans and other items. Srikanta and Puttaraju both uttered sweet nothings to endear themselves to him, and he was getting tired of their flattery. Then there was Giridhara, who kept asking him for instructions on rituals. He remained perpetually distracted and tired, until the previous night, when Jahnavi had prepared a potion for both of them. He didn't know what she had put in it, but it had worked. Now, as he prepared to go to Maravali yet again, he ran into Nanjunda outside.

"You had asked us not to disturb you, so we waited," said Nanjunda. "We've caught a thief."

"Why are you bothering me? Take him to Chandrabhanu.

Let him worry about this," Prabhakara Swami ordered him. Petty burglary being rare in Maravali, they were usually dealt with by the village council.

"This one is unusual," Nanjunda said. "A *Turka*…inside the estate. We thought you may want to see him for yourself."

Prabhakara Swami followed him to the barn, where a man was on his knees and tied up to a post with his turban. His hands were tied behind his back, and Narasimha's foot pressed down on the man's neck. He could hear the man's labored breathing. He asked Narasimha to release his foot from the man's neck.

"You!" he recoiled, surprised to see it was Azam Khan.

The last time he had seen the *Turka*, Rajanna was telling him something. Rajanna had just threatened to expose him as a spy, and he had pleaded for his forgiveness. But in his mind he had already decided Rajanna needed to die. Now, as the two walked away and Azam Khan glanced back at him occasionally, Prabhakara Swami had wondered whether Rajanna had told him about his dual identity. *Letting him live would be folly.* He had told Kaala to kill both Rajanna and his bodyguard. *So how did Azam Khan escape if Kaala managed to kill Rajanna? And does he know I was the one who ordered Rajanna's death?*

Fear gripped him for a moment, then he pulled himself together. *You are in control right now. Azam Khan is on his knees, at your mercy.*

He noticed the satchel strapped across Azam Khan's shoulder. *He must have stumbled on to it in Aadarshini's room. He is not just a petty pilferer, yet he picked it up. Why? How did he survive the assassination? Why is he here?* He tried to organize his thoughts, but there were far too many questions bouncing inside his muddled head.

"Go outside, you two. I will call for you if needed," Prabhakara Swami ordered. He turned to Azam Khan, who now looked at him with scorn.

"What are you doing in Madhuvana?" he asked.

Prabhakara Swami was amused at his prisoner's impertinence.

"Don't you know? I live here now," he responded insouciantly. "The more appropriate question is, what are *you* doing here, desecrating a Brahmin home?"

"*Live* here? This is my master's home, priest. His family still lives here. Have you no respect?"

"Alas," he said, "Rajanna's widows have perished, and his son is missing. I am here at the family's invitation. So what are you doing here, Azam Khan?"

"My master had sent me on an errand," he said. "When I returned, I got news of his death. I came here to check on his family. I..."

Prabhakara Swami interrupted him.

"You certainly took your time, didn't you? Don't slight my intelligence, Azam Khan, and I won't undervalue yours. You could have asked anyone in Maravali about the family. From what we hear, Rajanna died over an *amavasya* ago. Why come now, like a thief in the night? You know you aren't allowed inside Madhuvana, despite your loyalty to your master. You can be hanged for this transgression. No, Azam Khan, you came here for something else. Perhaps it's this satchel?"

Azam Khan glanced at the satchel. Prabhakara Swami bent down and whispered in his ears, "Is this yours? It's surely not mine. But others will surely be interested in what it has to say. Someone left it at the temple. Is this what you came here to get? Good. It will implicate you as a treasonous Afaqi! And then, of course, I will take the satchel back from you."

Don't waste time on self-pity. Think. Focus on getting out of your predicament, nothing else.

Rajanna's timeless maxim throbbed unceasingly within his head. He had to get out of his plight. He just didn't know how.

The last time he had seen Prabhakara Swami, Rajanna had told him to keep watch over the priest, but he hadn't said why. The following day, he had left for Masulipatnam. And now that he was at the priest's mercy. He realized there was more to him than he had thought, as if he was hiding something sinister. *Think, Azam Khan, think!* He decided to see how Prabhakara Swami would react to the truth. *When all else fails, confuse them with the truth!* Rajanna would say.

"I will not lie, O priest. I was not with Rajanna. I was here in Maravali. The satchel was given to me by a messenger and it was to be handed over to Rajanna. I haven't looked inside."

"But I have…keep talking," ordered Prabhakara Swami.

"Rajanna died and then dreadful events unfolded at Madhuvana. I was able to help Aadarshini escape, but we lost Raghu. I had left her by the river, but when I returned, she had disappeared. I have been waiting for her, and lost patience. I thought she had come back to Madhuvana. That, Prabhakara Swami, is the truth. It's up to you to believe it or not."

He could see from the priest's expression that he had thoroughly unnerved him. He was pacing across the floor, rubbing his forehead. He decided to press home his advantage.

"Wait," he added, "There is one more thing I forgot to mention. We were going to run away together to a land far away. That I swear is also the truth."

The priest stepped closer and slapped him across the face, over and over, till his lips split and his gums bled. He managed a taunting smile despite his predicament.

"I asked you not to disrespect my intelligence," Prabhakara Swami said, "and yet you persist. You have the impertinence to slander a chaste woman, your master's wife, a widow, a sati."

He thinks Aadarshini is dead. So she didn't go to him. Where is she then?

"What do I do with you, O insolent *Turka*?" Prabhakara Swami continued. "I can have my men beat the truth out of you, or I can establish the truth as I want it to be and mete out Vijayanagara justice to you. Yes, I think that's what I will do. The laws are clear about what happens to those who do what you've just admitted to."

"Do what you want, priest," he said, knowing well he had got under his skin. "I will restore Madhuvana to its rightful heir."

"Till then, *Turka*, Madhuvana is mine. It doesn't matter who owns it. Ownership is an illusion. What matters is that I am here, and I plan to be here as long as I want. I too will dedicate myself to finding Raghu. But I will raise him, and through him, I will rule Madhuvana."

"Not as long as I live."

Prabhakara Swami spit on his face and slapped him again. He called for Nanjunda.

"Give him water, and something to eat. Watch him closely. Don't let him talk. I will be back soon." He then stormed out of the barn.

Azam Khan was relieved. The priest had probably gone to get the other men of Madhuvana. *Good.* He knew them all. They'd never hand him a death sentence. He would lean on another of Rajanna's timeless tenets. *Let your silence speak for itself, for you will be less likely to say something stupid.*

Prabhakara Swami took a deep breath before bursting into the central courtyard, shouting hysterically, "Srikanta...Puttaraju...Kanteeravaa! Where is everyone?"

Everybody rushed out and asked what the din was about. Prabhakara Swami told them Azam Khan had broken into Madhuvana and was now in his custody.

"Impossible. He never comes into Madhuvana," a shocked Srikanta said.

"He must have come back to tell us about more about Rajanna's death. We must ask him why it took him so long to come back," said Puttaraju.

"I've dispatched someone to fetch Chandrabhanu," said Prabhakara Swami. "He must now discharge his duty as the head of the village council and the arbiter of justice. It is best that we wait for him before we begin interrogations. You've all known Azam Khan for years, but trying to enter my wife's room at night is not an offence I take lightly. Let the law take its course."

Chandrabhanu soon arrived in his palanquin. Prabhakara Swami suggested the trial be conducted outside Madhuvana. "We don't want the women and servants to witness this spectacle," he said. Everyone agreed. The men walked out to the large banyan tree outside, while Nanjunda and Narasimha brought a tied-up Azam Khan to the scene. As soon as the others saw the state of Azam Khan, they began to talk amongst themselves.

"Why have we tied him up like a common criminal? And what happened to his face? Why is it bruised? His lips are bleeding. His face is swollen. This is outrageous. Who are these two bullocks dragging him here? They are not from Maravali. What are they doing here?" Chandrabhanu furiously asked.

Prabhakara Swami hastened to explain who Narasimha and Nanjunda were. "You may recall that I had requested my superiors to send us two elephants to organize the festival. They've sent these two men. I plan to use them to run errands and send them back soon. It is they who apprehended the *Turka*."

"Trust our emperor's underlings to not know the difference between an elephant and a bullock. But must we treat Azam Khan in this manner?"

Prabhakara Swami did not react.

Chandrabhanu asked the two for their testimony, then asked them to stand away. "Azam Khan is not the sort to run away," he said.

Azam Khan stood upright now, looking straight at the men who sat under the banyan tree. Kanteeravaa was the first to question him. "I ask this on everyone's behalf. Why didn't you bring us news of Rajanna's passing? Weren't you with him?"

"No." Azam Khan shook his head.

"Why?"

"Because Rajanna had sent me to Honnavara on an errand."

"Is there any truth to what Prabhakara Swami just said about your intrusion?"

Azam Khan didn't say a word.

"Let me be direct," Chandrabhanu took over. "I have known Azam Khan since he arrived here as a thirteen-year-old. He is loved by all here. He has never offended anyone. He has never entered

Madhuvana before, despite serving Rajanna all his life. Rajanna trusted him with his life. So would I. It saddens me that he is being treated like a petty criminal. Just because he doesn't say anything in his defense doesn't mean he is guilty. I say that we treat him with compassion. If he entered Madhuvana, he must have a reason."

Prabhakara Swami fumed within. He realized he had miscalculated how others would view Azam Khan. He thought he could lay Raghu's disappearance on Azam Khan too, but now he saw that no one would consider it seriously. He switched to a different gambit.

"I agree," he said. "I too have admired Azam Khan's commitment to Rajanna and Madhuvana. But we all make mistakes. Perhaps he lost his sense of proportion after Rajanna's death and acted impulsively. I too would like to set him free."

The others looked at him puzzled.

"A good suggestion, Prabhakara Swami," said Chandrabhanu. "We all make mistakes."

"Wise," added Kanteeravaa.

"However, would that be a just ruling?" Prabhakara Swami then added, his words coming out slowly, measured. "After all, my wife could have been defiled in Madhuvana, that too by a *Turka*. I cannot overlook this. We cannot overlook this. It would not be just, not here in Vijayanagara."

"I understand, Prabhakara Swami," admitted Chandrabhanu. "I suggest..."

Prabhakara Swami interrupted him. "I suggest we set him free, but we must banish him from here, which we have every right to do. Let him say his farewells to all and his family here. My men will take him to the edge of our *jillé* in Pavanagiri. He must never be seen here again. A village crier must announce this decree in all villages. I believe this is an adequate outcome for this man's transgressions. If everyone agrees with my proposal, I am willing to forgive him. Let him begin life anew elsewhere. After all, with Rajanna gone, what purpose does he have here?"

The men discussed his proposal and acquiesced to it. Each of them requested to speak privately with Azam Khan. "To say a private farewell," they professed.

Prabhakara Swami watched patiently as Srikanta, Puttaraju, Chandrabhanu, and Kanteeravaa took turns walking Azam Khan a little away, their arm around his shoulders. He couldn't hear them, but he could see all of them sympathized with him. When everybody was done, he turned to Nanjunda and Narasimha. "Treat him well along the way," he said, making sure everyone gathered heard him.

He then walked to Azam Khan and whispered in his ear, "You are finished, my dear *Turka*."

"We'll see, priest" Azam Khan whispered back.

The council dismissed, Prabhakara Swami walked with Azam Khan, Nanjunda, and Narasimha till a little down the trail. Then, he asked Nanjunda to wait while the other two kept walking. "Take him through Maravali and to see his family. Ensure nothing happens to him. Don't let him linger. Once you are out of the *jillé*, slit his throat and leave him for the animals."

Nanjunda looked at him surprised.

Prabhakara Swami scowled, "Just do what you are told to do."

It wasn't till much later that he realized he had neglected to bring up the matter of the satchel during the trial. And then he had forgotten to take back the satchel before sending Azam Khan off to his death. He cursed himself for being careless. *It doesn't matter now*, he then told himself. *Azam Khan is a dead man; the satchel will disappear with him.*

Things looked bleak for Azam Khan. He knew he could unfetter himself from the rope with which his hands were shackled. He could also overpower one of his two burly captors. But he didn't stand a chance against both of them. He needed some luck, which he had learnt over the years, was a commodity the gods dispensed frugally. He had to keep his wits about him now. *At least the priest forgot about the satchel,* he thought to himself.

"This road will take us into Maravali, but you already know that," Azam Khan addressed the two a little after Prabhakara Swami left them. He pointed to a skinnier trail to the side. "And this trail bypasses Maravali and takes us straight to the other side. You can drag me through Maravali and strip me of my dignity, or you can treat me with respect and take me home to say my farewells. I can tell you are decent men, so the choice is yours."

Trust in the basic goodness of men, Rajanna would often say. He thought this was as good a time as any to test that premise.

Nanjunda said, "Lead the way, but don't get too adventurous."

Azam Khan thanked them and began walking down to the other side, where Mohammedans and others of low caste lived across a brook. When they came upon it, he turned towards them. "I vow not to ask any more favors, but that's my home." He pointed across the stream. "Do what you want with me, but spare my family the pain of seeing me in these."

The two surprised him again by unshackling him, and letting him cleanse himself in the stream. They held him from both sides, and began discussing the best way to get to Pavanagiri. Azam Khan found it amusing that he was both their guide and prisoner, for neither seemed to be familiar with the region. "Since we are on foot, we should be in Pavanagiri by evening on the fourth day. There are plenty of serais and taverns along the way," he said.

Hashim and his wife sat on the portico and ran out when they saw him. Azam Khan knew his captors wouldn't enter a Mohammedan's home. Nonetheless he offered them food and drink, which they refused.

"We will wait outside. Don't take too long," said Narasimha.

Inside, Hashim and Ammi broke into tears. "I told you that woman would mean nothing but trouble for our son," Ammi said.

Hashim quickly composed himself.

"I will mourn you later. Let us first talk about how to get you out of your predicament. Are they taking you to Pavanagiri? Good. There will be plenty of opportunities to set yourself free." Hashim suggested a variety of options. "I have no doubt they have orders to kill you. The priest is not a fool to let you go free with an axe to grind. Better you kill these two before they kill you. There is no shame in self-preservation."

"They've treated me honorably," said Azam Khan, "and I will do the same. But don't worry, I will not let them kill me either."

When it was time to leave, Hashim and Ammi blessed him. "Inshallah, we will meet again, son," Hashim whispered in his ears.

The trio resumed their walk towards Pavanagiri.

"You may shackle me now if you wish" said Azam Khan once they had crossed the brook. Nanjunda instead tied the rope around Azam Khan's waist and held the other end, switching with Narasimha as the day went on. The two kept talking amongst themselves, mostly about life in Maravali, the women, the food, and the rains. Azam Khan remained quiet. That night, they slept in an open courtyard at a serai. The two took turns staying awake to watch over him.

Azam Khan knew it would be impossible to give them the slip. He couldn't sleep either. His thoughts kept going back to the trial, and the conversations the men of Madhuvana had with him.

Kanteeravaa had said, "After you cross into Pavanagiri, keep going till you reach the sea. Go home." He had slipped Azam Khan his gold chain as a gift.

Srikanta and Puttaraju in turn had sought his support.

"I will be visiting our trading partners soon," Srikanta told him. "I will be back in a year to take charge of Madhuvana. Look for Raghu. If you find him, keep him with you till I return. I will need you the way Rajanna did. Don't let the priest bother you. I need him here for the time being to curb Puttaraju's ambitions."

Puttaraju's ambitions too had become clear.

"Find my uncle," he had said, referring to Shamanna. "Tell him I sent you. We could use a man of your valor to help us rule Madhuvana."

Chandrabhanu in turn had offered a practical advice. "The sultan in Bijapur has begun reprisals against Afaqis. Over three thousand Afaqis from his military, rendered adrift, have joined the rebel forces on our side of the border. They could use a leader who is one of their own and knows these parts well. Go to the police chief of Pavanagiri.

Tell him I sent you. He will put you in touch with the right people. Forget about Maravali. I see nothing but turmoil here for the near future. Fight for a bigger cause. Fight alongside Rama Raya. Rajanna would approve of that."

Now, as he sat back and reflected upon what they had said, he realized Madhuvana was in the middle of a succession struggle much like the empire. Fighting for the rebels was always an option, but his first duty was to Rajanna and his legacy. *The boy needed to be found!* Without him, the vultures would tear at Madhuvana. He wondered where Aadarshini was. He hoped she hadn't reached out to the priest, who he now knew had his own designs.

By the fourth day, all three of them had run out of conversation. They walked listlessly, each hoping the dreary walk would come to an end. They couldn't have been gladder to find a serai around midday. It was early and there were no diners yet. Nanjunda and Narasimha sat on a bench under the tree in the courtyard, while Azam Khan stood nearby. A man with a dusty turban and a dirty beard emerged from the path. He hitched his horse to the tree and sat next to Nanjunda.

"A prisoner of yours, I presume," the man said, pointing at Azam Khan. "I can see the rope around his *Turka* waist. What has he done?"

Nanjunda did not respond.

The serai owner came out and announced the midday meal was ready. The four ate in silence on the portico floor. After the meal, the man in the dusty turban reached into a pouch, retrieved a small stack of betel leaves laced with *sunna* and wrapped around areca nuts, and stuffed it into his mouth. He offered some to Nanjunda and Narasimha. The three chewed quietly while Azam Khan sat a short distance away.

"Your prisoner looks strong," the stranger said. "Looks like a beast capable of negotiating steep hills and waterways to move goods across the land, just the sort that's good in my trade. I would like to buy him."

Without waiting for a response, he placed a hefty pouch on the floor, where they could reach out and touch it.

"Gold coins," he said.

Nanjunda and Narasimha looked at each other, clearly surprised by the proposition. They spit out the crimson juice from the betel leaves and ordered Azam Khan to get up and follow them. As he walked past the stranger, Azam Khan watched him wipe the juice dripping from the side of this mouth and belch.

"Looks like destiny has smiled on you two," Azam Khan said. "That's more gold coins than you'll earn in your lifetime. What will you do?"

"What would *you* do if you were us?" Narasimha asked him.

"My advice would be to take the gold. Go back to Prabhakara Swami. Tell him I tried to escape and that you hunted me down, cut my throat and left my body in the woods. Take my tunic and soak it in blood. I will not return to Maravali anytime soon and embarrass you. When your tenure with Prabhakara Swami is over, start a new life. After all, we are just hirelings, so we need to watch out for ourselves."

"What about you?"

"Let me worry about me," replied Azam Khan.

The two stepped away to talk privately.

The meal over, the stranger paid the serai owner, belched loudly again, and prepared to untie his horse.

"Wait, stranger," Narasimha hollered and ran up to him. "We accept your offer. He is your *Turka* now."

Nanjunda nudged Azam Khan towards the man. The stranger handed him the pouch, and he beamed as he gleefully felt its weight.

"Use it wisely," said Azam Khan. "And thank you for treating me with honor."

Nanjunda and Narasimha didn't look back. Azam Khan watched till they were out of sight, then turned around to the stranger.

"Are you sure you didn't pay too much for me, my dear Rudra?" he said, grinning from ear to ear.

"For a friendship as precious as ours, I'd say I struck a great bargain, my dear Azam Khan," he replied, and rushed to embrace him.

"How long since our paths crossed? Three, maybe even four years! You look well," Azam Khan said, hugging him back.

"I remember. We were escorting Rajanna across Bijapur. Oh, how time flies," Rudra said. "I see you still haven't lost your penchant for getting into trouble. And you still smell terrible, like a horse that's rolled around in its own dung."

Azam Khan had to laugh.

"How did you end up at this serai?"

"Your Allah's will, perhaps. Kismet!" Rudra rubbed his fingers across his forehead. "I have been recruiting new informers and getting rid of the ones we couldn't trust. I came towards Maravali, and thought I'd visit you. Hashim told me about your predicament. He told me the serais you would be passing through on your way to Pavanagiri. You were on foot. I had a horse. I caught up with you at the serai last night, but they were too many people there for me to make myself known. So I followed you, and when I saw the two stop at this serai, I thought it was a good time to strike."

Azam Khan thanked his stars. He had told Hashim the route he would be taking to Pavanagiri, and had hoped someone, maybe Dilshaad, would come to his rescue. He hadn't expected it to be Rudra in his wildest dreams.

"And what if those two bulls had refused your offer?"

"Then they'd be dead and I'd still have my pouch full of gold. But I am glad we settled it like we did. You know I abhor bloodshed," Rudra replied with a smile. "But you, my friend, have a lot to tell me."

"I hope you can drink like you used to," Azam Khan smiled.

After drinking late into the night, and informing Rudra about everything that had happened since the day Rajanna asked him to go to Honnavara, Azam Khan told him he needed to find Aadarshini and Raghu, for they were the keys to the imbroglio that was Madhuvana.

Rudra quietly said, "There is only person who will know what to do next."

"Sidappa!" cried out Azam Khan.

<hr />

Azam Khan is dead, Prabhakara Swami told himself repeatedly. His two elephants had told him the job was done, but it didn't seem to calm him down. He needed to tell the whole world.

When a trader stopped by the temple and asked him for directions to the nearest serai, he invited him to dine at his home. During the meal, he planted a story he hoped would be carried far and wide. "Be wary of brigands on the road. Why, we captured one just the other day, right in my home! A *Turka* by the name of Azam Khan. He was tried by a tribunal and banished from the district. I am told he tried to escape and was hunted down and killed."

The man would share the story with his fellow travelers at the serai, and then again at the next, until the legend of Azam Khan made its way across all the serais. *That's what people do*, he told himself. *Everybody loves a sordid tale.*

After the trader left, Prabhakara Swami sat by the riverside near Madhuvana and smiled at the setting sun. All was well in his universe. Rajanna was dead. So was Azam Khan. His secret was safe. Aadarshini was dead, but that was karma, both his and hers. And he had Madhuvana. His patient search for Rajanna's son hadn't yet yielded results, and although this was frustrating, he knew the boy would be found sooner or later.

As he watched a few boys herding their goats back home he suddenly felt a tinge of envy towards their uncomplicated lives. The seductive beauty of the scene made him think of Aadarshini, and he felt a terrible rage. Ever since Azam Khan had planted the notion that there was something going on between him and Aadarshini, he hadn't been able to control his mind from conjuring up vivid images of the two making love, filling his heart with venom. *I'm rid of your philandering Turka*, he shouted into the void, as though she was in front of him, naked, taunting him, *and if you were alive, I'd send you back to the dead too, you impious sacrilegious whore.*

"Somewhere in my heart," Azam Khan said, "I feel we will find Aadarshini soon."

The two trotted on their horses. Azam Khan had stolen yet another Arabian steed from a tavern. Rudra gave him a curious look.

"You've never been one to think matters through. Let your heart be; now's the time to think with your head," he scolded him.

"What do you think Sidappa will say?"

"To keep things simple. He will not beat around the bush. He'll tell you to forget about her, and remind you that she went off on her own. If she had ended up in the refuge of a kind family, she would have resurfaced by now. She probably lost her bearings and ended up with dacoits or gypsies."

"You've never met her, Rudra. That's why you speak so coldly about what might have happened to her. She'd choose death before dishonor," Azam Khan said firmly.

Rudra smirked.

"Azam Khan, you know what survival instincts can drive a person to do."

"What about the boy?" Azam Khan changed tack.

"The boy is most likely dead."

"What purpose does that leave me with?"

"I know you were drunk when you told me, but I like your idea of sailing back to Persia. Do it. There is life beyond Maravali and a world beyond Vijayanagara. With the turmoil at the capital, who knows how long our beloved Vijayanagara will even last? Take my advice. Visit Sidappa. Then sail away." As an afterthought, he added, "I must caution you though. You will never actually be able to leave. The scent of the mogra will haunt you forever, wherever you are. It's the émigré's curse."

"Inshallah I will come back and take you with me someday. But before I leave," said Azam Khan, "I have to teach the priest a lesson."

"I will not let you do that, my friend," Rudra was firm once again. "From what you've told me, Prabhakara Swami is not as holy nor as priestly as he appears to be. Control your urge. Let me understand him better. I will avenge what he did to you, but in good time. I promise you."

They were to visit Rudra's home in Champanhalli before going to Sidappa's. Rudra needed a few days to settle his affairs since he hadn't been home in a while. "It will delay us by no longer than a few days.

Then we will leave for Sidappa's. Hopefully Venkata will be home too. Imagine the three of us together again, after all these years."

"What is the rascal up to nowadays?" asked Azam Khan.

"Venkata has been helping our other friends navigate between safe houses here. He is good at this. He knows the trails like the back of his hand, and he can be ruthless with enemies. Sidappa sends him on missions frequently. Dangerous work, requiring both brawn and brain, but the man was born for such things. As you say, inshallah it will pay off for all of us."

Azam Khan was envious. He had accompanied Rajanna to several meetings with the Rama Raya's representatives, but only as a bodyguard. He had often told Rajanna he could do more for the rebellion, but Rajanna had never allowed it. *Who'd take care of me and my family if something were to happen to you?*

8

AADARSHINI DECIDED IT WAS TIME for her to act.

Sidappa had assured her Venkata would go to Madhuvana to check on Raghu. She had privately asked Venkata to take her along, and he had agreed. Then that morning, she saw Venkata riding away. *He was supposed to take me with him. Why would he go back on his word?* This wasn't the first time men had behaved perfidiously towards her, treating her as if her opinion didn't matter. She wanted to rationalize his decision, thinking perhaps it was for her own good, but she felt a part of her psyche wilt.

She came to the pond to clear her mind. She bathed, draped herself in a fresh sari, and let her hair free to dry in the gentle breeze. Keshava, the boy with the limp, sat with another boy at the far end. She waved to him, calling him towards her. Keshava limped towards where she was, while the other boy disappeared into one of the huts.

"I hear you run errands all over the region, Keshava. That must be so exciting, so full of adventure," she said as she dried out her wet sari on a flat boulder. Keshava nodded and beamed proudly. She asked him to hand her some stones to weigh down the sari.

"There, the sun will dry it no time," she said. "Keshava, I've always wanted to ask you, have you ever been to Maravali?"

She knew he had.

"Yes, many times," the boy replied. "I can usually get there well before dark."

"You are a brave boy, going so far by yourself," said Aadarshini and squeezed his cheeks gently, making him blush. "Will you do me a favor then? I need to send a message to someone in Maravali. But you must promise not to tell anyone, not even Sidappa."

"Yes, surely I can. I am leaving tomorrow. I have to go to several places. Maravali is on the way. But I will return in a few days. I won't tell anyone, I promise."

Aadarshini thanked the stars she had come across the boy that day itself. "Good. Meet me tomorrow before you leave, there by the big tree," she pointed at a banyan that stood on the trail leading away.

She stroked the boy's face and smiled, hoping the boy was charmed by her. He blushed, bobbed his head, then turned around and left.

It was cloudy the next morning. Aadarshini walked to the banyan quietly. She had decided to send Prabhakara Swami one of her anklets. Everyone in Maravali knew of the distinctive anklets that Rajanna's wives wore. And she had so often caught the priest staring at her ankles that she was confident he would know it belonged to her. The boy waited patiently, and she was glad he did.

"Go to the temple in Maravali. An old woman sells flowers outside. Give this to her and tell her to give it to Prabhakara Swami. Tell her to tell him these came from Sidappa's village. Don't say anything more, and don't talk to anyone else."

A short rumble of thunder interrupted her.

"I hope it won't rain," noted Keshava, looking to the skies.

"Here, take this with you." She handed him the palm-leaf umbrella she had carried with her. "And this is for you. Don't eat it all at once." She handed him a packet of curd rice neatly wrapped in a banana leaf. "Travel safe. Come back soon. And remember, this is our little secret. No one else must know."

She watched Keshava limp away and disappear into the trail. When she entered the hut, she ran into Sidappa.

"I hear the sound of just one anklet," he noted. "Did you lose the other one? It's inauspicious to wear just one anklet."

Does the old man know what I've done?

"Don't panic. It must have dropped somewhere around. Or it may have slipped off your ankle when you were in the pond. Have one of the boys dive for it. They like playing that game," said Sidappa and walked away.

Aadarshini prayed Prabhakara Swami would get her message and come quickly. *I hope he brings Raghu with him.*

Prabhakara Swami felt refreshed. These short visits to nearby villages that didn't have their own temples always enlivened him. He'd stay at the headman's and relish the adulation of the villagers. He'd counsel them on wide-ranging matters, from naming newborns to rituals to conceive a son. He'd hold court under a banyan tree or on someone's porch and regale devotees with stories from the scriptures. He felt good about himself after such visits; they kept him grounded in what he most loved to do – tell stories – and also deny his other less holy personas.

As his palanquin returned to Madhuvana, he inhaled the serene stillness that greeted him. A light afternoon shower had rendered everything green and Madhuvana sparkled liked the hermitage of his dreams. He was happy to be back. Those who lived in Madhuvana too seemed to be pleased to have him. They'd come out to the northeast courtyard, where he'd be performing his morning pooja each morning, before commencing their daily chores, and take his blessings.

He noticed an unfamiliar horse tied outside the outside portico. It had just deposited a fresh mound of dung at the doorstep, and he winced at the malodor. The sight of an unfamiliar horse at his doorstep was an unsettling omen for him. Whenever his superiors wanted him to move from one village to another, the orders were delivered by someone who'd hitch his horse at his doorstep. He braced himself. He had no desire to move from Maravali.

He was relieved, and surprised, to find Shamanna waiting for him on the swing inside. *So the brother-in-law is finally here*, he thought.

"Shamanna, what a pleasant surprise! Welcome to Madhuvana. It is nice to meet you again after so many years. When did you arrive?"

Prabhakara Swami joined him on the swing.

"I came a few days ago. Puttaraju has been briefing me about everything that transpired here. I was surprised to hear about Azam Khan. I never did trust the bastard."

"That horse by the portico," said Prabhakara Swami. "It is yours, I presume. You must move it elsewhere."

"Ah, yes, the smell," said Shamanna. "Come, Swami! It is an Arabian steed. You should learn to like that smell. It is the smell of power."

Prabhakara Swami laughed. Rajanna too had aphorisms about Arabian horse-fart.

"What brings you here? The family could have used your counsel all these days. There was much turmoil..."

"Yes. I didn't know of Rajanna's passing till I got Puttaraju's message. I am annoyed at the acrimony about who inherits his empire. I will put an end to that discussion soon."

And how do you hope to do that?

"I too was travelling when the family got the sad news. They have acquitted themselves admirably. I wish I was here in time to thwart the sati. But then, who has ever thwarted fate, Shamanna?"

"Yes, indeed. I wish I could have been here to perform the post-death rituals for my sister and Rajanna. Despite my misgivings about how he treated me, there was much to admire in the man."

Prabhakara Swami decided not to probe about his misgivings just yet. *He will tell me himself in good time.* Instead, he said, "Those rituals would have been the son's responsibility. You needn't burden yourself with that guilt. Alas, the boy has disappeared."

"So I hear. But why are you here, Prabhakara Swami? Don't you live in Maravali, behind the temple?"

"Indeed. But when I returned to Maravali, the infighting in

Madhuvana had intensified, and Chandrabhanu, Kanteeravaa and the others asked me to stay here and guide them on a range of matters."

"Such as?"

"Organizing the search for Raghu, for one. I have also impressed upon everyone that if they don't keep the family together, an outsider will usurp Madhuvana. I told Srikanta to meet with Rajanna's business associates. Without their cooperation, Madhuvana will disappear into the quicksand of history. Puttaraju is administering the plantation. Everyone now has a mission. I am glad you are here, though. You can now take over, and I can get back to my priestly duties."

He waited to see how Shamanna would respond.

"And what do you suggest I do once we find the boy?" he asked.

"I assume you will return home. The family will care for the boy. He is the heir after all."

Shamanna wiped the sweat off his brow. He got off the swing and began walking around. *The man wants to vent*, Prabhakara Swami could tell.

"Do you know," he began, "there was a time when Rajanna was close to insolvency? I, then a prosperous merchant in the Malabars, helped him reestablish his supremacy. He reciprocated by marrying my sister Kalavati. But over time, he outmaneuvered me and turned me into his vassal. I was content, though, until he took that little myna as his third wife, just because an astrologer told him she would bear him an heir. I was outraged. Could you imagine how my sister might have felt? I would have killed him had I been a lesser person. I stayed away after that, until I found myself in dire straits when Rama Raya's troops, while regrouping, overran my estate and appropriated it for their own use. I had no choice but to come crawling back to him. I swallowed my pride."

All this was news to him. He was amused at Shamanna referring to Aadarshini as a little myna. *How apt!*

"Yes," said Prabhakara Swami, "but he liked you, Shamanna. He always spoke fondly of you."

"Condescension is not love, Prabhakara Swami. Manipulation is not love," replied Shamanna. "I have given my blood and sweat for him. I have been loyal. And I have nothing to show for it. Nothing!"

Prabhakara Swami smiled. He had Shamanna where he wanted him, drowning in self-pity and needing a sympathetic ear.

"You are agitated, Shamanna. Talking about Rajanna can often do that to people. I do agree with you for the most part. Rajanna liked to own people, as he did things. But it's over now."

"You are right," replied Shamanna, "I am agitated. I have a lot on my mind. There is no need for you to leave Madhuvana. Your presence has had a stabilizing effect. If you and I cooperate, we can lead this saga to a reasonable conclusion."

"How long will you be at Madhuvana, Shamanna?"

"I will leave the day after tomorrow."

"Then let us both go to the riverside on the morning of your departure. We will perform the morning rituals and talk at length about other matters, perhaps even of your little myna. I want to see you off with a smile," said Prabhakara Swami.

"Yes, that would be nice. I know how bewitching Madhuvana can be at dawn. I will take your leave now. Let us meet at the riverside in two days."

Two mornings later, as the two settled themselves by the riverside, a myna whistled.

"The sweet little myna," said Shamanna. "Too bad she has left us. I would never have allowed her to go through sati."

"Yes. She was the delight of Maravali. I miss seeing her at the temple. Alas, I too came back too late."

"She took care of me when I was here – so pleasant, so young, and so luscious. She took good care of Kalavati too. I would have gladly taken her as my wife if she were still alive. People would laud my magnanimity. These succession dilemmas would be resolved in a twinkle of her eyes."

"You'd have to fight me for her hand, Shamanna," said Prabhakara Swami, pretending he was saying it in jest.

"No, you couldn't marry a widow and stay a priest anywhere in Vijayanagara, Swami," Shamanna reminded him.

Prabhakara Swami knew neither could Shamanna. "With her as my wife, would I need to be a priest?"

"No, but you'd have to be alive. And I wouldn't allow that."

As they enjoyed their moments of mirth, Prabhakara Swami pulled out two scrolls he had brought with him. They contained the names he had seen on the scrolls he had lost to Azam Khan. He had subsequently written down as many as he could recall.

"I found these in Rajanna's room. You may be familiar with some of the names. Perhaps they were his business associates. The names don't mean anything to me. Keep them if you think they may be of use to you."

Shamanna studied the list quickly and set them aside.

"The names don't mean anything to me. They could be anyone – serai owners, prostitutes, informers, runners, horse traders – anyone, except perhaps this one." Shamanna pointed at one of the names.

"Sidappa," Prabhakara Swami read the name aloud.

"A long time ago, a man named Sidappa used to be Rajanna's bodyguard. He lost his eyes in a fight while protecting Rajanna. Azam Khan replaced him. But I've not heard Sidappa's name mentioned in over a decade. Did Rajanna ever mention his name to you?"

"No, never."

"Then Sidappa would have died by now," said Shamanna. "If he were alive, he'd surely have come to Madhuvana to pay his respects to Rajanna, and you'd have noticed him. Besides, Sidappa is a common name among these people. The one on your list could be someone entirely different."

He handed the scrolls back.

"Your desire for Madhuvana is understandable, Shamanna," said Prabhakara Swami as they made their way back towards Madhuvana, he on foot, Shamanna on his horse. "Your anger towards Rajanna notwithstanding, I suggest you and I focus on finding Raghu. It doesn't matter who finds him. However, if I find him before you do, I will be glad to hand him over to you, but I'd need to be appropriately rewarded."

"How, may I ask, would you want to be rewarded, Prabhakara Swami?"

"I will hand Raghu over to you in exchange for the rights to stay in Madhuvana. I don't seek material wealth. But build me a place by the riverside, a glorious *gurukula* where I can enrich young minds. I will turn it into a hermitage that will thrive for centuries. I don't care who prevails in Vijayanagara. I will have no trouble convincing the victor in the wisdom of letting my hermitage thrive. After all, religion is our people's favorite addiction. Take over Madhuvana. Do what you want with the boy – I would advise you to keep him alive in your custody. Take him into town during festivals. Let everybody see you care for him. They will worship you for your loyalty to Rajanna's legacy. You will need their adulation to live peacefully."

Prabhakara Swami could see Shamanna beaming.

"I like your proposal," said Shamanna. "I agree. Send a message to the temple in Beegralli, in the name of Bheema, when you find Raghu. We'll do the rest after."

As they neared Madhuvana, they noticed a boy using a palm-leaf umbrella to shake off tamarinds from the tree. When he saw them, he dropped the umbrella and disappeared along one of the other trails. The boy had a prominent limp and the comical sight of him scampering away like a monkey caused the two to guffaw.

"Do you want me to give chase?"

"No, let him go," said Prabhakara Swami. "He was probably trying to help himself to the tamarind. I hope he got some."

A pair of mynas began an earnest battle of tweets from the branches.

"May her soul rest in peace," said Shamanna.

"Travel safely, Shamanna. Our lives could change with a single message now."

Shamanna rode away. Prabhakara Swami turned to go inside, when, curious about what the boy had dropped before fleeing, he walked back to the tamarind tree.

Aadarshini had plenty to be anxious about. *Did Keshava deliver the anklets? How long before the priest came here? What will Sidappa do when he finds out I acted without his approval?* But the sun was gentle, and the breeze uplifting. Aadarshini tried to put away her anxieties and helped Sharada sweep the swath of tamped earth that circled the hut and made a platform perfect for sun-drying chillies, mangoes, and *sandigay*. Sharada was gently rubbing coconut oil into her mother-in-law's hair. Aadarshini spotted a rider fast approaching the hamlet, and saw that it was Venkata. He seemed distraught. As soon as he reached them, he jumped off his horse, and ran right past them towards Sidappa's hut. He rushed in and out of Sidappa's hut then asked them, "Where is he?"

"He went out for a walk with one of the boys. He couldn't have gone far," said Sharada.

"Find him," he ordered her. "Go around the huts. I'll go towards the fields."

Venkata mounted his horse and sped away. Aadarshini joined Sharada in the search for Sidappa. *Something was terribly wrong.* They peeked into each hut until they found Sidappa sitting in the sun outside one of them. They brought him back to his hut. When Venkata returned, Sidappa was pacing nervously. He fell at his feet.

"Appa," he cried out, "I have grim news. Azam Khan is dead."

Aadarshini could feel her stomach convulse. She took a deep breath, her head lolled back then slumped forward, and she let out a hopeless whimper. Sidappa slumped to the ground, tears pouring down his wrinkled face. Venkata too began to weep. Sharada and Padma ran to Sidappa. Before long, others had gathered outside their hut. Everyone waited for Sidappa to say something, but he remained silent, his hands on his head. "I have just been told that I've lost a son today. Allow me to grieve. We will talk some other time. Go home now. It's the same old tale. Life, then Death."

He asked Padma and Sharada to leave him alone with Venkata. Sharada tried to pull Aadarshini along, but Sidappa stopped her. "No, let her stay. She needs to listen to what happened. She may well have been responsible for the boy's fate."

Venkata then related what he had gathered at Maravali. "Everyone thinks she is dead. Her son is nowhere to be found."

"Raghu is missing?" gasped Aadarshini. She had thought Raghu would be in Madhuvana, being cared for by the family. Her heart began to palpitate. *Raghu was missing?*

Venkata ignored her.

"I was going to Azam Khan's home to tell him Aadarshini was safe with us when someone in Maravali told me a *ghoshaka* has been announcing that an intruder, a *Turka*, had trespassed into the priest's home in Madhuvana, and was tried by the village council. They banished him from the district. Citizens were warned not to give him refuge."

A new thunderbolt struck Aadarshini, temporarily numbing the shock caused by Raghu's disappearance. "Prabhakara Swami is in Madhuvana?" she was puzzled. "That's not his residence."

"Well, it is now," said Venkata, "the very home where Rajanna and his family once lived, *your* home. The family has sought his help to look for Raghu. They have asked him to live there till the boy is found."

"How in God's name would *he* know how to find Raghu?" noted Sidappa.

"The intruder was none other than Azam Khan. I spoke to several farmhands to confirm this. It was the priest who apprehended him, arranged a speedy trial and proposed his exile. Two bodyguards escorted Azam Khan towards Pavanagiri. The farmhands saw him being taken away."

Azam Khan, a prowler inside Madhuvana? Why did he go back? Did he think I had returned?

"But exile doesn't mean he is dead," offered Sidappa.

"I thought so too at first, Appa," said Venkata. "But on my way back, I heard travelers gossip at a serai that a man named Azam Khan had tried to escape his captors and was killed. His body was left for the animals. All taverns now know this tale."

"Animals!" Sidappa sighed.

"I went back to Madhuvana under the guise of seeking employment to see if the priest indeed lived there," he continued. "There is no doubt he does. I waited outside the door while his wife moved around like she owned the place. I left quietly."

"So much for your advocacy of the priest," Sidappa told Aadarshini. "Do you still want to beg for his help in getting back Madhuvana?"

Aadarshini, already having trouble holding back her tears, set free her deluge. "I sent Azam Khan to his death. He went back looking for me. I have his blood on my hands. And my Raghu, I cannot live without him. I have no reason to. Oh Raghu, I have failed you."

"Rajanna was always suspicious of this priest," Sidappa addressed Venkata, ignoring Aadarshini's harangue. "I know Azam Khan always showed respect to him. So when the priest caught Azam Khan trespassing, he could have sought his help to find Raghu. Instead, he sentenced him to death. Why? The priest knows more than he is letting on."

"Appa, you are thinking too much. Keep it simple. We have to avenge Azam Khan. I can go to Madhuvana right away and dispatch the priest to the gods. We will look for the boy after that. If he is alive, I will find him. Give me your blessings."

"Vengeance is the option of fools," said Sidappa, as if he was issuing an edict. "You will do no such thing. We must first let our anger subside. Then we will think. Only then will we act. Now, take me out to the pond. I want to be alone."

Venkata held onto Sidappa's arm and helped him to the pondside.

Back inside Sharada's hut, Aadarshini saw Sharada was crying.

"If you seek vengeance, wreak it yourself," Sharada said to her. "My husband will gladly lay down his life for Rajanna's family, but please don't use him to extract your revenge. Don't you have enough blood on your hands?"

"No, that is not what I want to do," she said, and tried to hold Sharada's hand, but she jerked herself free and left.

Aadarshini walked out to where Sidappa sat. She saw that he had been crying.

"I didn't know blind people shed tears," she said.

Sidappa laughed.

"I didn't either, till I lost my sight."

They were both silent for a while. Sidappa then addressed her, "Do you understand now what I meant by not trusting the priest? There is something not right with him. Rajanna saw it, and now Azam Khan has paid for it. But don't let his death blind you. We have to lull the priest into complacency. We need to learn what he is up to at Madhuvana. Let him think you are dead. Bide your time. There's nothing more satisfying than exacting revenge when your enemy least expects it."

Aadarshini was silent. *Oh Sidappa, how do I tell you what I have done in my haste? Keshava may have already told the priest I am alive. He may be on his way here by now!*

Sidappa began telling her about Azam Khan. "He was just thirteen when I first met him. He told everyone that Rajanna had rescued him and brought him to Maravali. But really, it was he who had rescued Rajanna. Azam Khan and his father were ambushed by bandits while travelling in the doab. They killed the old man, but the boy – his survival instincts were great even then – ran from the scene. The same bandits came upon Rajanna and Shamanna, who had been travelling. Their bodyguards managed to kill all but two before dying themselves, and Shamanna, by prior agreement, fled the scene. For Rajanna's trade to survive, it was important at least one of them survive such raids. It was Rajanna's turn to stay and fight. He managed to kill one of the bandits. Unfortunately, the surviving bandit got the better of him and was about to strike a lethal blow when someone appeared from nowhere and cut the assailant's throat, his warm blood splashing onto Rajanna. It was a thirteen-year-old Azam Khan, the dagger in his hand still dripping with blood. The dagger, which belonged to Rajanna, had been lost during the battle. He gifted it to the boy right there. Ever since, the boy has safeguarded it like a gift from God."

Sidappa paused. He turned his face towards her, like he could see her.

"And now, you possess that precious gem-encrusted dagger in its bejeweled sheath. I have to ask myself, why does Rajanna's widow have Azam Khan's dagger? Why does she weep for him? Why did he save her when he should've been with Rajanna?"

Aadarshini cleared her throat, floundering to say something.

"No," Sidappa raised his hand before she spoke. "Don't say anything that will disrespect my intelligence. Take me home now."

On their way back, he squeezed her palm reassuringly.

"I know how troubling Raghu's disappearance must be. Don't despair. We will find Rajanna's heir."

"Only if he is alive," Aadarshini's voice broke even as she said it.

"Oh, he is alive. Trust me. He is too valuable a piece to kill off so early in this game. Someone has hidden him somewhere. It's for us to find out who has and why."

* * *

Prabhakara Swami looked at the two items with great care. The palm-leaf umbrella felt familiar, and he was surprised to see a star etched on its handle, a star *he* had etched a long time ago. *My umbrella!* He had given it away to a woman when the cart passed her on the trail, on the morning he returned to Maravali. The other was a silver anklet tied up in a piece of cloth. He instantly recognized the piece of jewelry. He had seen it many times on Aadarshini's ankles. The unmistakable design with the sigil of a swan was unique to anklets worn by Rajanna's wives. He could feel blood rushing into his brain. *Aadarshini!* His heart fluttered with a fear he hadn't hitherto experienced. The din of the mynas got shriller. Unable to think, he began walking down the trail that took him to Madhuvana, shaking like a drunk.

That consummate liar! Azam Khan deceived me with the truth. He deceived me into disbelieving everything he said. He did save her from being cremated. He was indeed her lover. She is alive. She was in the storeroom. I passed her in the storm. And she sent me the umbrella and the anklet. Is she mocking me? Is she reaching out for help? Where is she? What am I to do now?

He staggered into Madhuvana and went straight to Jahnavi, who studied the anklet then put it away where Sarala or the other maids wouldn't pry.

"What am I to do now, Jahnavi?" he cried.

"You pretend to be a wise man, yet I have the misfortune of seeing you in this state," she was remarkably calm. "Think! The anklet by itself doesn't mean much, does it?"

He pulled himself together. "Yes, there is nothing to worry about. Everyone thinks she is dead. So she remains dead. I simply have to find her before she returns. I must ensure she remains dead. Nothing will have changed then."

"Yes," added Jahnavi, caressing his cheeks. "We'll soon find Raghu. We'll embrace the glorious future you have deftly negotiated with Shamanna. Find the boy with the limp. He will lead you to her."

A shiver went up his loins. He found Jahnavi's coldblooded assessment arousing. He came closer and placed his head on her bosom. She pulled him closer and continued talking, "Nature likes things in balance, just as Madhuvana now is. Aadarshini's reappearance will upset this balance, not just for us but for everyone in Madhuvana. She must not be allowed to do this. For the sake of the greater good, the sacrifice of a few is justified. Isn't that the way of dharma, isn't that what the epics teach us?"

"Yes. What needs to be done must be done," he replied coldly, as he pulled her down on the bed.

Aadarshini prayed hard. She prayed that Keshava hadn't found the priest, that the boy hadn't completed his errand. The possibilities were slim, she knew, for the snake was out of the bag. *Oh, why did I have to be hasty?* Aadarshini cursed herself.

Early one morning, however, her fears came true. Keshava stuck his head inside the hut and asked her to come out. Aadarshini rushed outside and followed him to the pond.

"The old woman was not at the temple yesterday. I waited for the priest. He didn't come to the temple. A passerby told me the priest now lives in a place called Madhuvana and told me how to go there. But when I got there, I saw two men at the gate. One of them was bald and on a horse, a black horse with a white tail. The other walked alongside. They spotted me. I panicked. I dropped what I was carrying, and ran away. I let you down. I am sorry."

Aadarshini was relieved. *At least he didn't reveal anything to the priest.* She stroked his cheek and thanked him. "You did well. I am proud of you. Now go home and don't talk about this to anyone." *I wish you hadn't gone to Madhuvana,* she thought, but she could do nothing about it now. She wondered who the two men were. What if one of them was Prabhakara Swami? *It doesn't matter. The priest will never know where the anklet came from. I am safe here.*

As she turned around, she saw Sidappa talking to Keshava and shaking his head. She wondered if he had overheard their conversation. *After all, the man's ears are like that an elephant's.* She considered confessing to him. But she chose not to. She'd made a mistake, but not much harm had been done.

Later in the day, as the three women prepared lunch in Sidappa's hut, Keshava entered with his father.

"You sent for us, Sidappa?"

"Yes, Nagaraja. This I say for the safety of all of us," said Sidappa, his words carefully measured. "Your dull-witted son has done something I had forbidden him to do. He ran an errand for someone without letting me know. He thought I wouldn't find out. And now his stupidity may have put us all in jeopardy. You must keep him hidden from the world for a while, till the next *amavasya* or two, maybe more. He is not to leave this hamlet without my permission. I will hold you responsible if he violates my order. Do you understand?"

Keshava's father nodded obediently. He apologized for his son's actions. Aadarshini was trembling, for she knew Sidappa would take her to task too. After they left the hut, Sidappa asked her to lead him to the pond.

Along the way, Sidappa began, "Do you remember when you first came here? Did you see any other settlements, homes, people, or any signs of human life along the way?"

"No," said Aadarshini, "just a barely discernible trail cutting through all kinds of forbidding landscape, uncultivated land, brooks, bushes, woods. It's a miracle I ended up here."

"You were lucky to find this place. Rajanna and I established this settlement here for a reason. It is difficult to get here unless one knows how to, or if they follow someone here," explained Sidappa, his voice somber. "You know Prabhakara Swami is no ordinary priest. If he finds your anklet, he'll deduce it's yours. He will look for Keshava high and low. When he finds where Keshava lives, he will find you. When he finds you, you are as good as dead. But then, so are we. You have disappointed me. I cannot protect you against yourself."

Aadarshini meant to ask him how being discovered would spell death to all of them. But Sidappa politely raised his hand and dismissed her. Distressed, she went back inside and lay down on a mat.

"Don't walk around with just one anklet," Sharada said coldly. "It's a bad omen, not just for you but for everyone around you."

Was that what she was? A bad omen?

9

THE RETURN OF THE ANKLET began to haunt Prabhakara Swami. His dreams now featured a wraithlike Aadarshini, wearing only the one anklet, and chasing him around Madhuvana. His mornings had been sullen, and as he sat on the swing that night, he wished he had a confidant other than Jahnavi. Puttaraju entered the courtyard and called out to him.

"I heard the creaking, Swami. You need to grease the hinges on that swing," said Puttaraju. "Don't you find that mind-numbing squeak annoying?"

He actually found the predictable rhythm of the squeak soothing. It reminded him of the swing in his childhood home, of uncomplicated times.

"I need to talk to you about something," Puttaraju continued.

"Come, sit. What's on your mind?"

"It's about the boy, Raghu."

Prabhakara Swami braced himself.

Puttaraju pointed to a woman snoring lightly on a mat at the far end of the courtyard, her face turned away from them.

"Who is that?" asked Puttaraju.

"That's the maidservant, Sarala. She was working late and Jahnavi asked her to sleep here instead of walking home in the rain."

Puttaraju lowered his voice. "As you know, it's been a while since the boy disappeared. Others may not agree, but I believe Raghu is dead. If someone wanted a ransom, we would have heard from them by now. What do you think?"

"The search is on. We must persist as long as we can. We will have to halt the search one day, but I don't think we are at that point yet."

"I suggest we should wait for one more *amavasya*, two at the most, then accept reality as it is and perform the boy's last rites."

"What is the rush?" Prabhakara Swami asked. "Shamanna didn't mention this to me. Did he discuss this with you?"

"Yes, we talked about how important it was to resolve succession matters at Madhuvana quickly," said Puttaraju.

"And peacefully," added Prabhakara Swami. "Puttaraju, if we don't find the boy any time soon, Rajanna's empire must move on. But let me warn you that if the boy were to materialize someday, you will have a war on your hands if you move too quickly. That's how these matters have been sorted out throughout history. Do you understand? You must have incontrovertible proof that the boy is dead before we declare him so."

"Yes, I know. But you and I both know Srikanta will not be back anytime soon. We cannot wait forever."

"Once the boy is declared dead, there will be other contenders for the Madhuvana throne, don't you think?" asked Prabhakara Swami.

Puttaraju changed tack. Instead, he asked, "What are your plans, Prabhakara Swami? Surely you were not planning to be here at Madhuvana forever. Where will you go after the succession is settled?"

"I am just a priest, Puttaraju, here temporarily at your request. I suggest you stop worrying about what I will do, and think about what you would do if your assumption about the boy is wrong."

"Yes, that I will. But we should settle this matter before *Deepavali*."

Prabhakara Swami knew that because of the recent deaths, the Madhuvana family would not be celebrating the festival this year.

"Yes. A new dawn for Madhuvana on *Deepavali* would be auspicious."

What is this snake up to? Prabhakara Swami thought, and yawned. *Is he is planning to double-cross both Srikanta and Shamanna?*

When he told Jahnavi about his conversation with Puttaraju, she simply said, "Concentrate on finding Rajanna's widow. Stop worrying about mosquitoes like Puttaraju."

The next day, Avadesha the weaver came to offer prayers at the temple. "Welcome. I haven't seen you in a long time," Prabhakara Swami greeted him. "I had sent messages some time ago to several priests. I was expecting a response by now."

"Yes, I remember," Avadesha said. "Unfortunately no one has responded. We are all anxious about Rajanna's son too. I will let you know the moment I hear from someone."

Taking advantage of the weaver's presence, Prabhakara Swami asked him to deliver a message to Bheema in Beegralli. The message was short: *The little myna lives.* The weaver asked him what it meant. Prabhakara Swami didn't explain. He just felt a sense of relief he wasn't carrying this secret all by himself.

That afternoon, the village crier came through Maravali beating his drum. A swarm of children followed him around, cheering. Prabhakara Swami asked Giridhara what the din was about.

"The *nātakā* troupe is in Vontikoppal," said Giridhara, visibly excited. "They will be performing the Ramayana at the temple there tomorrow. The *ghoshaka* promises there will be music, dance and drama. We should go too."

"Yes, perhaps we should," he replied, thinking back to his days travelling with such a troupe, and felt a gush of joy. He hadn't seen one of them perform in a long time. He came to a decision.

"Giridhara, notify the priest at Vontikoppal. Tell him that Rajanna's family will be attending the *nātakā*. So will you. So will Jahnavi and I," he said, and watched Giridhara beam. "I am sure there will be others who will go from Maravali. We shall all leave together." They'd all have to stay overnight, for there was no telling how far into the night the play would continue. But he knew that Vontikoppal citizens would gladly make arrangements for feeding and housing the visitors from Maravali in keeping with Vijayanagara traditions.

The news didn't take long to travel across to Madhuvana. Prabhakara Swami wasn't surprised to see grownups excited about the troupe too. The family had endured a prolonged period of mourning and needed relief. Everyone thanked him for instigating this family outing.

"It will do us all good," he told them.

The following day, a large group walked in procession towards Vontikoppal. They left after their midday nap and expected to be there before sunset. Children led the pack, women walked behind them, and the men trailed a short distance away. Behind them walked Nanjunda and Narasimha, looking out for everyone's safety. The troupe was performing in the large courtyard at the home of the Vontikoppal chieftain, and Prabhakara Swami found a spot in the front row along with other prominent citizens, all men. The stage was barely four steps away from him, hidden away by a makeshift curtain for now. He felt a refreshing sense of excitement pervade him and couldn't resist peeking behind to see what the actors were doing. On one side, boys had lined up in front of a man who dipped a rag into a solution of red vermillion and dabbed it around their mouths to impart a simian look. This was the monkey army, and he knew children always loved to play a part in it.

The show began. Prabhakara Swami was well aware that the actors were not constrained by a script and improvised as needed to deliver their histrionics. Some of the actors went on endlessly with their fiery speeches. By the time the monkey army was ready to cross the sea to invade Lanka, some of the children had fallen asleep. This was Prabhakara Swami's favorite bit. A singer alerted everyone about the scene by belting out an inspirational song about the folly of staying on the wrong path. Out of nowhere, a boy jumped onto the stage and ran across, then turned around and ran back and forth a few times, limping comically to impersonate the stride of a monkey. The other boy-monkeys followed and were soon prancing around the stage as they wished, amok, as a band of unruly monkeys might. The audience roared in laughter. So did Prabhakara Swami, till he noticed that the boy who had jumped first was the only one limping while the others weren't.

That's the boy!

He sprang up and stormed out to look for Nanjunda. "That boy, the one with the limp – find out who he is," he ordered. "Hurry now. I will wait here."

Nanjunda returned just as the performance was over and the crowd had begun to disperse.

"He is not from here. Some of these boys sneak away from their homes, play their parts and go back. I am sure their parents take them to task when they return. The boy you wanted to know about, he came with a few others. They don't live here. I am sure they will leave for their homes in the morning."

Prabhakara Swami briefly considered asking him to whisk the boy away and beat the truth out of him about where he lives. But he needed to be discrete. "Follow the boy. Find out where he lives. He shouldn't know he is being followed. Don't let anyone else know either." Nanjunda nodded.

Now that he had found the boy with the limp, he knew it was just a matter of time before he'd find Aadarshini.

"The monkeys were hilarious, weren't they?" Jahnavi asked him as they all walked back to Maravali the following day.

"Yes, they were," he replied. "Some more than the others."

<hr />

Aadarshini soaked her feet in the stream that meandered around the rice fields away from the huts. She often came here to purge her anxieties, which had increased even more after she heard about the priest's hand in getting Azam Khan killed. Sidappa had fallen ill, and Aadarshini blamed herself. *O Rama, please hear my prayers!* She had nursed the old man, but he remained feeble. Together with Sharada, she had walked to the stream for a brief respite. She needed it.

Sharada let out a sigh, her anticipation evident.

Aadarshini looked at her, puzzled.

"He is expected back by *amavasya*," she said. "He has promised."

Venkata had been travelling again, and as always, Sharada didn't know where he was.

"Yes, Sidappa too will start feeling better after he is back," said Aadarshini. She was about to say something more when she noticed Keshava limping up the trail.

"Keshava, come here," Sharada yelled out.

The women burst out in laughter as Keshava came nearer.

"What have you done with your mouth? You look like a monkey," said Aadarshini. "Where have you been? I thought you had been forbidden from leaving this place." Keshava told them about his escapade to the performance and begged them not to tell anyone. Aadarshini was amused. She thought of Raghu, who used to take off with the older boys for an adventure he was too young for. Sharada soaked the edge of her sari and washed the color off his face. "There you go, you look almost human now. Run. If someone asks, say you were sleeping in my hut, with us. It will be our secret," said Sharada with a twinkle in her eye.

Keshava beamed and went off.

"We have to get back to Sidappa," reminded Sharada.

As they walked back, they noticed a man loitering on the trail just outside the hamlet. They hid behind a bush when they saw him. The sight of a stranger near the hamlet took them both by surprise. In all the days she had been here, Aadarshini hadn't seen a stranger even once.

Sharada whispered, "I've never seen him before. He looks lost. Let's wait till he leaves."

The man walked further down the trail, along the bushes that kept the hamlet well hidden. He entered the cordon of bushes through a clearing, then emerged quickly and left. The women came out of hiding and sped back home.

"We should tell Sidappa," said Aadarshini.

"No, he is not well," said Sharada. "Let's not burden him right now. We'll tell Venkata when he returns."

Prabhakara Swami stretched out for a nap at his home in Maravali after having dispensed advice to a devotee with a string of bad luck in business.

"Fortune and misfortune are important to keep us grounded," he told the man. "When one visits, you gloat and are delighted. Then the other shows up to temper your arrogance. Such is life. Deal with both with equanimity."

He himself had good reason to gloat over the string of good luck he had been having. He had stumbled onto the boy by an accident. Nanjunda would bring him news of his whereabouts, which would lead him to Aadarshini. *The stars are in my favor*, he mused, as he drifted off to sleep.

A pungent stench woke him up. He stepped out to see what was causing the smell. Right outside his door was a horse that had just unloaded a generous pile of dung.

"Veeranna," Prabhakara exclaimed, taken aback by the unannounced visit of his employer. "What a surprise! I will have the mess cleaned up. Come, let me show you a better place to anchor the animal."

He rushed in to tell Jahnavi to make arrangements for Veeranna's stay.

"Why is he here?" she whispered back.

In all the years he had been in Veeranna's employ, this was the first time the spymaster had visited him at his home.

"I hear you call yourself Prabhakara Swami now. Nice name!"

Veeranna entered his home. "Beautiful," he said. "I can see why you are so attached to Maravali. It's easy to lose focus here."

"All by your grace, Veeranna."

Jahnavi readied a freshly cooked meal.

"You are fortunate, Prabhakara Swami," he said. "She is a fine hostess. She cooks well too. A man must be lucky as you are." He then turned to Jahnavi. "You like living here, child?"

"With your blessings, we have had a serene stay here," she replied. "We try to make the most of what we have. The people are nice. But we have learned not to get attached."

"Good. That's a wonderful attitude," said Veeranna.

The formalities now complete, Prabhakara Swami asked Veeranna if he wanted to rest.

"I have not come here to rest," the spymaster's voice took a turn for the stern. "Let us go someplace quiet."

"I know just the place." Prabhakara Swami led him to the temple. There were no devotees, and he locked the front door from the inside.

"Your insights have been of great help to me in the past, Prabhakara Swami," Veeranna began. "They have enhanced my value in the eyes of the royal council. But now I need you to help me hold on to my position. Needless to say, if I benefit, so will you, as you have in the past."

"What do you have in mind, Veeranna?"

"Not so long ago," he began, "my men captured a group of Afaqi mercenaries employed by the rebels. After the customary torture, they told us in a few days what you and others such as you haven't been able to deduce in years, about the movement of rebel troops, safe house locations, informers who are betraying our emperor Salkaraju, and such. We have recently inflicted severe losses on the traitors thanks to that information."

Prabhakara Swami was unmoved. "Of course, what an even match," he said. "You rely on torture, and I on deductive reasoning based on sketchy information from faceless informers." Guessing what was on Veeranna's mind, he added, "If this is about me enlightening you about how your royal masters can capture the throne, or about where they can find the missing heir, you've come to the wrong man. I have no insights to share."

Veeranna stood up and towered over him, standing so close that he could smell his breath.

"I am not asking, priest," said Veeranna. "I am giving you an order. Unless you've forgotten what it means to listen to one, and you need me to remind you."

A cold draft suddenly went down Prabhakara Swami's spine. He remained quiet.

"The Afaqi told us he and his accomplices had passed through

Maravali and stayed at a serai nearby. They had then walked a whole day to reach an inconspicuous cluster of huts. The area was enveloped by coconut palms and bushes so thick they could barely see the huts from the trail. They didn't see any other people or dwellings along their route."

"Hundreds of villages fit that description," he said.

"Yes," said Veeranna, "but these men were on the lookout for a safe house, since they were escaping Salkaraju's troops at the time. They had directions to a hamlet, but the Afaqi died before we could get him to tell us more. Since he talked about Maravali, I came in person, hoping you will be able to shed some light on the matter. Besides, I hadn't seen you in a long time."

"What do you want me to do?"

"Priest, you've been getting slow. It looks like you like the good life here. Now listen to me carefully. I want you to find out where the safehouse is. Find out who lives there, and what their role is. I will send you some men, soldiers who carry out orders most excellently. Lead them to the safehouse once you discover it."

"Then?"

"Then we do what we do each time we find such a safe house. We shut it down. We have to burn it to the ground, along with everyone who has been assisting the rebels."

Prabhakara Swami was shocked. The possibility of committing arson and mass murder of unknown persons was something he did not want to be part of.

"And what if I refuse to be party to this massacre?" he asked.

"Has the priest grown a conscience?" Veeranna laughed. "I need your help in locating this safehouse. Show the men how to get there. You have no other role to play. Your hands, and your karma, will remain clean. Besides, may I remind you that your holy avatar is a front for your real line of work! A conscience is not what I need at this juncture."

"I need time to think about this," he said.

"Take all the time you need. But I need an answer before I leave," said Veeranna, and rested against a pillar and shut his eyes.

Prabhakara Swami took a deep breath. There were far too many puzzles he was trying to solve at this time – Aadarshini, Raghu, and Madhuvana's succession struggles. Veeranna's request would leave him little time to pursue their solutions. Yet, in his mind, he knew his personal quests appeared to have a chance of success, and the drama being played out in Vijayanagara was far removed from his life. But he couldn't say no to the spymaster either. When Veeranna woke up, he had his answer ready.

"Veeranna, I will be glad to find this place for you. But, I must warn you it will neither be easy nor quick. People here are simple folk. They will sing the praises of whoever is on the throne, but their heart is with Rama Raya. There is little sympathy for Salkaraju around here, and no one here will snitch on the rebels. So finding the safe houses could take some time."

"That is all I ask. Just find the place for me," said Veeranna. After a short pause, he said, "You are losing your edge, priest. You have not yet bothered to ask me who you should be looking for."

Prabhakara Swami was embarrassed.

"Never mind. Like I said, it seems you like your life here. Sidappa – that's the name of the man I want you to find. Have you heard of him?"

His mind immediately returned to the scroll, and the names that were mentioned in it. *So the names likely belonged to those who operated rebel safe houses. Sidappa was assisting the rebels along with Rajanna.* He turned to Veeranna and said emotionlessly, "That will surely help, Veeranna. There are only a few thousand Sidappas here. It's a common name among these people. But I will see what I can do. If I come up with something, I will send you a message. But don't just ride into Maravali as if you own the place. No one here likes your caretaker king or his minions."

Veeranna prepared to leave.

"So be it," he said. "But be warned, priest, if any of my other men find Sidappa's hamlet before you do, you can consider our relationship terminated, and that it is time for Maravali to get a new priest." The spymaster rode away without waiting for a response.

Shamanna had told him Sidappa was likely dead, but if a rebel soldier had leaked his name to Veeranna, it meant he was alive. If he had the scroll, maybe it would be easier to decode the mystery. But then, did he really care? He thought he believed in an ideal – which is why he worked for Veeranna. But ever since he had ordered the death of Rajanna simply to preserve his secret, he had realized the only ideal that mattered was self-preservation. What good would it do to him if the current king survived, but he was no longer alive? For that matter, did it really matter to him whether Rama Raya or Salkaraju was on the throne?

That evening, however, all his worries were put to rest. Much to his delight, Nanjunda came to see him, and described the hamlet the boy with the limp had disappeared to. "He went home with other boys at first, all older than him. One by one, all went their own way. He stopped to speak to two women sitting by a stream. He then disappeared behind the bushes. I walked around and saw there were many huts built around a pond. The bushes keep them obscured from view. One of the women spotted me, so I pretended to be a lost traveler and hurried away. On my way out I sensed someone watching me. I kept walking until I was gone a fair distance, and then turned around to see who it was. It was the women who were at the stream. One of them had long hair, almost till her knees, while the other was much darker and shorter. The one with the long hair wore a single anklet. It was unusual, that's why I noticed it."

Aadarshini!

He was surprised at how vividly Nanjunda, who he viewed as pure brawn and not much more, described the journey. "I am impressed, Nanjunda. The precision with which you have described this hamlet, I could go there with my eyes closed. You must've been a poet in a previous birth."

"Do you want me to bring the boy here?"

"Not now. We can send for him when we need someone to play the role of a monkey."

Nanjunda laughed.

Later that evening Prabhakara Swami sat on the swing with Jahnavi.

"I've located her," he said, matter-of-factly.

She inched closer to him and kissed him, gently at first, then savagely. He could taste the metallic taste of blood in his mouth.

"You know what to do next."

"*Shubhasya sheeghrum,*" he whispered, and bit her earlobe gently. "Tomorrow."

"I will fast all day tomorrow and pray for your success – not even a sip of water."

Yes, don't waver. Just go there, do it, and come back. Don't get attached. She is dead to the world. And she means nothing to you, not after what Azam Khan said, he convinced himself.

"I'll leave at dawn."

10

PRABHAKARA SWAMI WOKE UP
early, well before daybreak. All through the night, he had tried in
vain not to think about Aadarshini. It wouldn't be easy. He squatted
quietly by the well while Jahnavi poured bucketsful of water over him.
She handed him a new set of clothes. He performed his morning
sandhyavandanam and draped the *angavastram* around his neck,
letting the ends of the stole hang symmetrically over his bare chest.

"You look like a king going into battle," Jahnavi said, beaming.
"Do you have everything you need?"

He patted the bag on his left shoulder. In it he carried food to tide
him over his walk, a towel, and a knife that had so far been used to
slice vegetables. He had neglected to pack it but Jahnavi had rushed
back and fetched it.

"I tested it this morning," she had reassured him. "It cut through
the gourd just fine. Her neck will surely be easier to slice through."

Prabhakara Swami smiled halfheartedly.

"I understand," she said. "Rama will keep you in His protection."

He walked away, tentatively at first, then briskly.

Based on Nanjunda's description he thought he could reach the
hamlet by midday. With each step, however, he became more aware
of the tension that gripped him. This was the first time he would be

meeting Aadarshini one-on-one. Whenever he had visited Rajanna, it was the senior wives who'd greet him. Aadarshini would do so only if Rajanna asked her to. When she came to the temple, she was always with an entourage. She'd listen to his discourses inattentively and giggle a lot. When she smiled, her dimples would glow. And when he distributed *prasada,* she'd extend her hand but would never say anything. But these instances were enough for him to fantasize about her.

And now that he had decided to kill her, he realized how unprepared he was. He had invoked the *shubhasya sheeghrum* logic and seduced himself into expediting the task. But this had given him less than half a day to think through the details, and most of that had been taken up by lovemaking. He thought about whether there was an analogous example from the scriptures for his act, hoping that would provide him succor. In those tales, men had slayed female demons numerous times, but those demons were all evil, unlike Aadarshini. *Don't waver,* he repeated to himself, and instead began planning the act. *How will I find her?* Rushing into the hamlet and going hut-by-hut would be foolish. He'd wait to accost her somewhere, preferably at the stream that Nanjunda had described. She would surely come there sometime in the afternoon. He felt sorry if another woman accompanied her; she would have to die too. *Killing them both won't be easy. They'll attempt to run away and raise an alarm. I'll kill Aadarshini first. I will let the other one run away.* He spontaneously broke into a sprint to see how quickly he could get away. *The others will first have to digest the event, and then compose themselves before giving chase. They will never catch me.* He brought out the knife and inspected it. Jahnavi had sharpened it. He felt his neck to find the spot where he would slice her neck. He imagined blood gushing out of Aadarshini's neck and felt a sharp pain in his chest. *Don't think too much. Just do it!*

It was a little past mid-day when the river, which he had been following all along, took a turn away. A tiny stream took off from the river and irrigated the farms along its path. *Almost there,* he thought. He took off his *angavastram* and tied it around his waist. He followed the stream, looking for a big tree. A little ahead of him, a woman sat with her feet in the stream. She appeared to be staring at the sky. A light wind had blown her sari flap, and her breasts were exposed. *Is that her?* He stood still, savoring the sight, and strengthening his will. *This will be quick and easy.* He took out the knife and cast away the bag.

Then he did what he hadn't intended to do. He called out Aadarshini's name.

The woman stood up with a start. She draped herself hurriedly when she saw him. Then she went limp and dropped to the ground. He dropped the knife and ran to her, soaking one end of his stole in the stream, and squeezed water on her face.

"Aadarshini," he whispered.

***

Aadarshini, Sharada, and Padma had been taking turns looking after Sidappa, whose hacking cough had taken a turn for the worse. It was Sharada's turn in the afternoon, and Aadarshini quickly left for the stream to get some rest. She had barely put her feet in the stream when she heard a familiar voice call out her name.

She saw the knife glint before she saw the priest, and her legs gave way. When she came to, Aadarshini could see him standing not far from her. She wanted to scream, but it would be of no help. She was too far away. None would hear her scream. She was on her own. She considered running away, but didn't think she would get very far before he caught her. *He has come to kill me!*

She rose to her feet slowly and asked him, "What are you doing here? What do you want?" She tried to remain firm, but the tremble in her voice gave her away. "I am not alone. Sharada will be here any moment. What do you want?" she repeated.

"You sent me the umbrella and the anklet," he smiled arrogantly and pointed at his knife. "It is obvious why I am here. But why are *you* here, in this hamlet in the middle of nowhere? How did you get here? Who sheltered you? Who saved you from sati?"

An unfamiliar confidence took over Aadarshini as the trembling subsided. She looked into his eyes. "What are you doing in Madhuvana, in my home?"

She didn't expect him to answer her.

"The family asked me to stay and guide them. I am their priest. I was duty bound to accept," he said.

"Good," she said. "So guide them. Take me back with you. I am prepared to return with you right now. Tell them about the umbrella and the anklet. Tell them it was a cry of help, that you rescued me and brought me back to restore me to my rightful position. That is the righteous path, isn't it...*poojya swamigaaru!*"

The honorific *poojya* had a touch of mockery in it, sufficient to sting him whenever she said it. She continued, "We will summon the village council. They will be pleased to see the infighting come to an end. The drama will end. Dharma will be served. Can you do this for me...*poojya swamigaaru?*"

"I am afraid I cannot do that," he said.

"It's the right thing to do, *poojya swamigaaru*," she said. "Be strong. Take me back. I promise I will make place for you at Madhuvana. I know there will be others who seek to possess it. Help me remove them. Don't forget, I hoped you would rescue me from my fiery fate. I prayed. I waited. You didn't return in time. Now here I am, appealing to you in person. Redeem yourself. Who are you afraid of?"

She could see he was distressed. His nostrils flared, his face was red.

"Just as I thought, *poojya swamigaaru*. It is not the wimps in Madhuvana who are the problem. It is you. You haven't told them about the umbrella and the anklet. You want Madhuvana for yourself, don't you?"

"It's not that simple, insolent woman," he said.

Aadarshini didn't relent.

"Of course it is simple. You have made it complicated. Madhuvana is what we all want. As long as I am alive, none of you can have it. As Lord Narayana is my witness, I will not let any of you have it. Till a few moments ago you, the puppeteer, held the strings. The gods only know how but you made the family dance to your tune. But the umbrella and anklet threw everything off balance, didn't it? You came down here to kill me, didn't you? But if you had killed me as soon as you got here as any self-respecting assassin would have, all would have been well by now. You would be on your way back to Madhuvana."

Aadarshini noticed him fidgeting.

"What a predicament, *poojya swamigaaru*. You lost your nerve. How pitiful. And now you stand here, powerless in front of a woman."

Aadarshini pointed at the knife.

"And look at that pathetic implement of male power," she said. "It just lies on the ground, flaccid. Was that what you would have killed me with? Look at you, a priest turned murderer. Who pulls *your* strings? Is it Srikanta? No, he is too docile. Is it Kanteeravaa? No, he is too old. Is it Puttaraju? No, he can't even defecate without permission from Shamanna. Is it a woman, perhaps?"

She noticed him wince.

"Ah, yes, a woman," she declared, then laughed mockingly. "Your wife, I presume? God bless her, at least she has vision – an impaired one, but a vision nonetheless. Go ahead, slice my throat, and fulfill her desire. Show her you are a man."

Aadarshini was relishing this.

"You could have sent someone else to do your dirty deed. Yet you came yourself. I know why. No one but you knows I am alive. No one was to know that I had risen from the ashes. How brainless could you be, O priest? I have been living here since the last *amavasya*. These people here are loyal to Rajanna, and therefore to me. They know it was you who had Azam Khan killed. They know I sent you the anklet. Don't you think they would know it was you who had me killed? They will come looking for you to the far ends of the universe if anything happened to me."

Aadarshini glanced towards the huts, hoping someone would emerge. Much as she enjoyed this, she knew she couldn't keep this up much longer.

"Heed my advice. Take me back to Madhuvana. I am not a vengeful woman. I give you my word I will let you live with dignity, in Madhuvana if you wish. If you kill me, it will only complicate things for you. Or you can just turn around. Go tell your puppeteer you did what you came to do. Then leave Madhuvana. For when I come, and I will, you will have several reasons to fear me."

"Enough!" he roared, loudly enough to startle Aadarshini.

He walked past her into the stream and rinsed his face.

Aadarshini picked up the knife.

"Enough!"

Prabhakara Swami cursed himself for hesitating when he did. *She's only a woman*, he told himself, *take charge!*

"You were such perfection in fantasy, Aadarshini," he muttered, as he stepped out of the stream.

He noticed the knife in her hand.

"So you think you can kill me? How naïve can you be, woman? Go ahead. Find out for yourself if it is easy to take a human life."

He wiped his face dry and cast aside his *angavastram*, exposing his bare chest. He walked to within a step of where she stood.

"Come," he pointed at a spot below his ribs. "Plunge it in with all your strength." He could see her hands tremble. "But then," he added, "you will never know where to find your son."

The knife clattered to the ground. She went on her knees, reeling in shock.

"So I suggest you heed *my* advice," he mimicked her words. "Forget about Madhuvana. Stay invisible, and out of my sight. I promise I will restore Madhuvana to Raghu. God willing you will be reunited with him too."

"No," she cried out. "Don't do this to me. I cannot live without Raghu. How can you be so cruel? Doesn't a mother's anguish mean anything to you? You are our priest. We trusted you. Tell me what you want. I will do what you ask. Just let me have Raghu."

Her sari slid off her shoulder, exposing one of her breasts. Shaking his head in disgust, he ordered her to drape it back on. She obeyed quietly.

"I have nothing against you or Rajanna or the family," he said. "You were all generous patrons. But the gods give the undeserving their bounty. Rajanna died. You died. Madhuvana was for the taking. The vultures appeared. They sought my advice. But they too didn't deserve Madhuvana. Trust me, the boy is safe. But he is not in Madhuvana."

Aadarshini was on her knees, crying uncontrollably.

"Listen to my advice. Remain dead. Disappear. If you are impatient, I will send Raghu back to you a portion at a time. I have to get back to Madhuvana now. Do as you please."

Aadarshini grabbed his feet and begged him to take her to Raghu.

"Ah, humility at last," he said. "If I were you, I'd disappear. Who knows I may change my mind and come back with others to finish what I've left undone today?"

Prabhakara Swami then stepped over her, taking care his feet didn't touch her, and huffed away. He was troubled by his decision to leave her alive. He saw her wiping her face and stand up.

"*Swamigaaru*, you better hurry back to Maravali, and run away as soon as you can. For if I find you there when I return, I will make sure the entire world knows who you are, and I will leave you to die for the vultures. Oh, *poojya swamigaaru*, remember who I am, for I am Rajanna's widow, Raghu's mother, and Madhuvana's queen."

He looked at the hatred in her eyes, and in a flash, he knew he couldn't just leave. The woman had the gall to taunt him again, despite all he just said! He needed to humiliate her. Her arrogance would lead her to her doom. After all, hadn't the wench thrown herself at Azam Khan, a *Turka*? Fury clouded his mind, and he turned to face her.

***

Aadarshini didn't see the first slap that sent her reeling to the ground. Suddenly, she was on the ground, crouched in a fetal position, when she sensed him again. She looked up in shock. The priest towered over her, naked now. He spat on her, then she saw his foot coming towards her face. She put up her hands up in defense. He pulled her hair, slapped her once more. He then lay on top of her and violently ripped off her sari. She could hear herself say 'stop' before losing consciousness.

She woke up in pain, unlike any she'd felt before. Her breasts were sore. So was her neck. She could taste the blood on her lips where he had bitten her. Her legs hurt. She moved her hands down between her thighs, and let out a horrific shriek. She listlessly dragged herself back to the hamlet, went straight into the pond and soaked herself, trying hard to clean the disgust she now felt all over her body and self. She stayed in the water a long time then staggered towards Sharada's hut and collapsed.

"Ayyo Rama…" Sharada rushed to cradle her in her arms. "What happened?" She began to cry, and in between her sobs, narrated what had happened.

"Oh Deva, O Rama! A Brahmin woman…a widow…what has this world come to? Curses on that priest, that lecherous bastard, that *rakshasa*! May he die and his soul ripped apart by vultures in *naraka*!" Sharada hurriedly put water to boil. She soaked a towel and applied it where she could tell Aadarshini was hurting. "There is no justice… there is no dharma," Sharada kept repeating. "Say something Akka, show some anger, some emotion. We have to punish the *rakshasa*. We'll wait for Venkata to return. I will make him cut his head off."

Aadarshini, still numb and hurting, looked at her and smiled a demented smile. "No," she finally said. "There will be justice…but *I* will administer it. I have had enough. Prabhakara Swami, you went too far for your own good. Prepare to die!"

She asked to be taken to Sidappa and to be left alone with the old man. She told him everything that had happened and asked him for advice about how to go about her vengeance.

"Don't despair, child. You are safe here," mumbled Sidappa. His body was hot. "We will regain Madhuvana. We will find your son. We will prevail, just as Rama Raya will prevail in Vijayanagara. The heirs shall soon have what is rightfully theirs. You are a strong woman, a worthy wife to Rajanna."

"I have had enough. I will be strong."

"Good. You don't have any other option," he said, and broke into a coughing spasm.

"You mustn't talk now," said Aadarshini, calming down, and strengthening her resolve.

Padma returned and cradled her in her arms as a mother would.

"Is Venkata back yet?" Sidappa asked.

"He has been delirious all day," Padma whispered to Aadarshini. "I just hope he lives live long enough to see Venkata one last time."

Aadarshini held Padma's hand.

"Rest your head on my lap, Amma. We have to be strong," said Aadarshini.

"Listen," Sidappa mumbled. "The birds, they are trying to tell me something."

I should have killed her, he kept telling himself. *I have complicated matters. What have I done?* It was nearing dusk when he reached Madhuvana. Jahnavi waited for him outside. She followed him as he rushed past her and plopped himself on the swing.

"You look tense," she said.

"You will not hear from her again," he lied, and rested his head on her shoulder.

They could hear the rumble of the village crier's drums from somewhere far away.

"Listen," she said and held his hand gently, "destiny's drums!"

To Prabhakara Swami they sounded like war drums.

11

PRABHAKARA SWAMI WONDERED
what Aadarshini would do next. He tried hard to convince himself
that she couldn't storm Madhuvana. *If she could, she would've done it
by now instead of sending me the umbrella and the anklet. Who were the
villagers who had sheltered her?* He briefly remembered her mentioning
they were loyal to Rajanna and would come after him. Nanjunda and
Narasimha were effective as bodyguards, but would probably run if
they saw a horde heading towards them. True, he had sown the seed
of doubt by telling her he had her son. Aadarshini would not attack
him as long as she believed he knew where Raghu was. *She has waited
so long; she will deliberate some more.*

"You have been morose ever since you returned," Jahnavi said. She
joined him in bed. "What you did was brave. It must not have been
easy. Be proud. You deserve to smile."

She played with his tuft, teasing it as she moved her toes over his
calf. He gently pushed her away.

"What's the matter?" she asked.

He didn't respond.

"Do you want me to wear the anklet?"

She got up to get it.

The last time they had made love, the day before he went to kill

Aadarshini, she had worn the silver anklet. He had spent a lot of time whispering into it, kissing it as if he was seducing the anklet itself.

"It's gone! Where is it? It was right here." Jahnavi ruffled a few clothes around. "Don't forget, it is *amavasya* tomorrow," she reminded him as she continued to look for the anklet. "I have talked to the Madhuvana family. The homa pit has been cleaned and prepared. The firewood and other provisions are in place. I've sent word to Giridhara to take care of the Maravali families."

Prabhakara Swami was well aware that he had to perform the *shraaddha* ceremonies in Madhuvana. He was irritated at Jahnavi reminding him of his responsibilities, as if he was a child. He had already advised everyone that the upcoming *amavasya* was special and was to be dedicated to propitiating the departed souls, and that the rites of this *amavasya* were to be considered especially auspicious.

He lost interest in Jahnavi's allure and left the room. There was no question of telling Jahnavi the truth. She would nag him to death.

A frenzied Sarala ran like she was being chased by a leopard. She hopped over the narrow channel of water that demarcated her world from that of those she served. She kept running till she reached the thatched hut where she lived. What she found in Jahnavi's room was eye-popping and she had to tell someone about it.

Inside, her sister-in-law Lavanya who was visiting for the festival season was preparing the evening meal. Sarala's husband was out working in the plantation.

"You are home early," said Lavanya. "Is everything well? You are panting."

Sarala took a moment to catch her breath. She hugged Lavanya then kissed her on the cheeks.

"She is alive!" Sarala declared jubilantly. She then held up the anklet she had been clutching. "This, my dear Lavanya, belongs to my mistress. I had put it on her ankle the morning they took her away. And here I am, holding it once again in my very own hand. This could

NIGHTS OF THE MOONLESS SKY {159}

mean only one thing, Lavanya – my mistress is alive. Akka is alive!" She was unable to contain her excitement. "This morning, Prabhakara Swami's wife sent me to her room to fetch something. I noticed the anklet under her pillow. I was stunned. I picked it up and hid it in the cowshed. I came running here as fast as I could when I was done with my chores."

"Maybe the anklet fell off during the cremation, and someone found it and brought it to the priest's wife? It is very pretty," suggested Lavanya.

"No! The priest didn't come to Madhuvana well after her sati," replied Sarala. "No! I had put this on her myself. It fit her ankles snug and couldn't have slipped off. It's not easy to pull off with a jerk either. Someone had to take it off intentionally. Only the priest or the men who carried her away would have had the opportunity, and they wouldn't do it. They wouldn't dare take off a dead woman's jewelry. Aadarshini Akka is alive, Lavanya! I don't know how she survived, or where she is now, or how the anklet even got here. But I know she is alive. Where is she? Who brought the anklet? I don't know these answers, but we will see her return sooner or later. The gods have been protecting her."

<hr/>

"Starting today, we enter an auspicious period that is especially significant for women. Can any of you tell me why?" Prabhakara Swami asked the women and children. The *shraaddha* ceremony was over, and as the embers in the homa pit died out, he sat down to narrate a story for the children as he always did at the end of rituals.

"This *amavasya* is special," he continued. "Today, the gods and goddesses will start making preparations to send Durga to our world. Seven days from now, we will gather here again to welcome her. Let me tell you about this brave goddess. A long time ago, she came down from the heavens on her lion to fight the arrogant *asura* Mahishasura. She chased him on her lion while he fled on his buffalo. They fought for days till Durga slayed him. The universe was safe again. Ten days from now, on *Vijayadashami*, we will celebrate that."

"Did she also have four arms," a young girl asked, "like the statues in the temple?"

"Four arms? No, of course not," replied Prabhakara Swami. "That would not be enough to kill a powerful *rakshasa* like Mahisasura. She had a thousand arms and more, as many as she needed to kill the *asura*. Isn't that interesting? We only show her with four hands in sculptures because it would take forever to make thousands of hands, wouldn't it?"

The children giggled. He felt a little peace at their laughter, still buried in the guilt of his crime and wondering when it would come back to haunt him. With that, he ended his sermon. After lunch, he boarded the palanquin with Jahnavi and came to Maravali. As they approached their home, he noticed a stranger sitting on their porch.

The man waited for Jahnavi to enter before addressing him.

"I am here at Veeranna's behest," he said. "He has asked me to give you this and to make sure you read it immediately, in my presence. He wants a reply right away. I have been asked to wait here for your response."

He felt a chill in his groin as the man handed him a scroll. He asked the man to wait as he went inside and broke open the seal. It was signed by Veeranna with his name and his seal. He read the message:

> *You have served me well. Few others are both as scholarly and crafty as you are. However, your recent demeanor troubles me. You have become complacent, argumentative, and disrespectful. Our last conversation left me questioning your loyalty.*
>
> *You will recall that I had given you an ultimatum about what would happen if I found Sidappa before you did. This is to inform you that I have. You have failed to deliver. You must now face the consequences.*

*After the next night of the moonless sky, you are no longer
in my service, nor are you under my protection. All your
privileges will be withdrawn. A new priest will soon be
commissioned to serve Maravali. You must leave Maravali
and disappear. I must never hear from you again.*

*Tell the man who has delivered this message that you
understand and that you will comply. He will communicate
your response to me.*

Prabhakara Swami collapsed in the courtyard. Jahnavi rushed
to help him. She read Veeranna's letter, and then, without flinching,
stepped outside the door.

"Prabhakara Swami has taken ill," he could hear her say. "Tell
your superiors he has said, 'I understand. I will comply. I pray that
the festival of *Deepavali* brings happiness and prosperity to us all.'"

The messenger nodded and rode away. Jahnavi returned to her
husband. He looked up at her, and seeing the pity in her face, pulled
himself together. "I must send a message to Shamanna right away.
I will meet him at his home after the next *amavasya*. I'll tell him I
hope to discuss the matter about Raghu. Let him assume I have found
the boy."

"And how do you propose we find Raghu?" she asked.

"I think we are placing too much emphasis on him. I don't think
the boy is necessary. Forget about him. We have no choice but to
leave Maravali now. Let us bid farewell and leave with dignity. We'll
tell everyone we are going on an extended pilgrimage. We will go to
Shamanna's. Once there, I will put things back in balance. We will
rebuild our lives on Shamanna's estate."

"But sooner or later Puttaraju will come to seek Shamanna's
counsel. He will find us there."

"No! Puttaraju will be busy fighting with Srikanta over
Madhuvana, and he will likely lose," he said. "Shamanna will be
forgotten, or he will return to Madhuvana to stake his claim, and I

will in turn build a glorious hermitage with him that will stand for centuries."

Prabhakara Swami found Jahnavi's eyes lighting up.

"No more talk," he decreed and raised his hand. He walked out to the temple, and asked Giridhara to summon Avadesha. When the weaver arrived, he asked for a message to be sent to Bheema at Beegralli: 'It is time to talk about the myna chick. I will arrive after *Deepavali.*'

Twenty-eight days. That's all I have left in Madhuvana. Unless providence wills otherwise.

12

AZAM KHAN AND RUDRA SPED towards Champanhalli, trying to outpace the storm clouds that shadowed them all along. Rudra's few stops had turned out to be anything but short. With his involvement in multiple operations, there was no way they could have sped matters along.

The hiatus gave Azam Khan an opportunity to shake off his angst about an uncertain future. The thought of leaving Vijayanagara without extracting vengeance from Prabhakara Swami, and giving up his search for Aadarshini and Raghu, was troublesome. But he agreed with Rudra that it would be sheer folly to return to Maravali, for if he got caught again, there was only death. He looked forward to meeting with Sidappa. They were spending a few days in Champanhalli at the most. Rudra would take stock of the messages that had arrived when he had been away. *Inshallah we'll all be sitting by the pond with Sidappa, and perhaps Venkata too if he is around, and talk all night.* He recalled how Sidappa would often use the expression Inshallah. "It accounts for the unknown factor in our endeavors better than any other word I know," he'd often say.

It was dusk when they sighted Rudra's home. Azam Khan noticed a man sitting out in front.

"Venkata, you rascal," shouted Azam Khan, surprised and delighted to see his old friend here. "Whatever are you doing here?"

Venkata ran up to Azam Khan's horse and pulled him down, embracing him tightly, and weeping uncontrollably as he ran his hands over his face.

"Ah, so you've heard the rumors of my execution," he said, smiling mischievously. "Yes, it's really me. You should've known I am not so easy to kill."

"Oh, Lord Narayana," said Venkata, "Your ways are indeed mysterious." He embraced Azam Khan again.

"Save some love for me too, you fool!" Rudra thundered. "What brings you here? Is all well?"

"Yes, thanks to providence, everything is well now. I came here this morning, but was told you were expected to be home any day now. I'm so glad both of you arrived so soon. I have exciting news for both of you," said Venkata. Looking at Azam Khan, he said, "Your search is over, brother. Rajanna's widow is alive. She is safe. She is with us."

Azam Khan sank to his knees and said a prayer, then stood up and kissed Venkata's hand then his cheeks, saying *Alhamdulillah* over and over. The storm reached them, and the rain began to pelt down. The three hurried inside.

"What are we waiting for then? Let's not waste time here," said Azam Khan. "We can't keep them waiting. You can't keep me waiting."

"Calm down, my brash friend. There is no need to leave immediately," said Rudra. "Sidappa and Aadarshini both believe you are dead. They aren't expecting you to come galloping. And have you seen the rain outside? The three of us have much to catch up on. We will leave for Sidappa's tomorrow."

Azam Khan was disappointed, but held back his protest. They had been riding for many days now, and rest would do them all good. They sat around a fire inside.

"Tell me all about Aadarshini Amma. I have been worried for her. Is there no news about her son yet?"

Venkata then began to brief the two, leaving both of them gasping in awe. Then as Azam Khan told Venkata about his adventure, it was the latter's turn to shake his head in disbelief. Meanwhile Rudra organized the many messages he had received. "These scrolls contain details of every message that has gone in and out of here while I was away," he told them.

Azam Khan knew that Rudra received a copy of all the messages, whether it was sent via the weaver from Maravali or the one-legged old man who sat under the banyan tree in Jayapura. The messages sat in two piles. The first, Rudra told them, were not important.

"However, what I have learnt from the other messages is that Rama Raya's forces are gaining ground over Salkaraju. This could be misinformation, but if this is true, Rama Raya is winning, my friends. I'll have to dig deeper. It would be a shame that Rajanna didn't live long enough to see his favored king prevail." He continued, "We also have an interesting conundrum from Sidappa. Why don't I let Venkata elaborate?"

Venkata took over.

"When Aadarshini first told Sidappa about what she had been through, he sent me to Rudra to find out who had sent the message of Rajanna's death to Madhuvana. Sidappa wanted to know if you, Azam Khan, were not with Rajanna, what happened to the man who was?"

"Pratipa, that was his name," Azam Khan added.

"Indeed. So what happened to Pratipa, and why did he vanish?"

Azam Khan had discussed Pratipa's unusual disappearance with Rudra, who had said he would ask his people to investigate this matter. Venkata continued, "Aadarshini also told us that the messenger had brought back Rajanna's turban, diamond rings, and gold necklace. But there was one thing missing. She didn't mention Rajanna's *vrigodharam*. This seemed odd to Sidappa. He wanted Rudra to investigate. Unfortunately, Rudra was not here when I came, so I left him a message. Alas, he didn't see it till now."

Azam Khan stood in awe at Sidappa's attention to detail. The missing *vrigodharam* had bothered Sidappa but no one else, not Aadarshini, not the other wives, not the family, and not even Azam Khan. None of them had even thought of it. And it was impossible for anyone who knew Rajanna to see him without his imposing mustache and his walking stick that swung by his side as he walked around like a lion. The well-polished walking stick was a weighted bamboo staff that doubled as a lethal weapon. A solid cast-iron orb covered in ivory fit snugly in Rajanna's palm. Azam Khan had seen many an unsuspecting assailant dispatched to the heavens with one swift blow. Sidappa referred to it as Rajanna's *vrigodharam,* in honor of the mighty Bhima's legendary mace from the Mahabharata. Rajanna carried it with authority, as a sovereign carries a scepter.

"Perhaps the messenger helped himself to it. Perhaps he lost it. Perhaps it was left behind where he died," Azam Khan tried to offer alternatives.

"Perhaps," said Rudra, as if none of these explanations seemed reasonable to him, and asked Venkata to continue.

"A few days ago, Sidappa sent me here to ask Rudra to find out more about Prabhakara Swami. That was when I saw you, and I was beside myself with joy. How you and Aadarshini Amma survived your ordeals, only Narayana can explain."

Rudra now took over. He pointed to a bunch of scrolls. "Our friend Prabhakara Swami has sent over fifty messages to various priests, seeking information about a boy and a man on the move." He drew concentric circles on the ground, with Maravali at the center. All the temples that received the message were marked down.

"The bastard-priest is quite thorough," noted Azam Khan. "Look at the pattern. If he heard back from more than two temples where they spotted the boy, he could have pinpointed their travel path and caught up with them. It's too late now, though. The boy could be anywhere by now, or more likely, dead."

"Or sold," said Rudra. "But listen to this, none of the priests responded to our friend."

"Good," said Azam Khan. "Let us send him some fake responses, and send him looking into nonexistent haystacks."

Rudra smacked Azam Khan playfully on the back of his head and went on to discuss the next message.

"Now this one, also sent by our priest, was sent not long ago.

It says, "The little myna lives". He has addressed it to a Bheema in Beegralli."

Azam Khan was about to react when Rudra stopped him.

"No, don't think too hard," said Rudra. "The message itself is not critical. We know who sent it. What we need to deduce is who Bheema is and where Beegralli is. We now know the priest is not alone. He has an accomplice called Bheema, which is most likely not his real name."

Rudra rubbed his chin.

"The name seems vaguely familiar," he continued. "I will see if I can find some reference to Beegralli."

"Perhaps we should just ask Sidappa. The old man has a memory like an elephant," proposed Venkata.

"I have also been meaning to ask you about that satchel you are carrying. Perhaps you should tell me about that now," Rudra said to Azam Khan. "I can tell it has something sensitive. I'd like to know, in case it has implications for me."

Azam Khan then told them Rajanna had ordered him to hand it over to Sidappa if something happened to him. "This is the reason I wasn't with Rajanna on his last journey." He told them about his visit to Honnavara, and how he had lost it, then found it again in Madhuvana. "I am more surprised the priest did not realize the satchel was important – it must have been, for Rajanna told me not to give it to anyone. Thank Allah that he didn't take it from me when he had the chance. It was an oversight on his part, but what do we care why?"

"Prabhakara Swami has obviously looked inside the satchel…the seal is broken. Have you any idea what it contains?" asked Rudra.

Azam Khan shook his head.

"I did look inside but didn't probe. It was meant for Rajanna or Sidappa, no one else."

He wasn't surprised that Rudra wasn't upset with him. They were both trained to be discrete. Unless circumstances dictated so, secrets were meant to be secrets. But he could sense the time for secrets was running out.

Rudra asked him, "With your permission, I would like to look at the scrolls. If they were meant for Sidappa, he would have had to summon me to read them for him in any case." Azam Khan handed over the satchel to him.

Rudra pulled out the scrolls and spread them on the floor. After flipping back and forth numerous times, he appeared to be satisfied. "This list contains names of operators loyal to Rama Raya. The last name here is that of Sidappa, our Sidappa. It should say Rajanna, but Sidappa always insisted on Rajanna's name remaining invisible. This map shows the location of several safe houses. You'll notice that these three places are highlighted. These are safe houses run by Rajanna's men, of which Sidappa's hamlet is one."

He put the scrolls back inside. The rain had stopped, so they emerged out of the hut. They saw Avadesha briskly walking towards them.

"You've come a long way from Maravali, Avadesha," Rudra called out to him, then called for water for the weaver.

"Yes, Rudra," said the weaver. "I thought you should know Prabhakara Swami has asked I send this message to a Bheema. I came right away."

Azam Khan read the new message aloud: "It is time to talk about the myna chick. I will arrive after *Deepavali*."

"This was sent to Bheema?" he asked Avadesha.

"Yes, at Beegralli."

"When is *Deepavali*?" asked Azam Khan.

"The next *amavasya*," said Rudra.

"Let's hold the message. The bastard is up to something," said Azam Khan. "Whatever it is, it is surely worth interrupting."

Rudra nodded, and turned to Avadesha, "Make sure Prabhakara Swami doesn't receive any messages from now on, unless I have first seen the message."

Avadesha agreed. He paid his respects to the men and left.

That night, Azam Khan and Venkata slept under the stars, which twinkled in a moonless sky, while Rudra slept inside. As they looked up at the sky, Venkata said quietly, "I promised Sharada I'd be back by tonight."

Azam Khan felt bad, for he knew that the man was constantly on the move. "I am sorry we delayed your return to Sharada," he said.

"I know she'll wait all night for me," Venkata smiled. "But she will understand. We should all be thankful. You are alive. So is Aadarshini. By god's grace we will find Raghu too. We will reclaim Madhuvana for him. The stars are now aligned in our favor. It's not the first time I have been late."

Azam Khan knew Venkata was perpetually travelling across the land, striking up friendships with bandits, dacoits, and the like, often going along with them on raids. These new friends would augment an already vast network of informers that Rajanna and Sidappa had painstakingly recruited across Vijayanagara. Venkata could be coldblooded and ruthless when he needed to be. But this was the first time Azam Khan sensed a melancholic pining for his wife under the cold exterior as he sang off-key:

"Yet another night away from you …Yet another sleepless night pining…"

"Bandit songs, I presume," jested Azam Khan.

They were about to doze off when Rudra came rushing out.

"I have the answer!" he announced triumphantly. "I know who Bheema is. It is Shamanna. Bheema was a code name Rajanna used a long time ago when Shamanna and he were doing business near Beegralli. We should assume the message was sent to Shamanna. Beegralli must be where he gets his messages from. Do either of you know where Shamanna lives now?"

Azam Khan knew the answer but right now his mind was elsewhere.

"Yes, I do. Go to sleep, Rudra. We'll deal with this later."

———————✦———————

Aadarshini protected the lamp's flame with her palm and walked away from the huts. Dawn hadn't broken through, but the pressure on her bowels had become unbearable. She had tried nudging Sharada awake, but she hadn't responded. She had no choice but to go by herself.

Outside, it was dark. She walked a little away from the hamlet, past the big tree. At a suitable spot, she set the lamp down, filled a tumbler with water from the stream, and crouched in the darkness. She looked up at the night sky and smiled, then blew out the flame. *Glorious*, she said to herself, and marveled at what she beheld. All around her, glowworms frolicked in the *amavasya* starlight. A light breeze tickled the gentle stream and made it giggle. Next to the pond, the birds were chatting up a storm in the trees. *Unusual*, she thought, *they are up early*. Then, a crimson hue began to emerge above the top of the trees, and in another moment, the sky lit up and glowed a deep orange, with the crackling of burning wood now filling up the air. Plumes of smoke blocked out the trees, and she could hear the sound of galloping horses, until they began to come closer to where she was.

She quickly hitched up her sari and hid behind the tree. Ten, fourteen, sixteen horses passed her by, their riders covering their faces with turbans and holding swords dripping with blood. As the sound of the hooves disappeared into the darkness, she ran back to the hamlet.

There, the flimsy straw and-wood huts were all ablaze, great tongues of fire engulfing everything in sight. She felt the heat singe her, but she didn't care. She ran to Sidappa's hut, where the roof had caught fire. She ran inside, and saw three lifeless bodies. Padma was stretched out over Sidappa, as if she died protecting him. Her neck had been slashed. Sharada too lay nearby. The smell of burning flesh was new to her, but she immediately recognized it as such. Smoke filled her lungs and her chest began to hurt.

The fire now burnt hotter, and she realized the roof would collapse soon. One by one, she dragged the three bodies out of the hut and into the open, away from the circle of hell, away from the intense heat. She noticed that there wasn't a scratch on Sidappa. *He must've died in his sleep*, she thought. *No wonder he had stopped coughing*. She then went back to the huts to see if anybody had survived. But the dead were everywhere. Outside one hut, she saw a boy lying prone. *Keshava*, she screamed out to him, but the roof caved in, and she could only look helplessly as the hut was consumed by the swirling inferno.

There was nothing more she could do. She stepped away from the huts and gazed into the carnage, numb. She stood staring into the fires until they died, until the huts began to smolder in a pile of burnt wood and ash. No birds welcomed the morning when it came. Aadarshini staggered into the pond and washed herself. She could feel the soot inside her lungs. In the morning light, she saw that the bushes that once surrounded the hamlet and made it invisible to the outside world had been burnt crisp. Ash swirled around aimlessly. Only the coconut palms remained unscathed. The fire had cleared out everything in its way.

She stared in shock at the dead bodies, not knowing what to do. She wouldn't leave them and go away. To look for help would be futile. *Where would I even go?* She had heard that dead bodies start stinking quickly, but there was only the smell of burning flesh that remained, nothing else. Sidappa lay calm, but the violence of the night was evident on the terror-stricken faces of Padma and Sharada. In her desperation, she felt a terrible rage coming on. She looked to the heavens and screamed aloud, "Prabhakara Swami! You are a dead man!"

She continued hurling threats at him, cackling uncontrollably as she moved around erratically, not knowing what to do. Her harangue was interrupted when she noticed three horsemen galloping towards the hamlet. *They are coming back*, she thought. One of the horses sped towards where she was. *They have seen me.* Aadarshini turned and ran across the paddy field. The ground was soggy. The vegetation, while it provided camouflage, was difficult to run through. She tripped and fell face first in the slushy ground. She meant to get up and keep running but she could now smell the unmistakable odor of a horse breathing down her neck.

"It's a woman," she heard the horseman yell out to his companions, then everything went dark.

13

"AADARSHINI AMMA?" A SHOCKED
Azam Khan asked as he dismounted to help the woman, now laying
prone in the sludge. Her face was covered in mud, but he thought she
looked familiar. He wiped the mud off her face. *Ya Allah, it is her!* He
picked her up and carried her out of the rice fields towards the pond.

Venkata and Rudra rushed towards him. Azam Khan laid her
on the ground and tried to revive her. He heard Venkata cry out,
and turned around to see him cradling Sharada's lifeless body. Rudra
too had broken down, with Sidappa's head in his lap. Padma lay
unattended. In the distance, wild dogs had begun assembling outside
the smoldering village.

"What madness is this, Rudra?" Azam Khan let out a painful sigh.

"They are dead. Everyone. Everything is gone." Rudra's voice had
never had such lack of temerity. He pointed at Aadarshini. "She may
have seen it happen."

"That's Aadarshini Amma," he said. He picked up the remains
of a clay pot and filled it with water from the pond, and splashed it
on her face. As the mud washed off, she began to cough. As soon as
she opened her eyes, she withdrew to a distance, as if she were a hare
trapped amid wolves. She saw the rising smoke, Venkata cradling
Sharada, and let out a piercing scream. Azam Khan rushed to her.

"It's me, Azam Khan. Don't be afraid. It's me, Aadarshini Amma," he soothed her.

"Be gentle," cautioned Rudra, "she has seen a vision of *naraka*. She must be terrified. And she doesn't yet know you are alive."

Aadarshini's gaze was transfixed on Azam Khan.

"Yes, it is him, Azam Khan," said Rudra, his voice soft. "I am Sidappa's nephew, Rudra. You are safe with us, Akka."

Aadarshini didn't say a word. She looked at Venkata, who now held Sidappa while crying into the heavens. She raised a hand towards him, and then tipped over and collapsed to the ground. Azam Khan rushed to help her. He couldn't tell if she was unconscious or dead. He placed a finger under her nose.

"She's alive."

"She must be exhausted and terrified. She pulled Sidappa and his family out of the fire all by herself. What a woman! She is spent. Let her sleep. We have plenty to do," said Rudra.

They left Venkata alone and went to the huts to inspect the carnage, pausing several times to vomit, and to shoo away the wild dogs. Neither spoke a word. Not a single soul was alive, and all they could see was half-burnt, half-charred bodies. The hamlet smelled of burning flesh, as if a fire demon had visited here during the night.

When they returned, Venkata was addressing Sidappa's corpse while cradling Sharada. "I should've come back last night, Appa. We stayed in Champanhalli for no good reason. This wouldn't have happened. None of this would have happened."

Azam Khan put his hand on Venkata's shoulder and squeezed it reassuringly. He then addressed Rudra.

"Seventeen, including these three," he said, "...men, women, and children."

"We can bury them or cremate them," said Rudra. "Cremation will be easier."

"We will bury them," said Azam Khan.

"Let's get on with it then," said Venkata, almost matter-of-factly, as he stood up.

The trio masked their faces with their turbans to ward off the stench.

One by one, they carried charred bodies out of the huts and brought them closer to the burial spot they had picked, a patch of land by the fields where the soil was soft. They retrieved pick axes and spades from the huts and began digging seventeen graves. It was well past midday by the time the graves were ready. Aadarshini remained unconscious. Exhausted and hungry, Azam Khan went into the hamlet and brought back coconuts that had survived the carnage. They rested with their backs against the mounds of soil that had piled up alongside the freshly dug graves and ate quietly. He noticed that Venkata and Rudra had both fallen asleep. Bone-tired, he too found it difficult to stay awake.

He woke up to Aadarshini's voice. She had washed clean the faces of Sidappa, Padma and Sharada, and wrapped them in saris she had gathered from the huts. She was talking to them, telling them to sleep peacefully, and that she would avenge them. He shook the other two awake.

"She shouldn't be doing this," he cried out. He then walked to Aadarshini. "We are here now. You don't need to do this," he said to her, his tone stern. "You shouldn't even be near this place at such a time. You're a Brahmin woman, a widow. This is not a woman's work. Go to the pond and cleanse yourself. Burn the sari you are wearing. Find a fresh sari if you can."

Aadarshini looked at him, her face barely showing emotion.

"I thought you were dead," she simply said.

"No, I am not. How could I die? Rajanna would never forgive me if I did. I have to take care of you and Raghu, don't I?" he said.

Aadarshini quietly got up and walked to the huts. She returned clutching a bundle of her possessions which included a hand of bananas that peeked out of the bundle. She had donned a fresh sari that was pockmarked with soot.

"I have everything I need. I don't want to go back in there again," she said.

"No, you don't have to," said Rudra. "Sit here. We'll finish what we have to do and leave."

"We need to hurry," said Azam Khan. "Those wild dogs may return."

The men patiently lowered each corpse into the ground. Aadarshini stood at a distance and watched. Venkata performed the burial for Sharada all by himself, crying, caressing her burnt face, mumbling indistinctly as he gently poured fistfuls of dirt till it covered all of her. The three men then buried Padma. Finally, Azam Khan placed the satchel in his mentor's grave as they laid him to rest.

"Sidappa, as Allah is my witness," said Azam Khan, "your murder will be avenged."

"Whoever did this will pay, Appa," vowed Venkata.

"I will watch over these two for you. I'll try to guide them as you did, Sidappa," said Rudra.

"Listen," said Aadarshini softly from behind them. "The birds have returned."

The men said their farewells.

"Sidappa, we leave you with your companions."

"The coconut palms will watch over you."

"The birds will visit as always…and sing songs about you."

"…about your brave deeds…"

"…about your kindness…"

"…about your wisdom…"

The three men hugged each other. Aadarshini began to weep.

"We should leave now," said Azam Khan, "before dusk approaches." He watched Venkata kneel by Sharada's grave, take a deep breath, and wipe his tears. "A friend lives not too far," he said. "We can stay there overnight."

"No," said Rudra with a tone of finality. "We'll ride back to Champanhalli. We need to get away from here as quickly as possible. Our emotions are clouded. I cannot think right now." Then, looking at Aadarshini, he said, "She is in a daze too. We need to get her to a safe place before we can hear what she has to say."

"She can ride with me," Azam Khan offered.

14

THE AIR TASTED DIFFERENT TO
her now. The taste of soot had long gone, but not its memories.

The sun didn't emerge from behind the overcast skies for seven
gloomy days after their arrival in Champanhalli. Aadarshini, spent
physically and emotionally, kept to herself in a small room that was
assigned for her exclusively. A woman came in from time to time to
bring her food or to ask her if she needed anything. Aadarshini had
not said a word to anyone in that time. She left the room a few times
a day to attend to nature's call or to wash herself at the well in the
backyard. She'd avoided any eye contact with the men. She could
see into the courtyard through a small window, from where she had
occasionally seen Rudra sitting pensively or reading. She'd not seen
much of Venkata or Azam Khan. Only occasionally had she heard
voices, mostly muffled monosyllabic exchanges between the men.

Then the night before, something within her seemed to stir. The
first sign of it was a wave of fury as thoughts of the priest came to her.
She grit her teeth as she went to sleep, nursing that feeling, which was
better than the inert numbness she had felt all these days. That night,
she dreamt about Azam Khan. She woke up early, enlivened. She went
to the window. She could sense a voyeuristic delight in seeing Azam
Khan sleeping on the portico with the others. Then she wished away

those thoughts, and firmed herself up. *The time for wallowing is over,* she told herself. *These men will do anything for me. So make them.*

She walked out into the courtyard, took a deep breath and opened herself up to the dawn.

The old woman who had attended to her walked past her into the house. Aadarshini followed the frail woman into the kitchen.

"I am Rajanna's wife Aadarshini, from Madhuvana," said Aadarshini, in an attempt to get the woman's attention. For a moment she was surprised by the firmness in her voice.

The woman, around Cheluvi's age, nodded courteously then stepped down a short corridor that led to a bathing area that was partitioned from the kitchen by a short wall. There she stuffed wood into a clay stove, then blew into the kindled wood to stabilize the flame, coughing as she inadvertently inhaled smoke. The familiar smell began to trigger memories of that fateful day, but Aadarshini remained where she was. A large vat of water sat atop the stove. The woman came back to the kitchen with a stump of kindled firewood and stuffed that into a smaller stove. She set a copper vessel full of fresh milk to boil. Her chores done, she turned to Aadarshini.

"I know. The boys told me who you are. I am Nanjamma. I have been working here since before Rudra was born."

"Thank you for taking care of me. I am sorry I couldn't be of much help earlier."

The milk began to boil over. Nanjamma rushed to take it off the stove.

"One must not be distracted while in the kitchen," she said. "See, you made me spill the milk." She smiled warmly.

"It's a good omen," said Aadarshini. "You will soon have guests in the house."

"Well," said Nanjamma, "you are here. Enough guests for now. I have my hands full. It is nice to see you up and about. What a horrific experience you have been through."

Aadarshini tried to lend a hand with cleaning the spilt milk, but Nanjamma wouldn't let her.

"No, you are Rajanna's wife. He was like a god to us. It is my honor to serve you. You shouldn't have to lift a finger here. The hot water should be ready by now. You should bathe before the men are up."

Aadarshini followed her to the bath, and stepped into the sunken space. Nanjamma had been heating water on a fire, and together they lifted the vessel off the stove. She bathed without disrobing, carefully scraping her feet to shave away dead skin. Nanjamma came and went as she pleased.

"The boys told me about you. You are a brave woman," said Nanjamma as Aadarshini dried herself and was draping on a fresh sari she had just been handed. "I noticed the saris you have with you are stained with soot and mud. Throw those away. It's not becoming of Rajanna's widow to wear dirty clothes. Wear one of mine for now. We do not belong to as high a caste as you do, but Rajanna never treated us differently. He ate the food I cooked, bathed here, and even stayed with us for days on end."

Aadarshini nodded. Nanjamma's kindness and the warm bath slowly brought her back from lifelessness. She asked her where Rudra's wife and children were.

"He is a good man, caring, even-tempered. Many families have come with proposals but he has turned them all away. He doesn't understand that he needs a woman to care for him. He seems more at ease in the company of men. I just don't understand it," said Nanjamma.

"How do I look?" she asked Nanjamma after draping the sari and tying her hair.

"As you should," replied Nanjamma. "It's apt to see you energetic today. *Durgamba* will keep you in her divine protection."

Aadarshini walked out onto the portico. The men were up.

"Nanjamma, what have you done with the woman who accompanied us here?" Rudra laughingly yelled out to Nanjamma, prompting the others to smile.

Nanjamma came outside and scolded the men. "No milk or *kenda-rotti* for any of you till you bathe," she jovially decreed. "Enough of sulking. Even the girl seems sprightly now. Follow her example."

The men seemed to enjoy being ordered around by Nanjamma. After they freshened up, Nanjamma fed everyone a light morning meal of *kenda-rotti* baked in firewood. The men held the hot flatbread in their outstretched hands while Aadarshini dropped a small clump of freshly churned butter on the bread.

"You don't look like the woman we fished out of the paddy field," said Azam Khan.

"Yes, she does appear to have recovered some of her strength," said Rudra. "But looks can be deceiving."

Then, addressing Aadarshini, "If you need more time we can wait as long as it takes. The same goes for you too, Venkata. There is no hurry. We have to talk about troublesome matters. But we must first be able to think clearly."

"I will never get over what happened. We might as well focus on what we need to do next. Moping will not make things better," said Venkata.

"I agree," said Aadarshini, surprising everyone with the coldness in her voice. "I have waited long enough. We must not lose more time looking for Raghu. And we need to take back Madhuvana."

Azam Khan suggested convening on the portico outside.

"No," said Aadarshini. "Let us go to the cliffs outside." She could tell the men were taken aback, but nobody objected.

The river Upajala flowed below, a vast rock bed sloping gently towards a precipice. Aadarshini walked up to the edge to take a look. Not far below where she stood, the Upajala turned sharply around a steep bluff. *One slight push or a big gush of wind and I'll crash into the rocks below,* she thought. She felt dizzy and hurriedly stepped back.

As the men got comfortable, she sat down and faced them. The river was behind her.

"We have much to discuss. Let us begin," said Aadarshini, just the way she'd seen Rajanna take control of discussions. Before any of them could say a word, she began telling her tale, taking care not to leave anything out, until the moment she saw Azam Khan chase her down on a horse. When she told them about her rape, they winced.

Azam Khan and Venkata then repeated their stories. Finally, Rudra asked, "So what really happened at Sidappa's hamlet?"

"There should be no doubt regarding what happened," Aadarshini began confidently. "Prabhakara Swami came to kill me but lost his nerve. He defiled me. He threatened me. He said he'd bring others to finish me off if I didn't disappear. He said he'd butcher Raghu if I returned to Madhuvana. I wanted to seek Sidappa's advice but he was too ill. Venkata was away. There was no one I could talk to. As promised, the priest sent his marauders. The carnage was targeted at me. I have no doubt that man knows where Raghu is. You must help me extricate Raghu from his clutches."

She noticed Azam Khan shaking his head.

"You say he came to you five days ago before the carnage. But five days are not enough for someone like him to organize such a raid. The way the homes were burnt down, and the villagers killed, it looked as if they were soldiers. The holy man may be devious and dangerous, but he doesn't have the wits nor the skills to pull off such an atrocity. You say you heard horses, more than ten of them. I can assure you the priest wouldn't even know ten people who can ride one. If he had such influence and muscle at his disposal, he wouldn't be a mere priest at a temple. No, I don't think he did it. I am having trouble imagining why he would want you dead. You present no threat to him even if you walked back into Madhuvana right now."

Venkata and Rudra waited for Aadarshini to respond.

"Like so many others," she spoke slowly, "he too has had designs on Madhuvana. I had been declared dead by the time he returned. Raghu had disappeared. The family began to squabble. The situation was perfect for a man as intelligent and manipulative as Prabhakara Swami. He moved into Madhuvana, I don't know why, but it was then that I sent him my anklet. It was a foolish act, I admit, which is why I feel the guilt. It is because of me that everyone is dead. I was too big a risk to be left alive. And only he knew I was alive."

"How do you think he found you," Azam Khan asked, "if the boy didn't tell him the location?"

"I don't know…"

"Do we have any other evidence, other than Prabhakara Swami's word, that he has Raghu?" Venkata interjected.

"No," replied Aadarshini, "but a mother's heart can feel such things."

Azam Khan threw up his hands in the air.

"It's unlikely the priest has Raghu," he said. "He wasn't even in Maravali when the boy disappeared. I think he is lying. He was probably just trying to manipulate you."

Venkata slowly began to speak, "Razing an entire hamlet and slaughtering seventeen people, all just to kill you? I just don't believe the priest would have it in him to do so. True, someone wanted the hamlet to disappear off the face of Vijayanagara, but the priest had nothing against Sidappa. He probably didn't even know of him."

Aadarshini began to pace nervously now.

"Akka," Rudra finally spoke. "We don't dispute that Prabhakara Swami would like to see you dead. I give you my assurance we will punish him for his evil deeds, for what he did to you and to Azam Khan. But even I am not confident that the burning of Sidappa's hamlet was an attack on you. It was perpetrated by forces far more powerful, and it was not personal."

He explained about Rajanna and his safe houses, of the succession troubles in the Vijayanagara capital, and of Rajanna's involvement with Rama Raya.

"Somewhere in the torture chambers of Vijayanagara, some hapless soul likely spilled information about the safe houses. Sidappa's hamlet is not the only one; in the last week, two others have been razed. You'd do the same if the throne of Vijayanagara was at stake. Rajanna and Sidappa had chosen to be part of a ruthless game for the greater good of Vijayanagara. Do you understand?"

Rudra maintained a gentle tenor, but Aadarshini listened with indifference. She couldn't care less about the politics of Vijayanagara. Her mind kept returning to the priest's assault on her, but after Rudra mentioned other villages had also been burned down, she grudgingly conceded that Prabhakara Swami and the carnage were not related.

"As for Raghu," Rudra continued, "unless the priest miraculously ran into the boy somewhere in Madhuvana itself, I too find his claim dubious."

Aadarshini's heart began to sink. She had wanted to establish three truths: that she was the target of the carnage; that Prabhakara Swami was responsible for it; and that Raghu was in his possession. Two had already been invalidated. The third too seemed to be in jeopardy.

"So, where is Raghu then?" she asked.

Azam Khan replied, his tone cold, "As much as it hurts me to say it, I maintain that the boy is dead."

"Then what are we to make of the message Prabhakara Swami sent Shamanna?" Aadarshini asked. Rudra had told her about the messages they had intercepted. She asked him to repeat the message.

"The little myna lives," quoted Rudra.

"Can't you see? The 'little myna' is obviously Raghu," said Aadarshini. "He is writing to Shamanna that he knows Raghu is alive."

"But why bother telling Shamanna?" challenged Azam Khan. "If the priest knows where the boy is, all he has to do is produce him before the village council. They'd declare Raghu the rightful scion of Madhuvana. All other claims would be voided. The priest could stay on at Madhuvana, probably as the boy's guardian, till he comes of age. The village council would surely accept such an arrangement. No! It's been a while since the message. The priest has yet to produce the boy. What is stopping him? I stand by my inference. He doesn't know where Raghu is."

"But he did send the message. And to Shamanna," noted Venkata. "Why?"

"Yes, that he did," said Azam Khan. "But think about it. If we match the days, that message was sent right after he had received Aadarshini's anklet and learnt she was alive. He must have panicked. He needed someone to commiserate with, not just anyone but someone who knew what was happening at Madhuvana. Shamanna appears to be that person. He must have visited Madhuvana recently and met the priest. Perhaps the two of them conspired together?"

Aadarshini recalled Keshava telling her he had seen the priest talking to a man on a horse. *Could that have been Shamanna?*

"So," Azam Khan continued, "it is my contention that you all are wrong about who the little myna is. It is not Raghu, it is you, Aadarshini!"

Aadarshini gave him an angry glance. She had expected him to defend her, yet all he had done was reject her arguments one after another.

"Rudra," Azam Khan pressed on, "remind us what Prabhakara Swami's second message said."

"'It is time to talk about the myna chick. I can arrive after *Deepavali*,'" quoted Rudra.

"Isn't it obvious?" Azam Khan pointed out. "This time, he talks about a myna chick and not a myna. Here he *is* referring to Raghu."

"And...," said Rudra.

"I haven't speculated beyond this," said Azam Khan with a sheepish grin.

"So Raghu could instead be with Shamanna?" said Aadarshini.

Rudra asked Azam Khan not to respond. "No, let's stop this. We can speculate all day long. You, Aadarshini, should be happy that you are still alive. As for Raghu..."

Aadarshini interrupted him.

"We know that Raghu is invaluable to Prabhakara Swami, or to anyone who wants Madhuvana. I now concede that Prabhakara Swami doesn't have Raghu." She paused to see what the men would say. The three gestured for her to go on. "But what if Prabhakara Swami suspects that Raghu is with Shamanna? After all, he too has his eyes on Madhuvana, and his nephew Puttaraju was in Madhuvana when Raghu disappeared. The only way for the priest to verify this would be to go to Shamanna's. Desperate, he sends him a message saying he will visit after *Deepavali*."

"Well, Shamanna will not get that message. I've killed it," Rudra reminded everyone."

Azam Khan replied, "True, Shamanna won't expect a visit from the priest. I know where he lives. One cannot just walk there from Maravali…its far."

Aadarshini then said, "Yes, it may be far for the priest to walk, but what if *we* paid Shamanna a visit and surprised him? It is worth the trouble, isn't it?"

The men looked at each other, hesitant to respond.

"It's an interesting proposal. Somewhat desperate, but interesting nonetheless," said Venkata.

"Let us not get carried away," said Rudra. "Prabhakara Swami is free to speculate about Raghu and Shamanna as he wishes. But we cannot go off to see Shamanna based on Aadarshini Amma's imagination."

Azam Khan agreed with Rudra. But Aadarshini refused to surrender.

"Even Rajanna was impressed with Prabhakara Swami's logical precision," she insisted. "It is my opinion that his message indicates he believes Raghu may be with Shamanna. Perhaps he wants to validate this. Let us not dismiss this possibility."

"Some of us happen to believe Raghu is dead," said Rudra. "You are dismissing our speculation."

Aadarshini, crestfallen, looked at the men, her eyes pleading for their support.

"You men cannot relate to a mother's anguish," she said, "which is why you're against it."

"I think there is some element of truth in what she's saying," Venkata finally said. "We should consider paying Shamanna a visit. What do we have to lose? We will pay our respects to Shamanna, and if the boy isn't there, we'll leave."

Azam Khan pitched in, "I agree with Venkata. If Prabhakara Swami believes Raghu is with Shamanna, we should find out before he does. We can outwit Shamanna and bring the boy away, or do whatever else we need to do. It's a long ride. We cannot take Aadarshini with us. She will stay here, with Nanjamma."

"No," Rudra said, "Shamanna is crafty. If he has Raghu, the boy will be well guarded. If we fail, we could all die. Aadarshini will be stranded once again. Rajanna and Sidappa will not forgive us for such thoughtless bravado."

"Rudra, you are the most experienced among us. Propose a prudent path forward, or we could be sitting here arguing for days," said Azam Khan.

Rudra walked away. He began to pace along the precipice and think, before he finally said, "Here is what I think we should do. Azam Khan and I will go to Shamanna's. Venkata will stay here with Akka. While we are gone, Venkata, you will send word to our mercenary friends and your brigands to join us for an undertaking on Rajanna's behalf. We need not give them details. They will come out of loyalty to Rajanna.

"If Azam Khan and I come back with Raghu, we will assault Madhuvana and take it by force. Between us, we will have enough men to overwhelm any opposition we may run into.

"If, however, we come back without Raghu, we must accept destiny's verdict that the boy is likely dead and that Rajanna's dynasty has ended. Aadarshini's fight for Madhuvana must end too. The men will return. Venkata can stay here and help me. The winds are shifting rapidly. The rebels appear to be gaining. But there is no telling who fortune will favor at the end of the game. I have to survive regardless of who prevails.

"Azam Khan will sail away from Vijayanagara back to his homeland, as he has often dreamed of. Before leaving, he will find an ashram where Aadarshini can live with dignity and peace. This is her destiny.

"As for Prabhakara Swami, I swear on our ancestors that Venkata and I will make him pay for the crimes he has committed against Aadarshini and Azam Khan, but I will bide my time. Now is not the time to unleash a hurried vengeance that may have unforeseen consequences.

"Do you agree with what I've suggested?"

Aadarshini had listened attentively. She didn't fully agree with Rudra's caution, but she knew she was outnumbered. She wanted to see for herself whether Shamanna had Raghu, but knew the men wouldn't permit her. She kept quiet.

Rudra then addressed Azam Khan, "I will ride into Maravali today with Venkata. We will visit the village square, the temple, and a few serais to see if there is fresh chatter about the priest or about Madhuvana. We'll be back tomorrow or the day after. You two cannot come for obvious reasons. When we return, you and I will leave for Shamanna's. Are we all in agreement about what we have discussed here this morning?"

Everyone nodded.

Following lunch, Venkata and Rudra rode away towards Maravali.

It wasn't till the following evening that Aadarshini mustered sufficient informality to ask Azam Khan if he would take her for a walk by the riverside. She knew he wouldn't let her go there unaccompanied. The sky glowed orange in the dusk, and Rudra had been right about its beauty. At the cliff, boys at play ran up to its edge and jumped into the river below like daredevils.

"They'll swim downstream then walk back and jump again. The river is calm now, ideal for this sort of horseplay," Azam Khan said.

Aadarshini walked up to the edge. She didn't feel as dizzy as in the morning. She saw that the boys had chosen the rock to jump from carefully, for if they jumped from the left of it, closer to the bushes, they would have landed straight on the boulders strewn along the bank. But below, to the left of the rock bed, the river changed its course and calmed down, creating a large pool into which the boys dived.

"Can you swim?" asked Azam Khan.

"No," said Aadarshini, "but I suppose I can if I have to."

A thin stream of smoke rose into the sky from across the river. *Perhaps from someone's kitchen,* she thought. "Beautiful," she sighed, admiring the smoke undulating in the wind, accentuated in the colors of the setting sun.

"The smoke is from Dasappa's serai where the evening meal is likely being burnt," Azam Khan jested.

They walked back home in silence, he a few deferent steps behind her. She could sense he wanted to say something to her; he had cleared his throat several times, but when she turned around, he had remained quiet. She wished he would say something, if only to relieve the awkward but pleasant tension between the two, now that they were alone.

Back home, Nanjamma served them dinner and retired to the back, where her room was. Aadarshini looked up at the crescent moon that hung over the courtyard.

"Do you think of Rajanna?" she asked him. "Do you miss him?"

"All the time. I miss being by his side, but pining for him won't bring him back. He taught me not to mope. But how does someone not remember a man like him?" Azam Khan went silent, then a little later, asked, "Do you…miss him?"

"I'm learning to let go of his physical presence. It's been a while since I missed it, and some of those memories have begun to fade. But I suppose he will always remain an abstract presence, a guiding force. He taught me much. I miss him in many ways."

But even as she said it, she knew it was not all true. Her life had changed in unimaginable ways since his death, which now felt as if it had occurred in the distant past, and not a few *amavasya*s ago. She had thought of him many times, but she'd thought about Azam Khan too, and the afternoon they had their encounter. She lowered her voice to a whisper.

"Do you think of the time in Madhuvana, just after Rajanna had left?"

He looked at her and nodded.

"Too often, I am afraid. It fills me with guilt. I banish those memories whenever they surface, but they keep coming back."

She smiled.

"And you?"

She didn't answer. Instead, she stood up and walked back towards her room, leaving her past behind in the courtyard, and hoping Azam Khan would do the same. She turned around at the door, and Azam Khan smiled. He followed her inside, and quite unexpectedly, he went down on his knees, held her by the waist, and placed his face on her navel. She could feel the hair from his beard tickling her.

"You've been through much," he said, and then kissed her navel.

"So have you," Aadarshini sighed, pulling him up, letting his scent saturate her senses. She felt his scraggly face, and his arms, and even under the clothes, they felt rock-hard. She put her head on his chest and took a deep breath. He slumped back to the floor, pulling her down with him. She hitched up her sari and sat astride him, and they eased themselves into a rhythm that brought them a pleasure they had long denied themselves. She felt her nails dig deep into his chest, and his strong hands cupping her from behind. She hoped Nanjamma couldn't hear their sighs of pleasure.

Exhausted, they rested, her head on his chest, her fingers dancing around the crescent moon tattoo on his nipple.

"Do you think Shamanna has Raghu?" she asked.

"No," replied Azam Khan, taking his time. "I am sure he does not have Raghu."

"Then why even go there?" She felt her spirit sag.

"To please you," he said.

She liked that.

"If Raghu isn't with Shamanna, Madhuvana is lost to me forever. I will have to go far away. You and I will never get to punish Prabhakara Swami, to look him in the eye as he dies. We will be left to speculate for the rest of our lives whether Rudra and Venkata served him the justice he deserves."

"I want to kill the priest myself...but I trust Rudra. He will not let him go unpunished."

She bit into the nipple, causing him to let out a sigh of surrender.

"Then take me away with you. I do not want to live in an ashram for widows. Take me across the seas. Show me a new world. If Raghu is indeed no more, there is nothing left for me here," she whispered as he pulled her closer, their lovemaking now more frenzied. As they reached their climax, her tongue in his ear, she whispered, "Promise me you will take me to Madhuvana one last time before you take me away."

She waited for his answer, hoping he would just say yes.

"Why?" he asked.

"I want to see Madhuvana one last time…and I want to teach the priest and others a lesson."

"A lesson? What do you have in mind?" he asked sleepily.

He asks too many questions. Rajanna has taught him well.

She didn't answer, preferring instead to watch him drown in the blissful stupor she had plunged him into. They barely slept that night, oblivious of Rajanna, satisfying urges long desired. Her persistence paid off and he eventually promised to take her to Madhuvana.

Rajanna has taught me well too.

"No one should find out about this night," he mumbled before falling asleep. "It will be an irretrievable fall from grace for us."

"Yes, I will remember," she said.

They woke up well before Nanjamma came to work. Azam Khan smiled lovingly at Aadarshini, then walked out without saying a word.

Venkata and Rudra returned by the afternoon, but they didn't have much to say about Madhuvana. There were, however, other developments.

"The serais are full of tales about how the rebels are gaining ground," Venkata said. "Mercenaries loyal to Salkaraju are switching allegiances. Many soldiers have deserted. It looks like Rama Raya may win, but Salkaraju won't give up so easily. I've sent word to twenty of our associates asking them to come here. Even if ten of them arrive, we have sufficient forces, provided we find Raghu."

The following day, Rudra and Azam Khan rode away to Shamanna's home.

15

PRABHAKARA SWAMI DIDN'T THINK
it was necessary to inform the council his tenure at Maravali was to
end soon. *Let them find out in due course.* Instead, he waited impatiently
for Shamanna's response. As if the wait wasn't stressful enough, the
possibility of Aadarshini coming to Madhuvana tormented him to
no end. He was weary, and his sermons leading up to *Vijayadashami*
were bland, without the excitement they usually carried. Realizing the
need to calm his demons, he wanted to perform an elaborate cleansing
ceremony, perhaps his last one in Madhuvana. He could hear the
demons taunting him in his mind, as if they had no plans to cooperate.

Jahnavi tried to invigorate him. "Tomorrow is *Vijayadashami*. We
begin a new era," she said as they went to bed. "Wake up early. Do
your rituals by the river. Cleanse yourself. Then come back and start
your *homa*. I will have everything ready. All will be well. The gods
are with us."

The ritual required him to not come into contact with anyone,
human or animal, till he was done with the *homa*. The riverbank
would be desolate this early in the morning, and just the place he
needed. He reached early, disrobed, and stood waist deep in the water.
Facing the rising sun, he prayed for his rituals to be unhindered. He
donned fresh clothes and filled two copper tumblers with water he

needed for the ritual. But just as he was about to step off the river bed onto the trail, a dozen out-of-control goats ran amok, startling him. He lost his balance and fell back on the rocks. The tumblers fell out of his hands and rolled down the rock, the metallic ring mocking his piety.

The goats gathered around a young boy who appeared to be counting them to make sure they were all there. A long braided pigtail peeked out of his oversized turban, while his dusty *panchay* swung behind him, his torso bare.

A lowly goatherd, Prabhakara Swami fumed. He settled his *panchay*, went up to a nearby tree and broke off a skinny branch. He stripped it of its leaves. The boy looked at him in disdain, and his anger now knew no bounds. He walked up to the boy, pulled at his pigtail, and began to mercilessly beat him.

"You imbecile, do you realize what you have done?" He whipped the boy's behind without mercy. He would have to go back and get a fresh set of clothes, bathe again, and repeat the rituals he had painstakingly finished. The boy did not emit a whimper, but all the goats ran away and began to graze at the river bank.

A woman ran to him and fell at his feet, begging him to stop.

"Is he yours?" he asked.

The woman said she was Lavanya, Sarala the maid's sister-in-law. "*Prabhu*...he is my son. Please show him mercy. It was an accident. The goats didn't know. Please pardon him. Punish me if you have to. He is just a boy, *prabhu*," she pleaded.

Prabhakara Swami looked at the long gashes he had inflicted all over the boy's neck and back, some so deep they bled freely. He recoiled in horror, and turned his face away, unable to look the boy in the eye.

"Serves him right for being so careless. Take him away. Tell him to never come here in the morning. I will skin him alive if he does. The desecrating halfwit!" He felt powerless against the rage that possessed him. The woman ran to the river, sobbing as she soaked the edge of her sari then returned to dab the boy's wounds. The boy pushed her hand away and whistled to the goats to follow him. The goats obeyed. He put his arm around Lavanya's waist and walked away with her, erect.

"Put some *haldi* paste on the wounds," he shouted behind them. "Don't let them fester. Bring him to me if he doesn't heal in ten days. I will take him to a *vaidya*."

O Narayana, what have I become?

At home, Jahnavi, noting his distraught demeanor and disheveled appearance, asked him what happened.

"Forget the ritual," he said annoyedly. "The gods are busy now. The demons are in charge this morning."

It finally stopped raining in the evening. Aadarshini found herself looking at a sky filled with scattered light of the setting sun. She moved one of her tamarind-goats closer to the center, clustering them to keep them safe from Nanjamma's pebble-tigers.

The triangular grid on the floor had a handful of tamarind seeds and a few pebbles. It had been a long time since she had played *Aadu Huli Aata*, but she found herself enjoying the battle of wits with Nanjamma.

"Aha," said Nanjamma, when Aadarshini had asked her if she wanted to join her. "So do you want to be a goat or a tiger?"

"Will it make a difference?" asked Nanjamma.

"Not to me," said Aadarshini and smiled. "I will win as either. You'll see." She didn't want to tell Nanjamma this was the only entertainment they had on rainy days at the ashram of her childhood. She rarely played the game after marrying Rajanna, but that didn't mean she had lost her touch.

Soon three pebble-tigers and fifteen tamarind-goats faced off on the grid. One by one she placed her goats, ensuring there were few spaces Nanjamma's tiger could jump over her goats, hoping to trap them. Nanjamma was about to place a pebble to unleash one of her tigers when the front door burst open and Venkata huffed into the courtyard.

"I need to talk to you," he said to Aadarshini, who was contemplating her counter. "Please…right now."

She could see he was agitated. She got up and followed Venkata outside.

"Rajanna didn't die in a place called Loconda. He didn't die a natural death either," his voice trembled as he said it. "He was murdered in cold blood."

She dropped one of her tamarind-goats in shock, unable to react.

"I know who killed him, and I know who was responsible," Venkata added. He had gone to Dasappa's serai to check on whether the men he had sent a message to had arrived. He began to explain, "When I reached Dasappa's, four men were drinking in a corner. I knew three of them, brigands who I have worked with previously, ruthless men but honorable. But the fourth was a stranger, a bear of a man with a bald head wrapped in a green turban. He introduced himself as Seena's cousin, Kaala. Seena is a mercenary I have known for a long time; Kaala told me that he could not come because of ill health, and that he had come in his place because of Seena's loyalty to me.

"We continued to drink. The four of them began to babble all about their past adventures, as such men are wont to do. Soon, one by one they left the table and fell asleep on the cots outside, all except Kaala. He continued to talk. He asked us about our mission. I didn't tell him much, just that it would involve violence. He then boasted about a wealthy Maravali businessman and his bodyguard whose throats he had cut on the orders of the Maravali priest. He said he left the dead men in the forest and sent back the man's personal effects back to the priest. 'I sold their horses. They wouldn't be needing them any longer,' he boasted. When I asked him about the priest, he told me he knew they were both employed by Salkaraju's nobles. 'That's how I was sent to assist him. But there's not a lot of difference between us. The intelligent ones like him worm themselves into comfortable positions, while those like me end up doing the dirty work for them, work meant for real men.'"

Aadarshini could feel her heart racing. Suddenly, everything Sidappa had said about the priest fell into place.

Venkata continued, "I wanted to reach across the table and grab the man's throat, but that would have been imprudent at a tavern. Perhaps realizing he had said too much, he got up from the table. He reached under the bench and pulled out his walking stick, then staggered outside. I recognized it right away – it was the *vrigodharam*, Rajanna's mace. I sat paralyzed as I watched him plop his towering frame on a cot outside, his leg extending well beyond the cot. Engaging him in one-on-one combat was not sensible. In any case, he is here at our insistence, so he's not going anywhere."

Fury rose within her at Venkata's supposed nonchalance. This was Rajanna's killer he was talking about! "What makes you think the man will linger till the others are back?" she asked him. "What if he leaves? We can't let him get away. Why not use some of the other men to take this Kaala prisoner?"

Venkata calmed her down. "Yes, I have thought about that. But it's dark, and these men will continue to drink more. They will not be in any position to follow orders. Kaala will also not be sober enough to leave Champanhalli tonight. Besides, why would he disappear? He is looking forward to being paid handsomely for our mission. We will have him soon. But more importantly, we now know it was the priest who ordered Rajanna's death. Everything Sidappa had told me about him was true. He is a Salkaraju spy in our midst!"

Her mind began to reel. Prabhakara Swami had been in the employ of Salkaraju all along. Rajanna must have discovered the truth about him, and that is why he was killed. Sidappa had been right. She had been wrong to trust the priest.

She finally said, "I want to watch him die. I want him to name Prabhakara Swami before he does. And I want Rajanna's mace back."

It rained all night long. She couldn't sleep, troubled by the fact that the assassin was sleeping peacefully not very far, and that the priest had been behind all their troubles. She tried to subdue the pounding in her head, but like the thunder outside, it didn't relent all night. She stepped outside as soon as dawn broke, desperate for some fresh air.

She walked, lost in thought, and before she realized it she found herself near the cliff from where she and Azam Khan had witnessed a most enchanting sunset. The river below was swollen, and seemed as angry as her. The cliffs were foreboding, glistening after a night of heavy rain. She hadn't intended to walk this far. Then, as she turned around to head back home, she heard the unmistakable sound of metal banging on stone. *Someone is coming!*

She quietly hid behind a nearby bush. In the morning light she spotted a man of gargantuan size walking towards the precipice, the walking stick in his hand clattering against the rocks. The green turban on his head gave him away, but it was the walking stick that made her certain. *That's Rajanna's! That's Rajanna's vrigodharam!*

Kaala placed the mace on the ground and walked hazily towards the cliff. He hitched up his *panchay* and squatted precariously close to the edge, positioning himself to defecate peacefully into the raging waters below. She could tell his eyes were closed, and by the way he stumbled his way to the edge, she could tell the inebriation from the previous night still hung heavy over his head.

Anger gripped her. Here he was, Rajanna's killer, and Venkata had asked her to wait until Rudra and Azam Khan were back to do something about it. Images of him mercilessly slitting Rajanna's throat flashed in her head. She mustered all her courage, and let the anger drive her. *The only reason he was needed alive was to prove the priest's guilt, but what need did they have of it? Wasn't the violation of her body enough proof? Let the man die. We will see about the priest.*

When Kaala got up and tried to settle his *panchay*, she slowly crept up from behind the bush and ran at full tilt towards the unsuspecting man. Putting her entire weight behind her arms, she pushed him towards the edge. Kaala tottered and she watched as first his legs, then his hands went flailing in the air until his head hit the rocks below, and he bounced once, twice before disappearing into the raging waters. The green turban floated to the top, now stained with blood.

Aadarshini found herself savoring every moment. There was no telling where the body would end up. She turned around, picked up the walking stick and ran back home. She kept running – across the rock bed, through the street – until she was in the courtyard. She felt a perverse rush coursing through her. *Was this how men felt when they killed? No wonder they enjoyed it.*

Venkata was still asleep in the courtyard. Aadarshini tip-toed to the well behind, drew a few pails of cold water and bathed. She draped herself in a new sari, and sat in a corner of her room. She began to tenderly clean the walking stick, polishing the metallic orb till she could see her reflection; it felt as if she was born anew.

Rajanna, she addressed the mace, *you will never believe what your Aadarshini did this morning.*

"Where is Raghu?" Aadarshini asked desperately. Azam Khan had returned empty-handed from Shamanna's place, and he now told Aadarshini their journey had been futile. Shamanna didn't have Raghu! She sank to the floor, weeping distraughtly.

Rudra then recalled their travels. "When we reached Shamanna's village, we first asked around if any boy now lived with the merchant. No one knew about it, so I pretended to be interested in buying horses and entered Shamanna's home. But it was unusually lifeless, with very few servants around. Voices came from a room at the far end of the courtyard. Two old women sat by a cot, on which an emaciated old man, bald and obviously very ill, struggled in his sickness. They told me he was Shamanna. The women were dabbing his forehead with a wet cloth and didn't extend the customary greetings when they saw me. I had to wonder, did this man ride to Maravali and back recently?

"When I felt Shamanna's forehead, it was on fire. In his delirium, he didn't recognize any of the names I threw at him – Rajanna's, Aadarshini's, or even Raghu's. I asked the women about him. They told me he had been sick since he returned from Maravali. No one had diagnosed his condition. The women speculated that he ate some poisonous berries along the way.

"I asked them whether he had come back with a boy. I told her I came to take the boy home. She said there was no boy living in the house. I believe her. Shamanna is as good as dead. We must now admit Rajanna's dynasty has ended. We must accept Raghu's fate. The assault on Madhuvana is not necessary. We will send back the men, and get on with our lives."

"Wait," said Aadarshini and turned to Venkata. "Tell them what you found."

Venkata told the two about his encounter with Kaala.

"Let's go get the son of a pig right away. What are we waiting for?" Azam Khan was furious.

"I went back to the serai the morning after I met him. But he wasn't there. No one has seen Kaala since that night. I have searched high and low. But his horse is still here, so he may have left on foot. I lost him, brothers. I have failed us," said Venkata, visibly disturbed.

"Kaala has disappeared…after coming here all the way? Why?" Azam Khan wondered aloud.

"And why would he leave without his horse?" said Rudra. "Maybe he went to a woman and plans to spend a few days there? Let us check with all the whorehouses around." He was fuming now. "Kaala and Prabhakara Swami are both enemies of Vijayanagara, traitors to our nation. Kaala is only an assassin, and he will be punished for Rajanna's death. But the priest has been living among the good people of Maravali, and who knows how many other places, and has betrayed their trust by spying on them. I wonder whether he had known about Rajanna's allegiances. But I don't care. As far as I am concerned, people like him are responsible for carnages like the one that killed Sidappa and others. The reasons don't matter anymore. The priest and others like him are a threat to us all and to the future of our glorious nation. They must be removed. As Rajanna would often say, for the greater good of Vijayanagara.

"I know I had dissuaded all of you from wreaking vengeance on the priest, and I know you were not happy with it. But Venkata's revelation changes everything. Prabhakara Swami must be punished. Azam Khan, I leave you to decide how and when to do it. This is a matter of urgency, and not just a dispensation of hurried justice. We will kill the bastard. Azam Khan will leave after, as we have talked. He will find an ashram for Aadarshini before he leaves Vijayanagara."

"I have something to say," said Aadarshini.

Azam Khan had trouble looking her in the eye. He had promised to take her to Madhuvana. But that promise was made in the heat of lovemaking, and he didn't feel compelled to honor it now.

"I know what you have to say," he began to say. "I have not forgotten my promise. But you must be…"

Aadarshini abruptly turned around and walked into her room.

A ceremonial conch signaled the festivities at the nearby Champanhalli temple were about to begin. It was then that Aadarshini returned, holding Rajanna's mace in her outstretched hands, her hair fluttering in the breeze. She banged it twice on the floor, demanding their attention.

16

PRABHAKARA SWAMI, WALKING
all the way from Madhuvana to the temple, tried hard to rein in his
emotions. The palanquin bearers had not come to work yet again, and
he felt slighted, as if they were deliberately showing him disrespect.
He'd complain to Chandrabhanu, considering it was he who had
bestowed the palanquin to him. But he wasn't sure the man would
do anything. He had been away from Maravali a lot lately, and even
when he was in town, he seemed preoccupied.

He thought of the faceless informers who'd also stopped coming
of late. *Does everyone know of my fall from grace? Are rumors about
me afloat among these cockroaches?* He felt humiliated. Everyone in
Maravali seemed to be going about their lives without paying much
attention to him. That, he reasoned, could be because of Puttaraju's
whisper campaign that he would return to Maravali after *Deepavali*.
And then there was the goatherd boy, whose beating he couldn't get
off his mind. *No point wallowing in the past*, he told himself, *it's the
future where victory awaits you.*

But even the future tormented him. True, he would soon leave for
Shamanna's estate. *But will I have to kill the trader, or will Shamanna
give me a portion to live in? Should I take along the two elephants with
me? After all, I could not even kill a woman,* he mocked himself.

The other question was, should he continue being a priest? The role had begun to bore him; he could just as easily become a teacher, an astrologer, or perhaps even a *vaidya*. Fortune, he was sure, would somehow find a way to smile on him. It always had. He took solace in that.

He was surprised to see a group of priests waiting for him at the temple with Giridhara. He welcomed the men. Their dusty clothes revealed they had been walking for long. The men asked if they could stay in Maravali for a few days. He asked Giridhara to arrange for their accommodation and meals. "I hope you've eaten since you've arrived?" he asked, and they nodded.

"So what brings you to Maravali?" he asked. "You look troubled."

The oldest among them, a priest by the name of Shankara Shastri, whose *shikha* ran long and displayed his age, said they were all priests from near the capital, and they were now migrating south to find new life. He was perplexed. Priests were always in demand, he knew, but these men had stable positions close to the capital. "But why?" he asked.

"So you haven't heard about the events at Vijayanagara yet," noted Shankara Shastri.

"No," he replied. "The *ghoshaka* hasn't arrived yet, and we don't otherwise get news from the capital unless travelers like you pass through Maravali. Sometimes a *ghoshaka* shows up more than six *amavasya*s after the event. Is all well in Vijayanagara?"

Shankara Shastri chuckled. "The rebels have prevailed. Salkaraju could not match Rama Raya's stratagem. His spies had infiltrated Salkaraju's camps, and they offered his captains bribes, which they readily accepted. Then there were the rumors around the campfires. *A descendant of shepherds...that is who you sheep are fighting for.* Rama Raya bade his time. He knew he had to weaken the morale of Salkaraju's troops. Massive desertions followed. Then came the battle at Tungabhadra's banks, when Salkaraju simply could not hold his remaining troops. He fled the battlefield, but was captured and beheaded. His head was hoisted on a flagstaff for everyone to see. And his nobles, they were all executed or thrown in the dungeons to die. They say the young Sadasiva was safe in Rama Raya's custody all along."

Shankara Shastri had the zeal of a skilled storyteller, punctuating his tale with pauses and animated gestures. Prabhakara Swami was certain he was the first person in Maravali to learn of these developments, for if the capital was in chaos, he doubted a *ghoshaka* would be coming this side anytime soon.

"You know our kind, Prabhakara Swami," he continued, "our loyalties are malleable. We sing the praises of whoever wants their praises sung. We had been loyal to Salkaraju. Unfortunately, we misjudged the citizenry. When the rebels won, those we had served turned on us. Some of us then chose to flee and start afresh. It's a vast nation. And men of our ilk are always welcome. Kings will come and go but we, keepers of the faith, will flourish. The gods meant it to be this way, isn't it?"

"You are right, the people cannot function without us," he commiserated. "I have travelled far and wide. I will be glad to tell you of places that need learned people like you." But even as he said this, he was thinking of something else. The fall of Salkaraju would have ripple effects across the land. Had Veeranna been executed or thrown into the dungeon? Either way, there was little chance he would survive. Veeranna's edicts were no longer admissible too. That meant he no longer needed to leave Maravali.

Almost instantly, the pounding in his head eased. He didn't need to go to Shamanna's. Maravali would remain home for him, perhaps even forever. He was liked here, and he could be the temple priest as long as he wished. The one hitch was his own association with Veeranna, but those who knew about it were already dead. *No*, he concluded, *no one knows*. He acknowledged grudgingly that his stay at Madhuvana had come to an end. He had agreed to not stay beyond *Deepavali*. He thought it best to return to Maravali as promised and wait for a fresh opportunity. *It is only a matter of time*, he told himself. *The family is weak. I just need to be patient.*

And then there was Aadarshini. If she showed up with the newly victorious rebels, who would owe plenty to Rajanna, he was doomed.

He was certain it was only a matter of time before she would seek justice and revenge. He decided to negotiate with her. *I will go to her, I will be contrite, I will ask for her forgiveness. I will be sincere like no other nātakā performer has ever been. I will promise to restore her to Madhuvana. I will admit to lying about Raghu.*

He then remembered he had asked her to disappear. He hurriedly called for Nanjunda after the travelling priests settled in the temple's guesthouse.

"Go to that village where you found the boy with the limp. Tell him I have a role for him in a play. Ask him to come see me. And check who else lives there now," he said.

The following day, he was at the temple in Maravali when Nanjunda returned with terrible news. "The hamlet is ash. There is nothing there but debris. I came upon several graves. No one lives there any longer. Everything is gone."

He was stunned. *Is she dead?* He remembered Veeranna writing him that his men had found a safe house run by Sidappa. *Was this the place? Had Aadarshini been with Sidappa all along?* But he was relieved in part, because her blood was no longer on his hands. He allowed himself to feel sorry for her, but he told himself that everything was in balance now.

A herd of goats passed outside the temple, and he thought of the boy. He couldn't help notice the difference between the goatherd leading the animals, and the boy he had met at the riverside. He had taken the beating with uncharacteristic forbearance. He had looked him in the eye, not usual for a goatherd when he came face-to-face with a priest. He bruised easily and his skin was not as dark. He had walked away erect, and he wasn't remorseful for defiling a Brahmin. The gait, he now realized, reminded him of Rajanna. *Could that have been Rajanna's son? But why would he pretend to be a goatherd? No, it couldn't be…*

He told Nanjunda, "Go with Narasimha and round up all the goatherds in the area. Check for wounds on their back – gashes, bruises, anything. Bring all such boys to me." He walked back to

Madhuvana hurriedly, and stormed into the northeast section where Sarala was finishing her chores for the day. Jahnavi sat on the swing.

"You," he addressed Sarala angrily. "Your sister, the one with the boy, where is she?"

"Why, *prabhu?*" asked Sarala with polite subservience.

"You insolent woman, how dare you ask back?" he said and picked up a cane and hit her on her back. "Who is that boy?"

"The boy is my nephew," she started to cry. "He left with his mother after the beating. My husband accompanied her. They live several days away."

He hit her again.

"You miserable lying child of a whore," he barked. "Tell me the truth. Who is that boy?"

"I beg you, Swami," insisted Sarala. "He is my nephew. I can bring him to you if you wish."

"Then go," he said. "Go to your sister's home and bring him back. Or I will ensure…"

He didn't finish intentionally. He knew Sarala and her people knew the consequences of standing up to the likes of him.

Sarala was shivering.

"You know I cannot travel alone. I have to wait for my husband to return. I will beg him to take me right away. I will bring them back," she said.

"Good," he said. "I expect you to have the boy here by *amavasya.*"

"O Deva! Is this what I get for being of low birth? What am I to do? How do I get him back so quickly? I know he is my nephew. Kill me now, Swami. It will be a relief," she pleaded.

"No, I must first see the boy. Death will seem a relief compared to what will happen to you if you don't return with him. Now go!" He watched as Jahnavi went into the kitchen and returned with a kindled stick of firewood. She came up behind Sarala and struck her on the back. The maid yelped in pain.

"And don't you think I don't know you stole my anklet. Better bring that back too," said Jahnavi.

Sarala left the courtyard in tears. He briefly considered

accompanying her home to check for the boy, but he reminded himself he was a revered figure, and couldn't just enter the homes of the lowly. He hoped fervently the boy she'd bring back would be Raghu.

⁂

Aadarshini savored the moment. The three men were aghast – her protectors, speechless, staring at the *vrighodaram* she held.

Azam Khan was the first one to break the silence.

"Where did you come by this?"

Aadarshini smiled. She knew they had all recognized it right away.

Come by it? I didn't 'come' by it. I took it away from your master's killer, and sent him to a befitting death. It was exhilarating, she felt like saying but didn't.

"Kaala must've come here looking for Venkata. Perhaps he left it here. Thank providence you didn't encounter him or there is no telling what such a man might have done," said Rudra. He then looked at Venkata. "He will come back for this, I am sure. We'll nab him then."

No, Rudra, he is not coming back. I pushed him off the ledge as he sat playing with his testicles and defecating into the river.

Venkata came up to her.

"May I hold it?" he said, deferential as always.

She could see he was in awe. The orb glinted in the sunlight as she handed it to him. The men took turns examining it, like children who had encountered a new toy.

"We have to look for Kaala," said Azam Khan. "He will return for this."

She wondered if she should tell them the truth. *They will fawn over me at first then return to their condescending ways. This is their way.*

Deciding to seize the moment, she took a deep breath.

"We don't need to worry about Kaala anymore. I took care of it."

As she began recounting her encounter with Kaala, she felt a thrill course through her veins, almost as if she was reliving Kaala's death. By the time she was done, it was clear the men were in awe.

"Unbelievable!" gasped Rudra.

Azam Khan's eyes were wide open, and he opened his mouth to say something but didn't. After a silence that felt like ages, he finally said, "You shouldn't have gone that far out by yourself. Anything could have happened. We'd never forgive ourselves if it had."

Anything did happen, my dear Azam Khan, but not to me!

Venkata was on his knees, adoration writ large on his face. "Sidappa had told me there was something remarkable about you, although you were found in such a vulnerable state. He told me he could sense Rajanna's spirit in you. I now know that to be the truth. You are the true heir to Rajanna, Amma." The other two nodded.

Aadarshini didn't want to gloat. There was much to be done. "Let's not forget the true culprit is still alive. The priest must die, and soon."

The men agreed. Later that night, Aadarshini could hear them discussing what was to happen next.

"It's time to ride into Maravali and get it over with," Azam Khan said. "I have to kill the holy bastard before I leave Vijayanagara."

"Only three of the men we've sent for have arrived so far. We should wait for a few others, at least fifteen. It has only been ten days since we sent out the message. They could be on their way," Venkata reminded him.

"Three days then, four at most," said Azam Khan. "After that we'll go in. We'll keep it simple. We will ride into Maravali. The priest comes to the temple every day. We will wait for him, pick him up, do the deed, and return – we can be in and out in a day."

"Each day Prabhakara Swami is alive represents another chance he has to betray the citizens of Maravali," said Rudra. "We must move quickly."

And what about Azam Khan's promise to take me to Madhuvana? She waited for him to mention it.

"It's not that simple," reasoned Venkata. "What if the priest is unwell and doesn't come to the temple that day? It's a half-day ride to Maravali. Do we keep riding back and forth every day till he shows up? No. We have to be closer to Maravali, where we can camp discretely while we wait and watch."

"Venkata is right," said Rudra. "I know a place close by which can accommodate us and the men. It's a short ride to Maravali from there, so we can go in and out at will."

"Can we take her with us?" added Azam Khan.

"We'll leave behind a few men to protect her. Nanjamma will be here too. She'll be safe here," said Rudra.

"No," said Venkata. "This vengeance is as much hers as it is ours. We must take her along. She can stay where we choose to camp. She'll be safe with us."

Aadarshini had heard enough. She burst out onto the portico. The men sat up. She wasted no time in confronting Azam Khan.

"Since all of us want to kill the priest, I would like to be part of this discussion. To start with, none of you has been affected by his crimes as much as I have. So I want to be there when he dies. I want to watch him die. I am disappointed that you want to leave me behind." She looked at Azam Khan. "Because it means you don't hold up your word. This man promised me he will take me to Madhuvana before I join an ashram."

She could see the shock on his face.

"Have you forgotten your promise? Were you toying with my emotions? Doesn't a man's word mean anything?"

"Word?" Rudra was surprised.

"I asked him for three favors. First, he promised to take me back to Maravali one last time. Second, I would see Prabhakara Swami die. Third, he'd take me to Madhuvana so that I can teach them a lesson…"

Azam Khan jumped to his feet, clearly startled by her assertions. Rudra was visibly perplexed. Venkata shook his head in utter disbelief. Azam Khan started to say something but Aadarshini didn't let him.

"Don't you remember? Do I need to remind you where you made this promise? We were…"

"Yes, I remember. No need to remind me," he raised his hand and interrupted her.

Aadarshini felt relieved. She had counted on him not wanting their affair to be revealed, or that she planned to go away with him. She didn't know how the others would react. She was, after all, Rajanna's widow still. In any case, Azam Khan had all but admitted she was speaking the truth.

"Tell me again…what were you promised?" asked Rudra.

"I have three simple requests," she said. "First, I don't want to be left behind in Champanhalli. Take me with you."

"Consider it granted. You will come to Maravali with us."

"Second, I want to watch Prabhakara Swami die. I will not come in your way."

"No, I will not permit that. Don't ask me again," replied Rudra sternly. "However, you will have proof that the priest has died. Azam Khan will see to it. Will that be enough?"

Aadarshini nodded.

"And finally, I want to set Madhuvana on fire."

Rudra sank to the floor. Azam Khan was now looking at her in abject bewilderment, his mouth wide open.

"O Narayana, what am I hearing? How could this fool have made such a promise?" he looked at Azam Khan. "Madhuvana is Rajanna's heritage. Venkata and I have played in Madhuvana when we were children. Burning it down is sheer lunacy. Are we to be part of this madness?" Rudra looked at her and said finally, "This promise was made to you by Azam Khan. But Venkata and I will not set Madhuvana on fire. It is up to you and Azam Khan to do as you please. Venkata and I will have nothing to do with it." He then looked at Azam Khan. "You made a promise to Rajanna's widow. Now keep it. Let your honor compensate for your stupidity. After that, the two of you will leave Maravali. Do you understand, Azam Khan?"

"Yes, I do. We must do what has to be done," he said. He didn't seem happy with the way she had maneuvered the situation to get what she wanted. *But there was no other way,* she told herself.

"For that, I will always be in your debt," she told him.

Rudra said, "We need more men, however, for the task you have in mind. Let us wait until the others arrive."

Four days later, the four of them left for Maravali with fifteen others.

❧

Azam Khan was familiar with where they were to wait outside Maravali, an inconspicuous cluster of three small houses with a common courtyard. *Perfect*, he thought, *far enough from the village, close enough to ride in and out swiftly.* A barn in the back served as a stable for the horses. They had brought along three maids from Champanhalli, instructed to stay invisible. Azam Khan told the others to spread out across two houses. They would stay in the third.

"I walked this path not too long ago," said Aadarshini. "The priest and I crossed paths somewhere around here during the squall. I wasn't myself that day."

"I remember when you were carried down this path as Rajanna's bride...you were just a girl then," Azam Khan pointed towards Madhuvana. "And now you want to burn it down. How times have changed!"

"Yes, times have changed. I don't want to think of the past. Sentimentality makes one lose focus," said Aadarshini, quoting Rajanna.

"What about your anger?"

"Well-reasoned anger gives one a sense of purpose," she said tersely.

"And your lie...about my promise to help you set Madhuvana on fire?"

"I had to...or they'd have listened to you and left me behind in Champanhalli," and she walked away, putting an end to the tense exchange.

That afternoon Rudra laid out their plan.

"Killing Prabhakara Swami is our primary motive. The killing must be done in his house, not in public," he emphasized. "Let there be no spectacle in the streets. Venkata and I will continue living here. No one should connect us to a priest's murder. In fact, if possible, let no one know that the priest is dead. We know him to be a traitor and a murderer. We do not need to explain to everyone why he is dead. Let his death remain unmourned."

Azam Khan then explained what the men were to do.

"Rudra will draw out the priest from Madhuvana and into his home by the temple tomorrow. The house is unoccupied except when the priest comes home. I will lay in wait inside. Rudra and two others will wait outside Maravali. When Prabhakara Swami comes in, I will cut his throat. I will then meet up with Rudra and we will come back here.

"After that, we will do what I had promised her," he looked nervously at Aadarshini, "if she still wants to go through with it."

Prabhakara Swami had to smile, albeit cynically. Killing time was an activity he could not delegate to someone else. With each passing day, his anxiety worsened. *Amavasya* was just a day away. He had been uncharacteristically lethargic of late, and had found it difficult to overcome his sloth and discharge his priestly duties. He hadn't been to Maravali for more than a week now, and did not plan to go until the maid had returned with the boy.

Jahnavi had been supportive. She'd let him make love to her whenever he desired, and she had indulged him. But this too bored him now. His anguish, he knew, wouldn't subside until the night after the moonless sky. To keep himself occupied, he wanted to invoke the gods and cajole them with mantras. Now comfortably seated in front of the *homa* pit, he began yet another lengthy fire ritual.

But his thoughts were not on the mantras, which he could chant effortlessly even in his sleep. As he chanted without thought or feeling, he could hear his mind struggle with all the questions he had. It felt like a duet of two discordant musicians trying to outperform each other. He chanted louder. The voices in his head kept pace, and try as he did, he couldn't drown them out.

Why haven't the two elephants come back with news about the goatherds? Where are they?

He chanted some more and uttered *Svāhā*, pouring ghee into the fire. The flames danced each time he added the fuel.

The duel continued.

Do you think you have found the heir? All because a goatherd's gait reminded you of Rajanna's? Sounds flimsy, self-serving…

"Svāhā," he said, and continued chanting.

So many people were looking for the boy — maids, farmhands, relatives. Could the boy have been here right under everyone's noses and gone unnoticed? Improbable!

"Svāhā!"

What if Sarala doesn't return?

"Svāhā!"

What if Sarala brings the boy, and he isn't Rajanna's son?

"Svāhā!"

If the boy isn't Raghu, bow to your destiny. Stay on as a priest here. The struggle in the capital is over. Vijayanagara will prosper again. New opportunities will emerge. The same is true of Madhuvana.

"Svāhā!"

Do not let self-doubt cripple you. You were right to think about the boy. But any way you look at this, you are the victor.

"Svāhā!"

By the time he completed the *homa*, the voices in his head were exhausted. Jahnavi served him *gasagasay payasa*, his favorite sweet dish made with poppy seeds, cardamom, almonds, rice, saffron, jaggery, coconut, milk, raisins, and cashews -- a concoction he loved for its aphrodisiacal and slumber-inducing virtues. He gulped down several tumblers. The lovemaking and slumber that followed were both soothing.

He woke up around dusk to find a visitor waiting for him outside.

"My salutations to you, *prabhu*," the man said. "I was told by my master to deliver this message to you."

He could see the message was sealed. He asked the young man why he didn't leave the message with Giridhara.

"I am Paundraka, a runner for Avadesha. I simply follow his orders. He asked me to deliver this to you here at Madhuvana, so here I am."

He smiled at the mention of his name. "Did you know Paundraka is the name of Yama's buffalo? You should change that name," he shouted behind the runner who had turned around and started walking away.

Jahnavi asked him to open the message quickly. He broke open the seal and read aloud.

> *My respectful salutations to you, Prabhakara Swami. You do not know who I am, but since receiving the news of Rajanna's demise, my master and I have been caring for his son and heir Raghu far away from here. We chose to take the boy away on the night of his mother's impending death, intending to raise him till he was old enough to reclaim what is his. Our loyalty to Rajanna, and our distrust of the Madhuvana family, compelled us to do this.*

> *Alas, destiny has wished otherwise. My master is on his deathbed, and I can no longer care for the boy. I have therefore come to Maravali to seek your help. I would have brought the boy to Madhuvana, but my master has specifically cautioned me against doing so. I have been instructed to hand the boy over to you, and to no one else. My master trusts you to take the boy to Madhuvana and present him to the family.*

> *I came to your home by the temple but no one was home. I met a man named Avadesha at the temple, who said he could deliver a message to you. He doesn't know the contents of this message. I sealed the scroll myself. No one knows me here. I haven't interacted with anyone in the village either.*

I will come by your house again tomorrow, sometime after the mid-day meal. I pray that we meet and I can be relieved of this great responsibility with which my master has entrusted me.

In the event we are not able to meet, I will accept it as a sign from God to leave Maravali and seek refuge for Raghu elsewhere.

A rush of blood entered Prabhakara Swami's head. He hadn't intended to leave Madhuvana, hoping to wait for Sarala. But the message was unique. Was providence being kind to him again?

"Who could have sheltered Raghu all along?" he wondered aloud.

"Does it really matter?" said Jahnavi. "The message sounds sincere. After all it was Avadesha's boy who delivered it. Go to Maravali. Meet the man. If he has Raghu, bring the boy home. If Sarala comes when you are away, I will make sure she and the goatherd boy don't leave. Surely one of the two boys will be Raghu. My heart tells me so. We have nothing to lose."

He stayed up all night, trying to figure who had the audacity to kidnap Rajanna's son, keep him with themselves, and then return him in such an unexpected manner. The list of suspects was long. But it didn't matter. Once he had Raghu, the game was won.

❦

17

AZAM KHAN AND RUDRA LEFT FOR Maravali with two other men before dawn broke. They had been up early. Before they left, Aadarshini had given each of them the *prasada* she had specially prepared this morning.

"Durgamba will keep you in her divine protection. Come back victorious," she said, like a queen sending her troops into battle.

The slow dreary drizzle was just enough to dissuade one from venturing out into the open. She hoped Azam Khan would return safely. The last time he left her waiting, he never returned. *He hasn't said anything more to me about going into Madhuvana. Why?* And for the first time since she had reconciled to a new life with him, she felt an unnerving discontent.

Venkata cleared his throat to get her attention.

Prabhakara Swami stopped for a moment and looked back at Madhuvana sparkling in the post-drizzle light. The clouds had dissipated. He inhaled the petrichor and marveled at his good fortune. He quickly pulled himself together and aborted his incipient fantasy. *This wasn't a time to daydream.* He resumed his brisk march into Maravali. Nanjunda and Narasimha accompanied him, one in front and one behind, carrying some of his books and other religious paraphernalia he wanted dropped at the Maravali home.

Nothing seemed out of the ordinary outside the temple. He wished he had set out earlier. The slushy trail had slowed him down considerably. Cautiously hopeful about meeting the man who sent him the message, he expected the man would be waiting for him by now. He was passing the temple when he heard Giridhara calling out to him. Giridhara latched the front door, closing the temple for the rest of the afternoon, and ran to him.

"Prabhakara Swami, what a surprise to see you here! I was going to come to Madhuvana to talk to you about the festival. We need to talk about how we should organize it. Do you have a moment?"

"Ah, Giridhara! You are late in closing the temple today. All well, I hope? Going home for your nap?"

Giridhara grinned.

He turned to Nanjunda and Narasimha and told them softly, "Go home. Go in and put the books inside. If you see someone waiting for me, tell them I will be there momentarily. Don't let them leave."

He then turned to Giridhara.

"Tell me, Giridhara, what's on your mind? Keep it swift. I am in a hurry and cannot linger now. I will be back in the evening. We can continue our conversation then."

<hr />

Aadarshini looked at Venkata admiringly. He had lost his parents and his wife just days ago, and yet here he was, dedicated to her cause, putting his grief aside for the time being. *It's rare to find such loyalty*, Rajanna would often say.

Aadarshini decided to seize the moment.

"Do you think Azam Khan will help me set Madhuvana on fire? I think he has begun to waver."

"I'd waver at such a request too. Burning down Madhuvana is not necessarily the right thing to do. When your actions are not aligned with your principles, you don't have to go to the holy books. He is conflicted. But he will keep his word to you. Don't forget, you won't just set fire to the home. The cowshed will burn down too. The cows will die. So will the goats. And the men, women, and children – what have they done to deserve such an end? What does *your* conscience tell you?"

"Let me then ask you, Venkata – will you take me to Madhuvana? Don't talk to me about conscience. What about their conscience when they wanted to set me on fire? What about when they forced Cheluvi and Kalavati to commit suicide? What about them fighting for the scraps of Madhuvana after our deaths? They put everything on tradition. They separated Raghu from me. Now they want to rule Madhuvana. No! If I cannot have Madhuvana, no one else will. Would you forgive the demons who set fire to your father and mother and the lovely Sharada? So I now ask you, Venkata, will you take me to Madhuvana? I do not wish to wait for Azam Khan. I have seen the doubt in his eyes. If you refuse, I will go alone. I have nothing to lose now."

She stepped away to give him a moment to think. She saw him looking at the other men who were milling around. She wondered if they would take orders from a woman.

Venkata seemed to have read her mind.

"After how bravely you have lived your life, how you handled Kaala, and how you selflessly put yourself in harm and pulled my family out of the fire, you should have no doubts about my loyalty, Amma. I am at your service, just as my father was to Rajanna," he said. Then, pointing at the men, "They will lay down their lives for you, as will I. When do you wish to leave?"

Aadarshini smiled. The sun began to break out as the clouds cleared. The moment seemed right.

"*Shubhasya sheeghrum*" she replied. "Let us leave right away," catching everyone by surprise.

Azam Khan had been waiting impatiently for more than half the day, and now he hoped the priest would make an appearance soon. He had been sitting by the priest's door, stroking a hatchet, playing with a heavy cast iron pestle someone had left lying around. The front door, as all doors in Maravali were, was a heavy slab of teak that let out a painful creak when pushed open. He longed to hear that creak. He had thought about Aadarshini, and looked forward to informing her of the priest's death. *She'll be so delighted!* He hoped the news would convince her not to set Madhuvana on fire. *Instead, we'll go away together.*

The front door finally creaked and interrupted his fantasies. Azam Khan held his breath and brought out another knife. He rose up, a hatchet in one hand and knife in another, and hid behind the door. He wanted to strike before the priest's eyes adjusted themselves to the dark room. As soon as the man entered, Azam Khan struck swiftly. The hatchet mercilessly cut across the man's neck, spraying blood all over the walls and over him. The man fell with a thud, and Azam Khan could see he was dead even before he hit the floor.

Suddenly, a shadow cast itself across the door. He realized another man stood in the doorway, and before he could turn around and strike again, the shadow struck out at him. Even as he skipped the slash of the knife, he realized he may have made a mistake. *That was not the priest!*

The hurried lunge caused the man to lose his balance, but not before he stabbed Azam Khan in the thigh. He screamed in pain and went to the ground, pulled down by the weight of the man, but regained his senses immediately and plunged the knife in his hand deep into the man's neck. A rich bubble of blood erupted from the wound, and he twisted the man's neck just to be sure. Just as he pulled himself away from the two dead men and let out an exhausted sigh, he heard the door creak open again.

"You!" gasped Prabhakara Swami.

Azam Khan picked up the hatchet and tried to stand up, but the gaping wound in his thigh hurt him. He could see the priest turn around and run. Azam Khan picked up the pestle and aimed it at the priest's head, but it hit him in the legs and sent him sprawling into the dirt. He then began to limp down the street that led to Madhuvana. Azam Khan picked up a turban from one of the dead men's head and wrapped it around his wound. He could see the priest hobble down the trail. *Where else will the bastard go but to Madhuvana? I will chase him all the way there.*

18

A STRANGE NUMBNESS TOOK OVER her. Here was the banyan where she met Azam Khan. There, the tamarind trees swayed in the breeze, as if they were happy to see her back. In the distance, the banana plantations and the rice fields she walked through, and the jasmine vines she plucked flowers from almost every day. The gates of Madhuvana stood solemnly, as if they knew why she had returned.

She wished she didn't have to undertake this journey. She knew it wasn't going to be easy. Her right eyelid, not her left, fluttered briefly. *Good tidings*, she told herself. It was a hesitant flutter, but it would have to do for now. She needed her share of good luck now. The mace felt heavy in her hand as she sat side-saddle on Venkata's horse. The rest of the men followed her quietly. She felt the jewel-encrusted dagger that hung around her waist, and thought it too felt heavier than usual. Self-conscious at first, she had managed to shrug off the discomfort. They had taken a circuitous route that circumvented Maravali, so that they didn't run into anyone along the way.

Venkata gave the men a final briefing. Aadarshini adjusted her turban to ensure it fit snugly. She wrapped her face in one of its folds, and with a softly whispered *May the Goddess keep us in her protection*, they rode into Madhuvana, four horsemen in front. They passed the paddy fields, the banana plantations, the coconut groves and the tamarind trees, until she could see smoke rising from one of the terracotta roofs. She prepared her mind to set it all on fire.

The attack was unexpectedly noiseless. Aadarshini knew most of Madhuvana would probably be resting after the mid-day meal. The women, if they weren't in bed with their men, would be in the *zenana* watching over the children and trading gossip. She noticed a group of servants milling around outside. At the first sight of the horsemen, they scampered away towards the woods and disappeared. She wondered if this would present a problem.

"Don't worry about them," Venkata said to her. "They are sheep. Right now they are thanking the gods for sparing their lives. Some are probably just hiding and watching us."

Aadarshini liked how Venkata seemed to read her mind.

The men stormed into the central courtyard then dispersed into the homes. The few maids and farmhands they found were ordered to lie face down on the ground. Aadarshini waited in the central courtyard as the others began dragging out the occupants. She could hear shouts of protest from the men and shrieks from the women as they were herded out like goats. No one recognized her, not the women, nor Kanteeravaa, nor Puttaraju. She didn't see Srikanta and assumed he was travelling. *I can deal with him later.*

The men, women, and children were segregated. They were taken away to the barns and tied up, three man standing guard. The children had begun to wail, but Aadarshini ignored them. She felt a tinge of disappointment. She had expected the men to put up a fight. *Here they are, marching without as much as a bleat.*

The servants and farmhands were led away to the barn. Aadarshini was surprised to not see Sarala among them.

"We have cleared the place. There is no one inside," one of the men told her, "except for that one."

He pointed at what had been her home – Rajanna's home, Cheluvi and Kalavati's home, Raghu's home.

As she entered, she saw that Venkata had pinned a woman against a wall. His sword rested on her shoulder, precariously close to her slender neck. Aadarshini asked him to tie her to one of the pillars on the portico then went inside what had once been her room. She could hear the woman yell outside.

"What is this outrage? How dare you come in here? Who are you? Do you know who I am? Chandrabhanu and Prabhakara Swami will have your heads for this!"

So this was the priest's wife! Aadarshini thought. *She'd certainly made herself home,* she chuckled to herself. The priest was likely dead by now, and although Chandrabhanu was responsible for keeping the king's peace, by the time he found out, everything would have turned to ash and she would be long gone.

She placed Rajanna's mace in a corner of her room, pulled the turban to a side, and stepped out into the courtyard where Jahnavi could see her. She reached into the pouch around her waist and pulled out her anklet. She bent down and wore it, taking her time, watching the priest's wife squirm. "They come in pairs. They say it is bad omen to wear just one," she said to her, without looking her in the eye. "I believe you have the other one. I had sent it to your husband."

"You!" Jahnavi spat out in fury, finally recognizing her.

"Your husband set my life on fire," she said, looking her in the eyes with a cold fury.

Jahnavi let out a demented cackle. "You should be careful before you do anything rash," she said. "Prabhakara Swami will be back from Maravali any moment with your son. Don't you want to see your boy? Think, mad woman, think!"

Your husband is dead, she was about to tell her, when a familiar moo interrupted her.

"Take her away," Aadarshini said to Venkata. "We'll decide her fate later. Keep her away from the others. Cut off her tongue if she screams too much."

Venkata gagged her and led her away. Aadarshini hurried into the cowshed and embraced her long-lost friends. "It's been so long. So much has happened, and here we are," she patted Gouri, Amba, and Lakshmi and fed them each a handful of grass. "Don't panic," she assured them. "You'll be safe."

Venkata returned with six farmhands.

"I know them well. I trust them," he said. "Should we have them watch the trail for unexpected visitors?"

She was pleased he was asking her for permission. She nodded her approval and asked Venkata to have them take the cows as far away as possible. *To the other side of the woods, perhaps even outside the gates,* she suggested. She didn't want them to smell the burning of the only home they'd known.

She was now alone in the courtyard, and she braved herself for her final act. She began to think about Rajanna being murdered; about Raghu, whose whereabouts she didn't know, or whether he was even alive; about the cruelty of all the other men and women who hadn't hesitated to condemn her and the other wives to a fiery death; and about how invigorating it had felt to push Kaala off the cliff.

But nothing seemed to help. The fury she had once felt had subsided once she was home. She had also not realized what it would take to burn down Madhuvana. *Sarala, how I wish you were here to help,* she thought, for it was Sarala's job to light the torches every evening. She walked to the shed behind one of the homes where they had been kept. The torches, wooden staves with one end wrapped in cloth, were neatly laid out on the floor. They would have to be soaked in oil before being lit. A vat full of oil sat in one corner.

This is it! Aadarshini took a deep breath. In her mind, she broke down what she needed to do. She'd have to go to each section of the rambling estate, pour oil everywhere, then she'd have to set the homes on fire finally. She found herself panicking, unable to organize her thoughts.

She stepped outside the shed and stormed across the central courtyard and beyond the front door. She tossed aside her turban, and let her hair unfurl in the afternoon breeze. A little distance away, the woods seemed to be at peace. She wondered if people were watching her from the trees – 'sheep', as Venkata had called them. The process of setting her beloved Madhuvana on fire now made her despair. *This is too much work for one person.* She decided she'd ask the men to do it. *They are better at such savagery.*

She took a deep breath and was about to go back in when a sound rang out from the woods.

"Ammaaaa!"

Aadarshini tried to pinpoint where the sound had come from.

A figure darted out of the woods and ran towards her. She was blinded by the sun in her eyes. A woman ran behind, frenetically trying to catch up, and behind her were two others.

"Stop! Come back here," Aadarshini heard the woman cry out.

She stood stunned as the boy almost collided with her. He held her in an unyielding embrace, his arms tightly wrapped around her waist, his face buried in her bosom. She cupped the boy's face to look at him. Her hands began to tremble.

"Raghu?" she gasped, and collapsed.

***

Two of Venkata's men appeared in the courtyard hearing Sarala shout out for water as she and Lavanya carried Aadarshini inside. One forcibly pulled Sarala and Raghu away from Aadarshini. The other held back Sarala's husband and Lavanya.

"Bring some water, fool," Sarala yelled at the man. She jerked herself free from his hold and ran back to Aadarshini. She began to massage her feet. "Can't you see she is unconscious?"

The man appeared confused.

"You fool! Imbecile! She is my mistress," shouted Sarala, then pointed at Raghu. "He is her son. Go, hurry!"

The man returned with a pail of water. Sarala wet a corner of her sari and squeezed some water on Aadarshini's face, then rubbed her temple gently.

"Akka," she spoke softly into her ear. "This is Raghu, your son. He is safe. He has been with me all along." Tears dripped down her face.

Aadarshini slowly opened her eyes and steadied herself as she rose. She felt Raghu all over, pulled him close to her, and then looked up at the heavens, weeping.

A third man entered the courtyard.

"Venkata," she addressed him. "This is Raghu, my son, the heir of Madhuvana."

Why is my mistress here with all these men? Sarala asked herself.

"And this is Sarala, the person I trust the most in Madhuvana," said Aadarshini as she introduced her to Venkata.

Sarala felt elated.

"Thank you for your trust, Akka. I think I have earned it!" she beamed. Then, without waiting to be asked, she recounted the events that had unfurled the fateful night which was to be her mistress' last night alive.

"Akka, on that terrible night, after we put Raghu to bed and I accompanied you out of the *zenana*, all the women were arguing about how Raghu ought to be raised. None of them seemed to care for him, but everybody wanted him simply because he was Madhuvana's heir. But you appeared unmoved by them. I couldn't understand why. I didn't want Raghu to be raised by those women. I wanted to reach out to Azam Khan, but he would take Raghu away and raise him as his people do. All I wanted was the good of Madhuvana, for your sake, for Raghu's sake, for Rajanna's sake.

"It was then that I took matters into my own hands. You've cared for me so much, you've been so good to me, and you've never treated me like a maid. I couldn't help it. I am sorry. That night I stole into the *zenana* and told Raghu I was taking him to you. He came with me quietly. I took him to my husband who was waiting in the woods, and then returned to be with you. After they took you away to the pier, the men realized Raghu was not to be found, and they organized search parties. Fortunately, my husband was part of it, and he steered everyone away from where we live."

"He was with you? Right here in Madhuvana?" asked a shocked Aadarshini.

"Yes, Akka. Your son was remarkably comfortable living in our small hut, and didn't even trouble us once. First I couldn't bring myself to tell him what they had done to you, so I only told him you were in trouble. I told Raghu you would return to Madhuvana soon, and that it was important no one knew who he was so that he could take care of you when you returned.

"He is such a brave boy, he didn't question us even once! He went along with what we told him to do. We rarely brought him outside the house, and when we did, we made sure he wore an oversized turban and clothes that didn't distinguish him from other goatherd boys. We told everyone he was Lavanya's son. The goats seemed to like him. So did the goatherds. But as you can tell, he doesn't look like he's one of us."

Aadarshini smiled. "No, he has too much of Rajanna in him to pass off as a goatherd," she said.

Sarala continued, "But then, I overheard Puttaraju telling Prabhakara Swami that the search for Raghu should be concluded and the boy should be declared dead. The priest seemed to agree. I knew I could not keep him hidden forever here. I planned on sending him away with Lavanya for her to raise him. But a day before she was to leave, I discovered the anklet in that priest's wife's bed, and I knew you were alive. It was a message from the gods! I decided to keep Raghu with me for a few more days. And then one day at the riverfront..."

She pulled off Raghu's tunic. Aadarshini pulled the boy closer and made him turn around.

"Ayyo Rama!" she gasped at the sight of his wounds.

Sarala burst out crying.

"Don't cry, Amma. I am well now. I was never afraid."

"Who is responsible for this, Sarala?" Aadarshini sternly asked, shuddering as she delicately swept her hand over her son's scars.

Aadarshini listened patiently as Sarala described Raghu's encounter with Prabhakara Swami, the beating, and his ultimatum to her to produce the boy by *amavasya*.

There is no point seething over the priest's actions now. The man is dead! Aadarshini told herself.

Sarala sat with her head buried between her knees. "I had to bring Raghu to him by today. I delayed it as long as I could," she said, sobbing all along. "I had no choice, Akka. You know the fate of our lot if we don't obey them."

"Look what they did to Sarala," Lavanya showed Aadarshini the festering scar Jahnavi had inflicted on her back.

"My brave Sarala," Aadarshini said and embraced her. "You did this to protect my son. You raised him as your own son. I am forever in your debt."

Venkata cleared his throat to get her attention. Aadarshini asked Raghu to go with Sarala. Once Sarala and Raghu were safely inside, they began to talk.

"The sun will set soon," said Venkata. "We must hurry. It takes time to set ablaze a house this big."

Aadarshini shook her head.

"No. That will not be necessary now," she said. "Raghu is alive. Madhuvana belongs to him now."

"And the residents of Madhuvana ... what's to become of them?" he asked. "They will surely go to the village council. Puttaraju and his clan will surely undermine you every step of the way. Srikanta will return soon too. Raghu's life, and yours, will be at risk. Madhuvana will resemble the war in Vijayanagara – a long insurgency, an unnecessary war of attrition. Is that what you want?"

"The family will fall in line, Venkata, or we will make them," she said, remarkably calm. Now that Raghu was safe, she knew everything would fall in place. "Yes, we will have to trim some unwieldy branches, but a tree grows stronger if one cuts them off. Puttaraju and everyone loyal to him must die. So must some women. If Srikanta returns, he will meet the same fate. I don't want to wait to see if someone is loyal to me. We need not explain anything to anyone. We will have the village council cooperate. Don't forget, Rajanna *was* the village council. Chandrabhanu was a loyal friend, but an underling. Also, after he has digested the news of my trials, for which the priest will be held guilty, I will propose Raghu's hand in marriage to his two-year-old daughter when she comes of age. He will be delighted. As Rudra confirmed yesterday, there is now a new regime in Vijayanagara.

Rajanna has helped the victors extensively. I will ask Chandrabhanu to make the case to the governor that I should rule Madhuvana as regent until Raghu comes of age. He will agree; after all, his descendants will one day rule Madhuvana. Chandrabhanu will also be useful to make Srikanta conform when he returns."

She could see Venkata was enamored by her thinking.

"And yes, as for my life being at risk," she concluded, "I have you to protect it. I hope I can count on you."

"My loyalty to you and Raghu is just as Sidappa's was to Rajanna," said Venkata, smiling admiringly.

Aadarshini nodded.

"And now go and put Puttaraju and his cohorts out of their misery," she said. "Have the priest's wife taken away from Maravali. Ask her never to step foot inside Maravali again. Cut off her nose before she leaves. Tell her it is her punishment for what she did to Sarala."

Venkata left, taking Sarala's husband with him. Aadarshini knew it would take the rest of the evening, maybe more, for his men to fulfill her wishes. The shadows had grown longer, and the sun had dipped in the sky. She sat with Sarala, Lavanya and Raghu in the courtyard, holding Raghu tight.

"Sarala," she said. "Fill the *homa* pit with firewood. Light it. Tonight my son and I will perform a fire ritual to celebrate this auspicious night of the moonless sky. Send someone to Giridhara. Tell him to make arrangements to celebrate the return of Rajanna's heir. Bring some torches. Let us light up this place. It is the festival of lights, after all. It's a new beginning for all of us."

Just then, a farmhand came running inside.

"I was told to bring news of anyone coming towards Madhuvana. I just got word that Prabhakara Swami is on his way here," he said.

No!

Aadarshini's heart sank. *Azam Khan has failed!*

She grabbed Sarala's shoulders with both hands, and told her, "My brave Sarala, You've been a warrior. Let us fight one more battle together."

"Should I send for the men, Akka?" she asked.

"No," said Aadarshini. "We may not have enough time for that. Prabhakara Swami will be here any moment now. Here is what I want you to do..."

Sarala listened attentively.

"Raghu, my prince, be brave, stay with Sarala. Do what she asks you to do." She rubbed his cheeks.

"One moment, Akka," Sarala said, and pulled out the other silver anklet.

"It is inauspicious to wear just one anklet, Akka. Here, let me put this on you."

"Hurry," said Aadarshini and smiled.

The three of them left the central courtyard and went back into the northeast section. Aadarshini took a deep breath and walked into her room. She made herself comfortable in the far corner, with the mace and the dagger by her side.

Then, composing herself, she waited.

Prabhakara Swami was relieved to see the gates of Madhuvana. The evening sun had not yet had its final say, and at least Azam Khan didn't seem to be tailing him. He had expected it to be dark already, considering he had to limp here all the way. His ankle hurt; he didn't know what the damn *Turka* had thrown at him, but he hoped it wasn't broken.

He addressed the heavens, "Do something, O *nakshatras*. I have served you well. Give me peace." He pulled himself together and marched inside, surprised to see the *homa* pit aflame, a fire only he or his wife had the sanction to kindle.

"Outrageous!" he yelled out. "Who did this?"

From behind one of the pillars, a woman stepped into view.

"You!" said Prabhakara Swami, startled, as he recognized Sarala. Moments later, a boy dressed in traditional Brahmin attire walked out from behind her.

"Is that Raghu?" he asked, the surprise evident in his tone.

Sarala nodded.

So my intuition was correct. The goatherd was indeed Rajanna's son, he gloated for a moment. He could feel his anxieties melting away.

"Leave!" he thundered. "Leave the boy behind. Raghu," he turned to the boy, his voice softer, his hands outstretched. "Don't fear, son. Come to me. All is well. You are home now."

He saw Sarala whisper to the boy. Raghu hesitated for a moment then made a dash towards the northeast courtyard. Prabhakara Swami walked in after the boy, who ran into his room at the far end. A flaming torch rested in a bracket and lit up the courtyard. He entered his room cautiously, calling out Raghu's name. He saw a woman inside, her hair unfurled, her arms protectively wrapped around the boy. A lamp behind her cast a shadow that made her appear wraithlike.

"Who are you? Step forward," he demanded, ready to strike her.

The woman set the lamp on a stool. Its soft warm glow flooded the room.

He stood frozen, his eyes and mouth wide open. "Aadarshini!" he gulped.

Aadarshini banged the mace twice on the floor.

"Surprised, *poojya swamigaaru?*" her voice at once sensual and frightening. "You've blessed me and my family with a long life and boundless prosperity so many times. The gods must have been listening. I keep surviving."

He tried hard to clear his throat. He was rooted to the spot, wary of what she would do next. Aadarshini whispered into the boy's ears, and immediately he bolted past him out the door.

Prabhakara Swami stepped back and yelled into the desolate courtyard for help.

"Jahnavi! Puttaraju! Isn't anyone here? Where is everybody?"

"Don't shout, you pathetic priest," said Aadarshini, her voice raspy. "No one will come to your help. You will never see your wife again. No one is left to help you."

Terror stricken, Prabhakara Swami walked backwards. Aadarshini matched him step for step. She placed the mace on the swing and picked up a torch. He ran into the central courtyard.

Aadarshini called after him, "You have no place to go...*poojya swamigaaru*. It's over now."

He tried opening the front doors, but it was jammed shut from the outside. Frustrated, he turned to her. "Insolent woman, *pisachi*!" he shouted, in a freshly found defiance. "How dare you talk to me in this manner? Have you forgotten who I am? Who has put you up to this outrage? Was it you who desecrated the homa pit, you unchaste whore?"

Aadarshini laughed out loud. She let him babble, savoring the sight of the terror-stricken unhinged priest. Finally, she raised her hand to make him stop. In a calm voice, she began reminding him of his misdeeds, walking towards him.

"You abused Rajanna's generosity."

"His power and influence were ill-gotten," he defended himself.

"Your position in the community was bestowed by him."

"He was a patronizing autocrat. I fed his vile ego."

"You cast your eyes on his queen – me!"

"He was a debauch. He didn't deserve you."

"You coveted Madhuvana. You coveted his son's inheritance. And you conspired with others to make it yours."

"I would have raised his son as my own. I would have taught him more than Rajanna ever would have."

"You mercilessly beat him up. The wounds still fester."

"I did not know it was him. I thought he was just a goatherd. I will atone for that act."

"And will you atone for trying to kill Azam Khan?"

"There is no need for that. He is not one of us. He is a *Turka*."

"You wanted to kill me. You defiled me when I was unconscious. Wasn't I one of *us*?"

Prabhakara Swami mumbled something unintelligibly.

"And you killed Rajanna in cold blood," she continued. "Yes, we know! Don't act surprised."

"Rajanna was a traitor. I worked for the empire. I was only following my dharma. But someone else killed him."

"On your orders. Your actions led to my sati. I was almost burnt alive."

"As Rajanna's wife, that was your dharma, your duty, your path to moksha. Rajanna wanted it that way. No one can sanction death. Only one's karma can. The scriptures say ..."

He jumped a little, feeling the heat from the homa pit. Aadarshini had backed him up against the fire pit, the torch in her hand dangerously close to his face.

To her surprise, Sarala and Raghu came into the courtyard.

"Don't forgive him, Akka," said Sarala. "He almost killed your son. He stood silently when his wife scalded my back. And they wanted to take over Madhuvana. Push him in the fire. Do it."

"Will you take advice from a lowly thieving wench?" he shouted back. "Don't listen to her. She is inciting the demons within you. Beware!"

Aadarshini raised her hand.

"Enough!" she said, and thrust the torch towards him. He took another step back, trembling. His ochre garb was now drenched in his sweat. He slumped beside the homa pit.

Aadarshini looked at Raghu. The boy was terrified by the proceedings, she could tell. He looked on helplessly. She wondered what he thought about his mother's demonic avatar. Just then, the front door burst open, and Azam Khan stormed into the courtyard, his thighs drenched in blood.

He stood in shock. The hapless woman he had once desired and vowed to protect now stood like the goddess of death. Aadarshini was ready to push the priest into the burning pit. The priest groveled in front of her, sitting in a pool of his own urine. And at the other end of the courtyard, Sarala the maid held Raghu. As their eyes met, Raghu ran to him. He dropped his hatchet and hugged the boy.

"Praise the mercy of Allah!" said Azam Khan, and carried Raghu up in his arms. "My tiger cub is well. How we looked for you, how we prayed, praise the mercy of Allah!"

A beaming Raghu now rested his head on his shoulder. The boy looked away from his mother. Azam Khan didn't need to be told what was happening.

"Go ahead. Do it. This is not the time to waver. Allah knows he deserves it. Give him a taste of what it feels to be cremated alive. Give him death, as he has so mercilessly handed it to others. Do it, or let me do it!"

Aadarshini turned to look at him. Then she saw Raghu looking away, and sank to her knees, the torch thrown aside.

"I cannot," she cried. "I cannot let my son see me do this. I cannot do it ... I will not do it."

Azam Khan put down Raghu and asked Sarala to take the boy to the *zenana*. He ordered his men, "Watch the priest. If he tries to flee, chop off his legs."

Aadarshini was crouched on the floor, her arms around her stomach. She quickly composed herself, took a deep breath and stood up. "But we must all reap the fruits of our karma ... don't we, O *swamigaaru?*" she said. "Isn't that what the scriptures say?"

"He is yours," she turned to him. "Do with him what you want."

Prabhakara Swami prostrated himself at Aadarshini's feet. "Have mercy. What'll happen to my Jahnavi? Who'll care for her? She's with child..."

Aadarshini raised her hand.

"Take him away," she said with disdain. "Get him out of my Madhuvana."

Azam Khan called two men to tie the priest's hands and legs, and pulled him up a horse. He then rode away from Madhuvana, the men escorting the priest, ensuring he didn't try anything adventurous. They crossed the banana plantation, the tamarind trees, and even the stream that marked the boundary of the other side of Maravali. They were now deep in the jungles, beyond any trail.

"Where are you taking me?" Prabhakara Swami demanded to know.

Finally, the three got off their horses and dragged the priest down. Two of them began to dig a pit. Prabhakara Swami and Azam Khan sat watching them, under the terrifying flicker of a flaming torch.

"The stars," the priest said laconically. "It's all in our stars, *Turka*. Or who'd have thought you would still be alive? Go ahead and put me out of my misery. It's my fate, perhaps."

"Yes, there is no thwarting kismet," Azam Khan said.

"Azam Khan, listen to me. I can make you wealthy. I am a man of influence. I can get you a commission with the king's military. Let me go. My men once spared your life too. Remember?"

Azam Khan laughed shrilly.

"I am a wretched man, Prabhakara Swami. I have lost two fathers in one lifetime. Can wealth bring my father back? Can it bring Rajanna back? I don't deserve the wealth you promise me, priest. I don't deserve this new life you claim your men bestowed on me. I am a wretched man, star-crossed, cursed..."

He didn't bother finishing. Instead, like a bolt of lightning, he turned around in a flash and swung his hatchet, letting it cut across the priest's torso. As soon as he struck it, he knew the priest was a dead man.

Prabhakara Swami fell to the ground, coughing up blood. Azam Khan ordered the two to throw him into the pit, too deep for him to climb out.

"You'll live till dawn, holy man. Say your prayers. Think of your deeds. You have often said the body is impermanent. Let animals and birds feed on it. They will set your soul free. Maybe your sins will be forgiven. *Khuda Hafiz!*"

No one would hear Prabhakara Swami shrieking into the heavens.

Venkata and Rudra entered the courtyard moments after Azam Khan had left.

"What happened here?" asked Venkata, breathless.

"We were taken by surprise by Prabhakara Swami. There was no time to go find you or your men, so I took charge," Aadarshini said matter-of-factly. "Azam Khan arrived in time, so I handed over the priest to him. He was wounded. Find him. Someone needs to take care of him when he returns."

Rudra told her two men lay dead in Prabhakara Swami's house, and he had guessed that Azam Khan had followed the priest to Madhuvana.

She asked Venkata about the others.

"You'll never hear from them again," Venkata said plainly. "The farmhands are still tied up in the barn, so are the other family members. What should we do with them?"

"Untie the farmhands. Let the others remain there for the night. We'll bring them out tomorrow," she replied. "Have your men bring the cows back right away. I want Raghu to drink fresh milk in the morning. We are all exhausted. Tomorrow, we start afresh."

It was past dawn by the time Azam Khan returned. He joined Rudra, who stood silently at the entrance and watched the courtyard. Aadarshini sat on the swing, looking refreshed and wearing a crisp sari. The mace stood in one hand. Raghu sat beside her. On one side stood Venkata, much like he, and Sidappa before him, had once stood beside Rajanna.

Aadarshini told Sarala, "Let Madhuvana know of our return. We will begin with the farmhands and servants. They will need time to get over their shock. Gather them. Don't rush. Tell them Rajanna's son has returned to Madhuvana."

Once Sarala had left, Azam Khan hobbled inside. Aadarshini then asked Venkata to take Raghu outside. "I need to talk to Azam Khan privately."

When they were finally alone, Azam Khan said, "I set him free."

"Good," she said. "For now, we'll tell everyone he and his wife decided to renounce the material world and repair to the Himalayas. Let the truth emerge when it chooses to."

"Will you come away with me?" he asked after a pause.

"No, not anymore," she replied. "I have to make Raghu worthy of assuming Rajanna's mantle. I have to be here, don't I? Isn't this my dharma ... my *imaan*?"

Azam Khan couldn't look her in the eye. He knew it was time for him to leave Madhuvana. He stepped forward and held her in his arms. He could feel her pressing herself against him. He took a deep breath and let the scent of her tresses torment him one last time. This would be the last time, he knew.

Aadarshini handed him back his dagger.

"This is yours."

"Inshallah, till we meet again," he said.

"Inshallah!" she replied.

Azam Khan bowed, as a subject would bow to royalty, and left quietly. On the way out, he stopped to say goodbye to Venkata and Raghu.

"You be well," he embraced Venkata. He then picked Raghu up in his arms.

"Be brave, my tiger cub. Take care of this. Take care of your mother," he said.

Raghu began to cry.

The rising sun announced an end to yet another night of the moonless sky. Azam Khan wiped his tears.

Rudra put his hand on his shoulder.

"I think our work here is done."

The two of them quietly rode away from Madhuvana.

Aadarshini could hear the faint rumble of the *ghoshaka's* drum.

Finally!

She looked up at the azure sky and smiled. She rocked the swing back and forth to her heart's content, as she would when she was a young girl. Sarala walked in to break her reverie.

"The farmhands, the servants, they have been waiting since dawn to get a glimpse of you," Sarala reminded her.

She sat erect, as a queen would, and asked Raghu to come sit beside her.

"Yes," she said, rubbing her left eyelid to stop it from fluttering, and pulled Raghu closer to her. "Show them in!"

EPILOGUE

Rama Raya never became the emperor of Vijayanagara. After vanquishing Salkaraju, he governed the empire for over two decades as Sadasiva's regent, appointing blood-relatives to all administrative posts including principal forts, governorships, and courts. When, upon turning twenty, Sadasiva began asserting the right to rule on his own, Rama Raya had him imprisoned. As a courtesy, he was brought out in procession once a year for the citizens of Vijayanagara to see him. Even this courtesy was eventually discontinued. Sadasiva, however, remained the official emperor of Vijayanagara.

Unfortunately for Vijayanagara, Rama Raya became obsessed with securing the fort city of Kalyana, in Bidar territory to the north. Four of the five sultans who ruled north of the river Krishna, all offshoots of the once great Bahmani Sultanate, joined forces and challenged the army of Vijayanagara in 1565. Rama Raya, who was eighty at the time, personally led his forces into what turned out to be his last battle – the historic Battle of Talikota. He was wounded by a spear and captured by the forces of Nizam Shah of Ahmadnagar, who had him beheaded; the severed head was mounted on a stake and paraded in front of Rama Raya's troops.

Almost immediately after the debacle, Rama Raya's brother Tirumala moved the Vijayanagara capital to Penukonda. Sadasiva continued to remain an emperor till his death in 1570, when Tirumala ascended the throne. The Aravidu dynasty thus formally took over the reins of the Vijayanagara Empire, a dream that had gone unfulfilled during Rama Raya's lifetime. For a hundred years after Rama Raya's death, the Aravidus ruled an empire that slowly came apart. Though Rama Raya never became emperor, his grandson Venkata II and his great-grandson Sriranga III, did. They ruled from 1630 to around 1670, when history finally downed the shutters on the Vijayanagara Empire, its slow fall from grace brought on by Rama Raya with the defeat at Talikota, and its demise in 1670 surely presided over by his bloodline.

Following the Battle of Talikota, the city of Vijayanagara was sacked mercilessly for over six months by the victorious troops from the north. Within two years, the once grand city, which several foreign travelers had compared with Rome, lay in shambles, overrun by vegetation, inhabited by beasts and dacoits. Vijayanagara stayed hidden till 1800 CE, when it was surveyed by a British archeological team led by Colonel Colin McKenzie. It is now called Hampi and is today a UNESCO World Heritage site.

Aadarshini never met Azam Khan again. Madhuvana and Maravali disappeared into the pages of history.

ACKNOWLEDGEMENTS

I respectfully express my gratitude to my many friends who encouraged me during my quest to write a story that works. Ambassador A. Madhavan and Girija Madhavan of Mysore for spending countless evenings teaching me interesting words and feeding me bruschetta. Dr. Tom Butler, Suzan Dunlavey, Joanne Lazos, and Ray Reska for being who they are. My 'early readers', Dr. Vandana Nadig Nair, Satish Jhunjhunwala, Dr. Sanjay Rao, Dr. Naina Rao, and Armeen Ramabhadran, for candid feedback that shaped the telling of my tale. Amish Mulmi, one of the sharpest editors I've met. Celia Currin, a New York City angel from *Poets and Writers*, who introduced me to Amy Berkower (Writers House) who in turn introduced me to the legendary Al Zuckerman who then taught me how to tell a story properly. Mr. R. Mukherjee of Hindi High School in Calcutta who was my English teacher from a long time ago and taught me how to read. India's most illustrious historians Dr. A. V. Narasimhamurthy and Dr. B. Sheikh Ali, who taught me how to educate myself about South Indian history. The numerous writers who have written so vividly about life during Vijayanagara times - in particular, Dr. Sanjay Subrahmanyam for his insightful book about the political economy of commerce in sixteenth century South India, Dr. Richard Eaton for his wonderful book on the social history of the Deccan, and Dr. N. Venkata Ramanayya for his thesis on the political drama that played out during the times in which this story is set. All my friends and family around the world - so many, so precious, so supportive.

And most importantly, my wife Asha (which means *hope*) for patiently watching over me as this book took shape, and letting me be me. No Asha, no hope, no novel!

GLOSSARY

Aadarshini – one whose resplendency is unconcealed, available for all to see.

Aadu Huli aata – a game of "Tigers and Goats".

Agrahara – the name given to a section of a heterogeneous village inhabited only by Brahmins, or to a village populated entirely by Brahmins.

Akki-rotti – a type of bread made from rice flour, generally baked in a wood-fire or on a pan.

Alhamdulillah – Praise Allah.

Amavasya –The new moon day of the lunar month when the moon is not visible.

Angavastram – a stole, worn by men from the Hindu community, which is draped over the shoulders.

Asura – demon.

Ashtami – the eight day of each half (the dark half and the bright half) of the lunar cycle.

Ashram – a hermitage or a sanctuary for (usually) women, children, or the elderly.

Appa – Father.

Amma – Mother.

Akka – Sister (elder). But not necessarily related by blood.

Atma_hatya – Suicide. The murder of one's Self.

Ayyo – a typically South Indian exclamation used to express a wide range of sentiments - shock, surprise, sadness, amusement, happiness, disgust, and just about everything in between.

Ayyaaaa – an exclamation, similar to *Ayyo,* but not quite the same.

Ayyo Rama! – a typically South Indian exclamation similar to *Ayyo* but with the power of the gods added in. Used often for no rhyme or reason to emphasize just about anything – akin to *Oh My God!*

Ammamma - an exclamation akin to *mamma mia.*

Brahmamuhurtam – a period of around one and a half hours prior to sunrise.

Bhagavad Gita – a 700-verse Hindu scripture, appears as a central chapter in the epic *Mahabharata.*

Cowry – small sea shells once used as money. Now used to make handicraft, or as pieces in board games.

Chandala – a Hindu of low caste, someone who deals with the disposal of corpses.

Deepavali – the festival of lights symbolizing the spiritual victory of light over darkness, good over evil, and knowledge over ignorance.

Dharma – one's sense of duty; a 'right way of living'.

Doab – the tract of land that lies between two rivers, at the point where the rivers merge.

Durga – a goddess of war whose mythology centers on combating evils and demonic forces that threaten peace and prosperity.

Durgamba – "Mother Durga"; a respectful way of referring to Goddess Durga.

Gasagasay payasa – a pudding made with poppy seeds, rice, coconut, milk, palm jaggery, cardamom, raisins, saffron, cashews, pistachios, almonds.

Ghee – clarified butter.

Gopuram – a tower-like structure over the entrance gate or over the main temple – typically in South Indian temples.

Gurukula – a type of residential school in which the aspirants live near the guru, often in the same house.

Haldi – turmeric.

Hakim – a physician who uses traditional medicine (typically a Mohammedan).

Hanuman – a Hindu god who is an ardent devotee of the god Rama. His external form is that of a monkey but Hanuman possesses all the desirable qualities of an ideal human being.

Homa – a Hindu ritual in which making offerings into a consecrated fire is the primary action.

Imaan – Faith; Belief.

Inshallah – an Arabic statement meaning *if God wills it.*

Jahannum – Hell.

Jillé – Administrative district.

Kenda-rotti: A flatbread in which the dough is flattened between two banana leaves and baked in a wood-fired fireplace.

Khuda Hafiz – May God be your guardian.

Krishna Janmashtami – The *ashtami* on which Lord Krishna was born.

Kumkuma – a red pigment used by Hindu woman to make an ornamental round mark on the forehead.

Laadoo –ball-shaped sweets made of flour, ghee, sugar and other ingredients like chopped nuts or dried raisins.

Mantra – a hymn, an incantation.

Mahabharata – an ancient Sanskrit epic concerning the dynastic tussles between warring siblings. It is said that there is no subject of human experience that the Mahabharata does not address.

Mané Aliya – A son-in-law who lives under the roof of his in-laws.

Mangalasootra - a necklace that the groom ties around the bride's neck in a Hindu wedding ceremony.

Mogra – a type of jasmine known for its sweetly fragrant flowers.

Moksha – Salvation, release from the cycle of birth and death.

Nakshatras – heavenly bodies; stars.

Namaskara – a greeting similar to *Namaste*.

Narayana – a name for Vishnu, one of the three deities of the Hindu trinity.

Naraka – Hell.

Nātakā – A play performed for an audience; drama.

Panchay – a traditional garment worn by men, tied around the waist and extending to cover most of the legs.

Puranas - a genre of Indian literature dealing with myths, legends and folklore, told in story form.

Pisachi – a ghost, a demon, a non-human.

Pooja – an act of worship.

Poojya – venerable.

Prabhu – a respectful way of addressing someone if you don't know his name.

Prasada - a religious offering that is normally consumed by worshippers.

Rakshasa – a demonic being (male).

Rakshasi – a demonic being (female), evil with terrorizing looks.

Ragi mudde – a lumpy wholesome meal made of millet flour.

Ramayana – an ancient Sanskrit epic concerning the exploits of Lord Rama.

Sandhyavandanam - a religious ritual performed by Brahmins initiated through the sacred thread ceremony referred to as the *Upanayanam*.

Sandigay - a fried snack served as an accompaniment with meals

Shikha – crest; tuft.

Shraaddha - is a ritual to honor a deceased person.

Swamigaaru – A respectful way of saying 'Swami'.

Swargaloka – Heaven.

Sunna – a paste of slaked lime, often spread over a betel leaf to enhance its flavor.

Svāhā – an incantation, a denouement indicating the end of the mantra, usually said when making an oblation into the sacred fire.

Tauba – a vow to sin no more. A way of showing repentance, common among Mohammedans.

Thatha – grandfather or anyone of that age group.

Tulsi – (or Holy basil) is a sacred plant in Hindu belief.

Turka – an outdated pejorative curse word.

Vaidya – a physician who uses traditional medicine (typically a Hindu).

Vaikunta – abode of the creator of the universe.

Yaaru? - Who is it?

Yama – The Lord of Death.

Printed in the United States
By Bookmasters